Barry's Kiss

Lynden Mann

Copyright© 2024
Published by Boston Press
Email: Lyndenmannbooks@gmail.com
Cover design: Kirk Rundell
ISBN: 9798990795105

Chapter 1

For weeks, I felt nothing but latex—latex gloves on my shattered body.

I was so broken the x-rays looked like a jigsaw puzzle.

A bus hit me. I never saw it.

I was sitting at Bossy's café in La Rogue, Louisiana.

Jack and Margo Plummer, regulars at the café, were doting over their nine-year-old poodle, Tippy.

Witnesses said a city bus blew a tire. Jumped the curb. Plowed into the café like a bull in a china shop. The Plummers were killed instantly—crushed against a wall. Tippy was mortally wounded. He died after several minutes of yelping in pain.

Amid the carnage, bystanders could smell hair and flesh burning. It was me. I was trapped beneath the bus. Its hot exhaust pipe was pressed against my back branding me like a giant curling iron.

It was only after a tow truck pulled the bus away that someone spotted me. They screamed, turning away from my mutilated corpse…but I wasn't a corpse.

I was alive. Barely.

Four weeks earlier.

Gavin was asleep.
No, that's a lie.
He was passed out.
My lip wasn't bleeding, but fat and tender.
I snuck around the bedroom stuffing clothes in a pillow case. I thought about getting a steak knife and cutting off his penis as he lay naked across the bed. We were making love when he snapped. Cocaine took over. His passion turned to rape. His caressing hands balled into fists. He literally climaxed while beating me.

My name is Rozlyn Muer. I moved to Louisiana from Michigan to escape Gavin. I could say the abuse was my fault, but why defend a cheating scumbag whose addiction turned him into a demon.
I left in the middle of the night. My laptop, a few clothes, and my old Honda Civic headed south. I left my purse, my cell phone, my self-esteem.
I didn't know where I was going, I just had to escape. At a rest area near Toledo, I accessed their free Wi-Fi. I Googled a map of the U.S.
Playing 'pin the tail on the city,' I floated the cursor over the deep south. I clicked. The first attempt was a dud—the middle of an Arkansas swamp. The second click was in the Gulf of Mexico.
I cheated and dragged the cursor inland. The first town the cursor drifted over was La Rogue, Louisiana. A sleepy seaside town whose glory days have waned. Forty years ago, it was a bustling port town. Today, it's dotted with empty buildings and vacant lots.
Only diehards remain.

It took twenty-two hours to reach La Rogue. I arrived at 2 a.m. It had one traffic light flashing lonely and slow—just the way I felt. Without a soul in sight, I drove past a dark grocery store, a closed restaurant, and a gas station with two outdated pumps.

I slept in my car behind the restaurant.

I slept hard until a tap on my window woke me.

I was afraid, but thankful it was daylight.

A stocky old lady in masculine clothes was peeking in the window. Probably a homeless person wanting money. I only had four-hundred dollars.

I started my car and cracked the powered window.

"Are you okay, darlin'?" she asked with a bayou twang.

"Yeah...I was driving all night, just needed some sleep."

"Come on in. You can freshen up in the bathroom. I'll make you some breakfast."

Her offer surprised me. She looked like she didn't have two nickels, let alone a job.

I followed her into the restaurant. She introduced herself as Marta.

She owned the place.

The building was tired on the outside, but amazing inside—a retro 1950s bar and grill. Black and white checkered floor. Sturdy stools along a counter bar. Every wall was lined with red vinyl booths. Each booth had a tiny jukebox on the table. It was adorable.

The bathroom door creaked when I closed it. The light was dim, but the mirror was honest. I looked haggard and homeless. I laughed. I was haggard and homeless. I left Michigan in survival mode. I had no idea what I was going to do.

My humor turned to tears—even dry-heaved a few times. I was eighteen-hundred miles from home with no money, no plan—not even a toothbrush.

"Breakfast is ready," Marta called through the door.

"Ok," I politely muttered.

I wasn't hungry. I was numb.

At the far end of the counter bar, Marta slid a plate in front of me. Two pieces of plain toast with a cup of black coffee.

"I'll get you something else if you want, but I'm guessing you need something to settle your stomach."

She must have read my mind. Marta seemed like an all-knowing grandmother...wise as a serpent, gentle as a dove.

I nibbled at the toast.

I don't like coffee, but slurped it anyway.

"Want more?"

I shook my head 'no.'

"What's your name, darlin'?" she asked, leaning over the counter in front of me.

"Roz...Rozlyn."

"Where ya' headed?"

"Here."

Marta's psychic powers kicked in again.

"You don't know a soul in this state, do you?"

I shook my head 'no.'

"Rozlyn, I have a gut feeling you're a good girl running from some bad shit."

Was it that obvious?

Chapter 2

Angela groans through another wave of pain.

"You're having prodromal contractions. Buckle up, honey, they're about to get worse," the nurse says with a terse smile.

Smiling? Really?

"That chick has the bedside manners of a fucking gorilla," Angela hisses as the nurse disappears out the door.

"Babe, I know you're hurting, but don't talk like that."

My wife has a strong personality but a weak heart. The stress of labor is dangerous. She needs to stay calm.

The nurse pokes her head in the room.

"I'll give you something to ease the pain."

I nod with gratitude.

Angie refuses to look at her.

This is our first baby—a boy. We're going to name him Kyle.

The nurse returns with a washcloth.

"Hey, daddy, why don't you get something to eat while I take care of momma."

I kiss Angie's sweaty forehead.

"See you in a bit."

The two women watch me leave then look at each other.

The nurse has an odd expression—dark.

"What are you giving me?"

She doesn't answer.

She has no syringe...no pills...just a washcloth.

She gently wipes Angie's face—nose and mouth first. Something gritty sticks to her lips like salt crystals. She licks them, but tastes nothing.

"You'll feel better in a moment."

"You didn't give me anything."

An ugly grin grows on the nurse's face.

"This fucking gorilla always wins," she whispers and walks out.

A euphoric feeling rushes over Angie's body. Her pain instantly fades.

Chapter 3

"We need the trauma team in cube 9, STAT!"

In a blur of motion, they heave me from an ambulance gurney to an ER table. They cut off my clothes. The room goes silent. My world is dark, but my ears are open.

Someone pukes.

"Where in the hell do we start?" a woman whispers.

"Just keep her breathing."

A nurse, or more accurately, a shitty barber, shaves my head. The clippers are painful against my scalp. Globs of bloody hair fall to the floor. I want to scream, but nothing works except my pain receptors.

Countless hands grope my body. They try to be gentle. There's no way to avoid punishing me.

"One, two, three."

They roll me left. The pain makes me vomit.

"Up her morphine," the ER doctor says.

He runs his latex covered hand down my spine.

I spasm and moan.

"I know this hurts, honey. Just give me a few seconds."

"Cervical vertebras two through five are displaced," he says.

They restrain me with straps. My bed is jostled down a noisy hallway. They shove me into a machine that clicks and whirs.

"Oh shit! It's lodged in her brain."

I was filling my mouth with strawberry waffles when the bus hit. The impact slammed my face against the table. It drove a fork through the roof of my mouth into my sinus cavity. It punctured my optic nerve.

I'll never see out of my right eye again.

Chapter 4

I'm chewing my last bite of an over-priced hotdog when an announcement blares.

"Attention visitors…will David Rand—"

I don't wait for the message to finish. I'm already running.

Sprinting passed the elevator, I charge up three flights of stairs.

Angie's room is chaos.

A doctor is not between her knees telling her to push. He's hunched over her bare chest driving a needle in her ribcage.

"Come on Angela, take a breath," he shouts, draining the syringe in her heart.

I elbow through the crowd.

Angie's lips are blue—her belly filleted wide open from an emergency C-section. Our baby, bathed in amniotic fluid, is lying near her feet, the umbilical still attached to Angie's innards.

A nurse is pumping air into his lungs with an Ambu bag. Another is performing CPR, compressing his tiny chest with her fingertips.

"Angie!"

My scream startles everyone.

"Get him out of here!" the doctor barks.

"I'm not leaving!"

We lock eyes, coming to a silent resolution.

"Her heart stopped eight minutes ago. I can't get it started."

He tries for forty minutes, but Angie never revives.

Our baby is stillborn.

My whole world died today.

Chapter 5

"Rozlyn, I'm Dr. Briggman."

I open my left eye. The other one is *forked up.*

That's my inside joke.

Briggman is old. He looks like a seasoned sailor. Weathered skin, salty hair, faded brown eyes.

"You're extremely lucky. You're beat to hell, but holding your own."

I try to speak. Nothing happens.

"You can't talk. Your larynx is crushed. If you speak again, it'll be a whisper."

A tear melts from my eye.

"I've been assigned as your primary doctor."

Obviously, I say nothing.

"I'm going to spare you the grocery list of everything that's wrong and focus on the major issues. You're not paralyzed, but the nerves in your legs have been severely damaged. You have feeling in your legs, just no muscle control. With a lot of therapy, you'll walk again."

Another tear drips from my eye. Not sad, just hopeful.

"You'll be in traction a while. You have four twisted vertebras in your neck. Also, three cracked ribs, two broken arms…and a partridge in a pear tree," he humorously adds.

If I wasn't in agony, that might be funny.

"While your bones are healing, we'll do skin grafts to patch the burns on your back. After that, we'll focus on reconstructing your face."

He tweaks my meds. Everything fades.

Chapter 6

Yesterday was the third anniversary of Angie's death.

I went to work with a heavy heart.

I'm a veterinarian.

I was petting a hundred-pound mastiff in the lobby when she walked in—a woman in her early-thirties.

I did a double-take.

Angie?

Her resemblance to my wife took my breath away. At her side, was the cutest little boy. His dimples matched his mother's—matched Angie's.

She was a new client, came in to get her dog neutered.

I greeted her warmly, but my knees were shaking. When she introduced her three-year-old son, Benjamin, I broke. My son would have been the same age.

"Will you excuse me a moment."

I rushed to my office and puked in a trashcan.

"David, are you okay?" my office manager asked.

She could see I was struggling.

"I need to leave."

"Sneak out the back. I'll take care of things here."

I grabbed my keys. Forgot my wallet.

I had no recall navigating traffic. I thought I was driving aimlessly until I pulled into the parking lot of the hospital where my wife and baby died three years ago.

I didn't want to live.

I didn't own a gun and slitting my wrist wasn't guaranteed.

I decided to jump.

First Mercy Hospital is the highest building in town. Six-stories tall.

Head first into the pavement would do it.

Getting on the roof was easy. The hospital has a floral garden on the rooftop for patients and visitors to enjoy. It has a panoramic view of the Gulf of Mexico across the street. The only obstacle between me and death was an eight-foot security fence.

At 7:40 p.m., a security guard announced the garden was closing in five minutes. He politely held the door of the service elevator as patients and visitors exited.

I ducked behind a concrete flower box.

At 7:45 p.m., the guard scanned the area.

"The roof is secured," he said over his radio.

The elevator door slid shut.

I was alone.

In the waning sunlight, the sky was beautiful. Its orange glow off the Gulf of Mexico magnified its splendor.

Numbly, I walked to the roof's edge. I gripped the fence. It was a heavy construction fence made of diamond-shaped wire.

Eight feet up—eighty feet down—my pain will be gone.

The wire dug into my fingers. It was hard to wedge my toes in the diamond-shaped openings. It hurt, but nothing like the pain in my heart.

Atop the fence I teetered at waist level.

A row of prickly barbed-wire stabbed my hands. All I needed to do was lean forward. Gravity would do the rest.

"God, forgive me," I whispered.

I looked down. The view made me dizzy. An asphalt parking lot dotted with cars awaited my arrival.

"I'm sure my purse is here," a lady said as the elevator 'dinged' open.

The security guard spotted me right away.

"Sir, what are you doing?" he yelled.

I threw myself forward, but didn't fall. The barbed-wire snagged my clothes. I kicked and thrashed. The guard caught my ankles before I could free myself.

The woman tried to help, but was too short. All she could do was scream.

More people rushed onto the roof. Dozens of hands tore me from the fence. Bodies dogpiled on top of me. Fearing for my life, the security guard cuffed my hands behind my back.

When I came to my senses, I was in the psychiatric ward on the sixth floor of the hospital where I tried to end my life.

Chapter 7

"Rozlyn, why can't you be more like Darleen?"

"Mom, college isn't for me."

Darleen is my older sister, the golden child. She's the hero. I'm the zero. She's pretty, book-smart, has boobs. I'm scrawny and shy. Tend to make bad decisions—the wrong guys, the wrong friends. A constant disappointment to my parents.

I'm shocked when they walk into my hospital room.

"Oh, baby…" Mom chokes, unable to hold back her tears.

Dad cries too.

I have no idea what I look like. I'm sure it's awful.

"Roz, can you talk?" Dad asks.

I can't speak. Can't move.

He quickly catches on.

"Blink once for *yes*, twice for *no*. Are you able to talk?"

Blink. Blink

"Do you know who we are?"

Blink.

"You must be Rozlyn's parents?" Dr. Briggman asks, diverting their attention.

I try to listen. All I hear is medical jargon.

"Fractured maxilla...shattered zygomatic...ruptured sinus...torn optic."

I fade out.

When I open my eye, the room is dim. It's nighttime.

A dark figure is standing in the corner. I try to see who it is, but can't lift my head. I'm trapped in a neck brace.

The person stands there for several minutes, then disappears.

Chapter 8

My psychotherapist, Dr. Moore, classified my suicide attempt as "abbreviated traumatic amnesia." That's a fancy way of saying I have no memory of trying to kill myself.

I read the report filed by the security guard. It sounds like he's talking about someone else...some crazy person.

That was four days ago.

I'm lightly sedated, but don't need drugs.

I'm heartbroken, not suicidal.

Unfortunately, Dr. Moore won't release me from the hospital. He says it's not punishment. He just wants to see if I exhibit any neurotic behavior.

On a positive note, he must not think I'm too crazy. He enrolled me in an in-house work program. The Resident Service Program (RSP) allows select patients to do odd jobs in the hospital. It's a win-win for everybody. The hospital gets free labor and us crazy folks get a little freedom.

Some workers are assigned to the cafeteria, others do laundry. I drew the short straw. I'll be cleaning restrooms. I don't mind. It's better than staring out a window all day.

The job is routine. I go to the janitorial closet. Fill up a bucket with hot water. Load the cart with cleaning supplies and follow a map taped to the cart.

RSP workers wear green nametags. It allows staff members to easily identify us. We also get to wear scrubs so we don't look out of place as we move through the facility doing our jobs.

I guess putting us in straight-jackets would be a dead give-away.

Chapter 9

Each day of pain bleeds into the next.

A plastic surgeon harvested skin from my thighs to patch the burns on my back.

The procedure will leave scars in both places.

There goes my modeling career.

My room has no mirrors. Apparently, they don't want me to see myself.

Each morning, a nurse empties a large syringe into a PEG tube inserted in my stomach. This is how I eat. With a shattered jaw, I won't taste food for a long time.

"How do you want your eggs this morning, scrambled or over-easy?"

She always says the same stupid thing.

I see Dr. Briggman twice a day.

Same old stuff.

"You're getting stronger...it'll take time...blah, blah, blah."

The only major change is my method of communication. I used to blink to answer questions. Now, I'm able to move two fingers—my thumb and middle finger on my right hand.

Thumbs-up 'yes.'

Flip you the bird 'no.'

When my parents visit, I tend to flip off Mom a lot. I think I'm secretly repaying her for all the condescending bullshit she's shoved in my face over the years.

At night, they up my pain-meds to help me sleep. I rarely wake up. The few times I have, I've seen a shadowy figure standing in the corner of my room. I raise my thumb hoping to get a response, but he or she never comes close.

Chapter 10

I'm allowed to leave the psych ward twice a day.

In the morning, I clean restrooms on the first three floors. In the afternoon, it's floors four and five. I can clean the sixth floor anytime. It's the psych ward. I live there. I usually do it late at night. It gives me something to do, plus most of the patients are asleep so no one is pissing on the floors.

The first time I cleaned after-hours, I had the pleasure of meeting Bart Edmond, the night-shift supervisor.

He interrogated me for ten minutes. He didn't believe I was authorized to be out of my room after-hours. All he had to do was check the Resident Service roster.

He's weird. Tall. Skinny. Quirky personality.

He constantly prowls the halls checking for unlocked doors. When he finds one, he hurries in like a DEA agent raiding a Columbian drug lord.

I think he's a psych patient himself.

Chapter 11

"Hello, Mrs. Muer?"

"Yes?"

"This is Gavin, Rozlyn's boyfriend."

Bev strains to be polite. She suspects he abused Roz.

"Oh...hi, Gavin. How are you?"

"I'm okay. Have you've heard from Roz?"

"No."

"Hmm…I don't know where she went."

"Well, you know her—free-spirited, always disappearing somewhere."

"Yeah, that's true. Anyway, if you hear from her, tell her to give me back the $2,000 she stole."

"I don't know what you're talking about."

"Listen, Bev, if I don't hear from Roz in a few days, I'm going to the cops."

She abruptly hangs up, shaking.

Chapter 12

It's been eight days since the accident.

I've been moved to long-term recovery. This area of the hospital looks like a low-income nursing home. Nothing modern—gloomy. It's all the city will provide as they squabble with attorneys. The city does not want to pay my medical bills. Their bus ran over me, but they say the café is at fault for providing sidewalk seating.

I hate bureaucratic assholes.

Long-term recovery is staffed by a skeleton crew.

My daytime nurse is Joseph Mersk. I like him. He keeps the embarrassing stuff to a minimum. I need to wear diapers, but he's quick at changing them.

Presto-change-o—he's done.

I don't know how he does it so fast.

When he bathes me, he always looks away while cleaning my girl parts.

My nighttime nurse is an old Russian woman.

Sova Garbisch-*whatever*.

Her nametag looks like a bunch of backward numbers and letters.

I call her Gargoyle. She's creepy. Stooped shoulders. Uncaring eyes.

She talks like a Soviet spy from an old James Bond movie.

She rarely says a word. She's most unpleasant when changing my diaper. Rough. No bedside manners.

I can't wait for my broken arms to heal.

Never take for granted wiping your own butt.

Chapter 13

I've been in the Resident Service Program for three days.

This morning, I'm outside ER cleaning restrooms.

The hallway is empty except for my cleaning cart.

With a bucket of soapy water, I step into the women's restroom.

"Hello? It's the cleaning guy. Anyone in here?"

"Give me a minute," a voice shouts from a stall.

"Oops…sorry."

Before I retreat, a set of double doors burst open behind me.

A noisy entourage spills from the emergency room.

A husky medic with broad shoulders shoves my cleaning cart against the wall. He's dragging a bed behind him. A nurse holding an I.V. bag is keeping stride. The bed is flanked by two doctors—one on each side of the patient.

The swarm disappears down the hall.

The double doors to ER are still open. Beyond them is an exit to the outside world. I could easily walk out.

"We don't pay you to daydream," a chubby man with a clipboard growls. "Get your ass to cube 9 and clean it up."

"I don't work here," I mumble.

"Clean it up!" he barks, not listening.

I push my cart into ER.

The chubby man closes the double doors behind me.

I have no idea where "cube 9" is located.

I feel out of place as I move past several busy cubicles where the real world happens. Heart attacks. Auto accidents. Drug overdoses.

At the far end of the aisle, I find cube 9.

It looks like a tornado hit it.

Rubber gloves everywhere. A pile of greasy clothes in one corner. A puddle of puke or baby shit in the other. The most disturbing sight is the hair—clumps of blood-matted hair strewn everywhere.

A car accident? Was someone thrown through a windshield?

I slip on my rubber gloves—the same ones I use to clean toilets.

I scoop up the clothes and toss them in the trash.

They smell like gasoline and exhaust fumes.

I mop up the nasty puddle and soak the area with bleach.

I sweep the hair, but it's stuck—glued to the floor by its owner's blood. I use a dustpan to scrape it up. When I dump it in the trash, a glint catches my eye. Tangled in the wad of hair is a necklace. A heavy necklace with a medallion. Inserted in the medallion is a jewel—a ruby, the same birthstone as my wife.

Is this a sign, Angie?

"If you would have committed suicide, you'd be with her now," a dark demon whispers in my ear.

I ignore the taunting voice and examine the necklace.

Three initials are engraved on the back…RRM.

I'd like to find its owner. Sometimes a trinket of our past gives us hope for the future.

Chapter 14

He smiles and nods.

Says please and thank you.

Well groomed. Thin build. Friendly.

Not handsome. Not ugly.

Average.

He blends in.

That makes him dangerous…a demon hiding in plain sight.

He's not a serial killer.

Not a thief.

He's a hands-on guy…a molester…a sexual pervert.

He works at First Mercy Hospital. It's rife with opportunity.

Teens and children are his preference, but he's flexible.

His pattern is consistent. With untethered freedom, he roams the hospital looking for victims. When he sees a potential target, he'll watch a few days, mostly at night. When he's ready to strike, he's fast. It doesn't take much to sedate a person if you know what you're doing. Once they're drugged, he does his dirty deed.

He currently has his eye on a girl in ICU. Thirteen, maybe fourteen. She's battered and bandaged, beat to hell.

The more immobile, the bigger the thrill.

ICU is tough to infiltrate.

She'll be moved to general care in a few days. Until then, he'll keep an eye on her.

Chapter 15

I had my first reconstructive surgery today.

They removed bone fragments from my cheek.

They'll reform my face with synthetic implants.

I'm still foggy from anesthesia.

Gargoyle is taking my vitals.

"I'll increase your meds to help you sleep," she says with her heavy Russian accent.

I give her a groggy thumbs-up.

"Hey, Sova," someone shouts. "Mr. Gordon is having chest pains."

Gargoyle hurries away.

The commotion in the hall fades as my door glides shut.

I wait for the pain meds to kick in.

Nothing happens.

My face is throbbing.

Maybe Gargoyle forgot to up my meds before she left?

Sleep evades me.

Visions haunt my mind.

"Hi, Sweetie, I have a surprise for you when you get home."

"Are you naked?"

"Gavin, your mind is always in the gutter."

"Yeah, so what. Be naked when I get there. I want to do the wild monkey dance."

That's his code for sex.

The apartment door bangs open. Gavin stumbles in. He's high.

Per his request, I'm naked on the couch trying to look sexually pleasing despite my scrawny body.

He staggers over, eyeing me from head to toe.

"Put some clothes on, you skeletal bitch!"

He slaps my face.

I wake up panting, my eye wet with tears.

Joseph, my daytime nurse, is touching my face. I translated the pain of his touch to a nightmare of my ex-boyfriend beating me.

"Sorry, Roz, didn't mean to wake you. I was checking your bandages."

I give him a thumbs-up.

"Everything looks good. I'll see you in the morning."

Joseph is a great guy. He's not even on the clock but comes in to check on me.

The morning light is brutal. Between my nightmare of Gavin's abuse and Joseph's unexpected visit, it was a long night.

"Good morning," he sings out.

If I could smile, I would. Joseph is always in a good mood.

"Time for breakfast," he says. "You're having waffles," referring to the contents in my feeding syringe.

I jerk with fear.

I was eating waffles when the bus hit me. Joseph doesn't know that. Just the thought terrorizes me.

Flitting around my bed, he gently washes my face with a warm washcloth. Reaching under my gown, he wipes my chest and armpits. My arms are entombed in heavy casts so there's nothing to clean.

Chatting about the weather and such, he discretely spreads my legs. Without looking, he peels off my diaper, cleans my crotch, and redresses me.

He's so fast and efficient, I never feel naked.

Chapter 16

"Nice to meet you, David. My name is Krista. You're gonna enjoy this assignment. It's easy."

Dr. Moore, my psychotherapist, extended my responsibilities. Instead of cleaning toilets, he's assigned me to work with an orderly on second shift.

Today is my first day.

"The first part of our shift is crazy busy," Krista says. "After eight, it becomes a snooze-fest. I usually go to the visitor's lounge and read. No one goes there after hours. At midnight, our shift is over. Any questions?"

"Do I have to stay with you all night?"

"You're supposed to, but I'm not anal about it. If you want to wander around and keep yourself busy that's fine with me."

Krista is right about the job description. From 4 to 8 it's a zoo. After eight the building turns into a morgue.

The nightshift is sparse—a handful of doctors, a few-dozen nurses, and one maintenance guy.

The first two days, I hang out with Krista in the visitor's lounge.

By day three, I'm bored to tears.

"I'm going to find some busy work."

"Knock yourself out," she mumbles, glued to a four-hundred-page novel.

It's weird having so much freedom. After two weeks of being under tight observation, I feel liberated.

I dig in my pocket and pull out the necklace I found in ER four days ago.

I want to find its owner.

No…I *need* to find its owner.

First step, where to look?

The hospital has six floors. The first and sixth are off the menu. The first floor is ER. The sixth is the psych-ward.

I decide to start on the second floor and work my way up.

The second floor goes fast. It's pediatrics and geriatrics—children and old people. The necklace was tangled in a wad of long brown hair. No one on this floor.

I take the stairs to the third floor.

It's general care and post-op.

Under the guise of a janitor, I go room to room and empty waste baskets. The tricky part is getting far enough inside each room to see the patient's hair color.

It took less than an hour.

There were only seven patients with brown hair. Five men and two women. Both women had long hair. The owner of the necklace would be bald or partially shaved.

The elevator 'dings' open on the fourth floor.

I step out.

The sound of a crying infant stops me dead. This is the floor where Angie died…the maternity ward.

I fade into the elevator and slump against the wall.

The door closes.

I don't push any buttons, just ride up and down.

30

Occasionally, a person enters.

They talk—I don't.

It makes them uncomfortable. Most can't get out fast enough.

When my soul returns, I go to the visitor's lounge where Krista is devouring her book.

"If you don't mind, I'm going to call it a night. I don't feel good."

She actually looks up, concerned.

"Are you okay?"

"Yeah, just tired."

I ride the elevator to the sixth floor—my floor.

Bart watches me with his suspicious eyes.

I go to my room.

I'm usually a back-sleeper. Not tonight. Tonight, I curl in a fetal position and cry myself to sleep.

Chapter 17

Far at sea, a monster is moving across the water.

The placid ocean gave it life. The sun intensified its strength.

Mel Gibson—not the actor—is watching.

He grabs his phone.

"Hey, Rich, it's me. We've got a monster off the coast of Haiti."

The monster's name is Jenise. A few days ago, she was a tropical storm in the Caribbean Sea. Today, she's a raging hurricane.

"What are we looking at, Mel?"

"A CAT 3...gaining strength."

"How did she get so strong without us knowing?"

"I have no idea. I've never seen a storm develop this fast."

"Okay, I'll let you know when we're airborne."

"Thanks Rich...fly safe."

Mel works for NOAA...the National Oceanic and Atmospheric Administration. He tracks severe weather. Richard Wells is a hurricane hunter. He and his brave crew fly airplanes into hurricanes to collect critical data.

They risk their lives so millions will be saved.

Chapter 18

Krista's routine is so rote we could do it blindfolded.

From 4 to 8 p.m., it's super busy. One minute after eight, her butt is parked in the visitor's lounge with her nose in a book.

I'm still on a quest to find the owner of the necklace. I was derailed last night when I went to the fourth-floor where Angie died. I think demons will forever haunt me when I go there.

The elevator opens on the fifth floor. This area is long-term recovery…people in for the long haul.

Like every floor, it's a ghost town after hours.

I step from the elevator.

"Watch it!" a woman barks.

A nurse pushing a cleaning cart nearly runs me over.

"What are you doing?" she suspiciously asks, her Russian accent adding to her intimidation.

"I'm…I'm here to do custodial work."

"We don't need you—leave," she huffs.

She looks familiar.

I want to ask if we've met, but don't want my ass chewed.

I step back in the elevator, easing away from the glaring nurse as if she were a hungry lion. I press the 'door close' button. She gives me the stink-eye as the door glides shut.

Her shitty attitude isn't going to stop me. Taking the elevator to the third floor, I sneak up the stairs. I glance down the hall hoping Miss Congeniality is not around.

Rushing to the nearest room, I peek inside.

It's occupied by an old man. He's surrounded by so many machines it's hard to see him. Definitely not the owner of the necklace.

I trot to the next room.

Another old guy. His TV is on, but the sound is off. Doesn't matter. He's snoring like a hibernating grizzly.

The third room looks lonely. It's occupied by a small person lying in an over-sized bed. The bed is not nestled against the wall, but dead-center, allowing medical personnel to approach from all sides.

The patient is a female. I'm guessing early-teens based on her tiny frame.

Poor thing looks miserable. Both arms entombed in heavy casts. A stiff neck brace digging into her shoulders. Her face is grossly swollen with a patch over her right eye.

I step in the room, but keep my distance.

I can't see her hair color. Her scalp is wrapped in gauze.

What happened to her? She looks helpless.

Pity overwhelms me.

I abruptly leave and join Krista in the visitor's lounge.

I flip through a magazine to distract my mind, but can't un-see the poor girl on the fifth floor.

I'm not sure if I'm curious or morbid?

I want to see her again.

Chapter 19

"Good afternoon, ladies and gentlemen, this is your captain speaking. We'll be arriving at our destination shortly. Please make sure your seat-backs and table trays are locked in their upright position. Also, if you have any carry-on luggage, please stow it in the overhead compartment at this time. Thank you for flying Hurricane Hunters airlines."

Richard Wells has a good sense of humor, but takes his job seriously. As captain of the C-130 hurricane hunter aircraft, he knows their mission is dangerous.

The crew departed from Florida at 9 a.m.

It's currently 12:44 p.m.

Billowing clouds loom on the horizon. Hurricane Jenise is seventy miles away.

"Wow, those wall clouds are pushing 60,000 feet," Wells says to Bruce Somski, his co-pilot. "That's got to be a record."

"NOAA says she's getting meaner by the minute," Somski says.

Jenise is not big geographically…only a hundred miles wide, but her tight formation makes her powerful, like an F5 tornado on steroids.

Twenty miles from the wall cloud, the plane starts to dance in the turbulence.

At ten miles, she jumps and jerks like riding a rodeo bull.

When they enter the wall cloud…

"Let the games begin!" Wells announces to the crew as the plane shakes violently.

Pea-sized hail and heavy rain pelt the windshield. Doesn't matter. The visibility is zero, obscured by thick clouds.

"Tell Mel we're ready to drop the first Dropsonde," Wells says.

Dropsondes are Pringle-sized canisters they eject from the plane. They collect weather data inside the hurricane to help predict its path and strength.

Somski relays the message to Mel at NOAA.

"Drop four…one on each corner," Mel radios back.

Traveling counter-clockwise into the storm, Wells gives the green light to the crew.

"Bombs away!" someone says, jettisoning the first device.

Inside the plane, several computers update.

-Wind speed- 155
-Barometric pressure- 28.22, and dropping.
-Temperature- 58F (climbing)

At the south end of the storm, the second Dropsonde is released.

-Wind speed has increased to 169
-Barometric pressure has dropped to 27.40
-The temperature is still climbing.

These numbers mean nothing to the average Joe. To a trained meteorologist, they're indicators Jenise is gaining strength.

On the east side of the storm, the third Dropsonde is released.

    -The wind speed is raging at 185

    -The barometric pressure is approaching a record low.

    -Temperature- 72F and climbing

Golf ball-sized hail pummels the plane. The lightning is constant. The aircraft is pitching and falling like a violent rollercoaster. Wells and Somski hardly notice. They're talking about the NFL pre-season.

On the north side of Jenise, the fourth Dropsonde is released.

    -Wind speeds are over 200 mph

    -Barometric pressure is hovering at 26.10

    -Temperature, 81F…holding steady

After circling the hurricane twice, Wells exits the wall cloud and heads home.

Somski receives a bleak message from Mel at NOAA.

It's short and disturbing.

"Haiti is in trouble."

Chapter 20

My parents came for the weekend.

They're heading home today.

"It's gonna be a muggy day in Michigan," Dad says."

I miss Michigan summers. They're beautiful.

Green, alive.

Unlike me. Beat to shit—living in misery.

"Gavin called," Mom blurts.

My body stiffens.

"I told him I didn't know where you were."

I give her a thumbs-up.

Thanks, Mom. Thanks for keeping your mouth shut.

A rare event.

"Dr. Briggman said your next operation is Tuesday," Dad says, purposely changing the subject.

I lift my middle finger.

"I know, more pain," he says sympathetically.

Dad understands me.

"Gavin said you stole two thousand dollars from him."

I give Mom a stiff middle finger.

Gavin never had money—never worked. All he did was sponge off me.

"We won't be back till Labor Day," Dad says with a tight jaw, glaring at Mom.

"Gavin said he'll call the cops if you don't return his money."

"Beverly, shut up!" Dad huffs. "She didn't steal anything from that lying bastard."

I love my dad.

He'd kick Gavin's ass if he were twenty years younger.

Chapter 21

Krista made me stay in the visitor's lounge all night. She heard a rumor her boss might pop in. I'm not supposed to wander the hospital unsupervised.

At 12:02 a.m., the elevator opens on the sixth floor.

I stroll passed Bart. He glares at me with his shifty eyes. I want to raise my hands and surrender. Okay, Bart, you caught me. I'm smuggling drugs into the psych ward.

Suspicious bastard.

I go to my room…603.

It feels cold. Not the temperature. The atmosphere.

I toss and turn.

I can't stop thinking about the person one room away. Not the person to my left or right, but below me. Room 503 where the battered young woman is lying. I've only seen her once, but can't stop thinking about her.

I think she's afraid.

I wish I could comfort her.

I slip out of bed and peek down the hall.

Bart is gone.

The stairwell door is propped open with a broom.

Where in the hell is he? He's not the type to violate rules and leave the ward unattended.

I quickly dress, taking advantage of the open door.

I scurry down a flight of stairs to room 503. Like the previous visit, I stand in the shadows.

Her eye is closed, but wandering beneath the eyelid.

She's probably dreaming.

She jerks and moans.

She's definitely dreaming.

I build my courage and step to the foot of the bed.

There's a gentleness about her. An angelic glow despite her battered face and wired jaw.

Panting with fear, her eye pops open. Her dream must have been a nightmare.

I want to console her, but remain frozen in place.

She moves her hand. Actually, her thumb—pointing it upward like a 'thumbs-up' emoji.

I'm too nervous to respond.

I slip out the door, hoping she didn't see me.

Chapter 22

It's just after midnight.

The staff is thin…a skeleton crew.

A man, leaning against a wall, is waiting.

He's got his eye on room 213.

Two days ago, a ten-year-old girl was admitted with stomach pain.

Appendicitis.

Her mother has not left her side…until now. She just walked by talking on her phone.

"…yeah, she's asleep. I'm gonna run home and take a shower."

Dressed in blue scrubs and holding a clipboard as a prop, the man joins the mother in the elevator.

He looks like a nurse.

"So, how's Madison doing?" he casually asks.

He got the child's name and medical info from a roster at the nurse's station.

"She's doing great," her mother says with a tired smile.

"That's awesome…appendicitis can be scary."

"Sure is. Thank God, they gave her a sedative to help her sleep. I need a break."

The man struggles to suppress a smile. The staff didn't drug Madison…someone evil did.

The elevator opens at the lobby.

He politely nods, allowing the mother to step out first.

"Have a good night," he says.

"Thanks, you too."

"I will…I definitely will," he grins.

He steps around a corner and watches the mother leave.

He anxiously trots up two flights of stairs to the second floor. His heart is pounding with excitement.

The hallway is empty.

Madison's door is open.

He hurries in and closes it.

He steps close.

"Madison," he whispers.

She doesn't answer.

He vigorously shakes her shoulder.

She's out cold…drugged.

Smiling with satisfaction, he pulls out his cell phone to record the event. He'll make a lot of money selling lewd images online.

As he loosens Madison's gown, the door opens.

Her mother hurries in.

"Forgot my keys." she frowns.

He nods, pretending to check his phone.

The mother heads for the door, but freezes.

"Weren't you in the elevator with me?" she curiously asks.

"Yeah."

"How did you get back here so fast?"

"I got a text from the nurse's station," he says, holding up his phone. "They wanted me to check her vital since they gave her a shot."

The mother stiffens.

The man's story isn't making sense.

The nurse who administered the sedative gave her a pill, not a shot.

Continuing his façade, he grabs Madison's wrist. He stares at his watch for ten seconds, then writes something on his clipboard.

"Her pulse is good," he says with a smile.

He doesn't have a stethoscope, but places his hand on Madison's chest. She's far from puberty, but he appears to cup her left breast.

What in the hell is he doing? the mother scowls.

"Her heartbeat is strong. She's a beautiful girl. Going to be a little hottie when she grows up."

His words sound perverse...his expression creepy.

"She'll be out for a while. You'll have plenty of time to go home and take a shower."

The mother's gut tightens.

She never said anything about taking a shower. All she said in the elevator was needing a break.

"I'm gonna stay," she says, pushing between the man and her daughter.

"You won't have another chance," he presses. "You should go."

"I'm staying," she growls.

His jaw tightens with frustration.

Visibly agitated, he leaves.

When the door glides shut, the mother sees the clipboard sitting next to the bed. There's one page attached heavily inked with random doodles...smiley faces...tic-tac-toe boxes. Among the drawings she sees something disturbing. Vulgar illustrations of private body parts.

Among the obscene sketches, she sees '213' written dozens of times—her daughter's room number.

She hurries toward the door with the clipboard, but collides with the man as he rushes in.

He shoves her against the wall, glaring angrily.

"You talk, you die," he hisses.

He grabs the clipboard and darts out.

Stunned, the mother is too afraid to leave.

By the time a nurse shows up, the man is long gone.

Chapter 23

A leggy meteorologist smiles at the camera. Her makeup is heavy. Her hair obnoxious blonde. A snug dress accentuates her over-sized implants. Her injected lips are over-shadowed by fake lashes that flutter like oriental fans every time she blinks.

Her appearance is gaudy. No one cares. Everyone is more concerned about hurricane Jenise.

"The Dominican Republic is getting hammered," she says with a gleam in her eye. "Jenise is bearing down on Haiti with wind gusts in excess of 200 mph. If the storm maintains its present course, it could bring catastrophic weather to the Gulf region. We'll keep you updated as the storm continues to move north."

Chapter 24

I had another surgery.

Just woke up. Been unconscious for ten hours.

They removed one of my ribs. It was shattered, creating a dangerous barb. There was a risk it could puncture my lung.

Oh well…one less bone for Gavin to criticize.

I think it's Thursday.

Not sure of the time.

There's a clock on the wall. I can't see it. If my I.V. stand is in the right place, I can see its reflection, but it's backward. Two o'clock looks like 10 o'clock, and so on. I have to really concentrate to flip the image in my mind.

Around 11 p.m.—or maybe 1 a.m., my door opens.

Joseph? Gargoyle?

I don't hear footsteps, but a man appears at my side.

I can barely see his face in the dim lit room.

He's wearing blue scrubs.

His nametag says, 'Dr. Barry.'

Something is printed beneath, but the text is too small.

His eyes are blue—piercing blue with dark hair. He's unshaven with a heavy shadow. Maybe he's the surgeon who operated on me this morning?

His lips never move, but his eyes speak.

They convey trust.

He leans close and looks into my eye…my only eye.

I feel a connection, like he's looking beyond my marred countenance into my soul. He seems to understand my pain.

Without a word, he gently traces his finger across my forehead.

A gush of warmth oozes through me.

I close my eye.

It's the first time in weeks I've been touched. Not with latex covered hands, but flesh to flesh.

His fingers are soft—the hands of a surgeon.

I open my eye.

He smiles and leaves.

Was I dreaming?

Chapter 25

Haiti is a poor nation. Cite Soleil is the poorest city. Rickety huts. Dirt streets.

Disease.

Starvation.

Violence.

Death has many faces in this tropic slum. Stray dogs are better off than children. Dogs can scavenge for food—children can only beg.

Two days of torrential rain has brought more suffering to this impoverished place. The shantytown looks like a swamp. Drainage canals have over-flowed their banks flooding thousands of huts with raw sewage.

The inhabitants have no idea the pouring rain is a prelude to greater destruction.

Chapter 26

"Goodnight, David."

"G'night, Krista. See you tomorrow."

It's exactly midnight.

That girl lives by the clock—punctual coming and going.

Today's shift was okay. I stayed busy, but my mind was elsewhere. I couldn't stop thinking about the girl in room 503.

I tried to visit, but the nurse with the Russian accent chased me away. She probably thinks I'm a pervert.

The elevator opens on the sixth floor.

I nod at Bart as I pass by. If he stares any harder my soul is going to burst into flames.

Without closing my door, I undress and crawl in bed.

Bart strolls past and glances in. My lights are off. He can't see me watching.

A few moments later, I hear a *clack* in the hall like someone dropped a broom.

Curious, I peek out.

Bart is gone—again.

The stairwell door is propped open with a broom—again.

Where in the hell does he go? He constantly sneaks out after midnight.

I crawl back in bed, but struggle to sleep.

The girl in 503 haunts me—in a good way. I wonder how she's doing? Poor thing was having a bad dream last time I visited.

Visited?

Stalk is a better description. All I do is hide in the shadows and watch her like a creepy vampire. I don't know why I'm reluctant to step close. Maybe I feel unfaithful to Angie, like 503 is stealing my attention.

That's stupid.

503 is battered, bandaged, and broken. What would I be attracted to?

A faint noise in the hall disrupts my wandering mind.

I peek out.

Bart is putting the broom back in the janitorial closet.

It's 1:30 a.m.

Hmm?

The next few days, I spy on him.

He's like Krista—lives by the clock.

He's out the door at exactly 12:10 a.m.

Comes back on the dime at 1:30 a.m.

Chapter 27

Gavin is slouched in the driver's seat of his car. His overgrown bangs hang over his eyes like dirty curtains. He's spying on Roz's parents. They're loading luggage in their car.

Where you going? he questions.

He follows them to Bishop Airport, the closest airport to their home. When they pull into the 'Long Term Parking Lot,' he hurries back to their house. He breaks-in through the back door of the garage.

Snooping room to room, he searches for clues of Roz's whereabouts. He finds nothing, except a hundred-dollar bill tucked in a drawer. He stuffs it in his pocket.

A little rum-n-coke tonight, he smiles. Meaning, a few lines of cocaine and a bottle of Bacardi.

He wanders back to the garage. An over-flowing trashcan catches his eye. Buried beneath a blob of spaghetti sauce he sees a brochure for Hertz rent-a-car.

'Welcome to Louisiana,' it says in bold print. An address at New Orleans International Airport is stamped on the back.

A greasy grin grows on Gavin's face.

"Are you hiding in Louisiana, Roz?"

Chapter 28

Bart just did his nightly disappearing act.

I have roughly an hour to visit the girl in 503.

If I'm caught, I'll lose my privilege working with Krista.

It's a chance I take.

Her room is dimly lit—as usual.

Taking a deep breath, I build my courage and step close.

Her left eye...her only eye, locks on to me.

I didn't expect her to be awake.

We say nothing, but our eyes speak.

I can tell she's broken, not just outside, but inside, in her soul.

So am I.

She seems lost...missing something in her life.

Me too.

I sense she wants to live.

I hesitate to agree.

Do I really want to live? Will the suicide demon tempt me again?

Her brown fawn-like eye compels me to respond.

I hesitate, but finally agree.

Yes...I want to live.

Without realizing it, I find myself caressing her brow, the only part of her face not bandaged or bruised

She closes her eye, expressing relief, like someone scratched an itch she couldn't reach.

When she opens her eye, her gaze pierces me.

I feel vulnerable.

I abruptly leave.

I don't want her to see me cry.

Chapter 29

Replacing bandages.

Surgeries.

Injections.

Pain. Pain. Pain.

Today, a new element of torture was added—physical therapy.

DAMN! A bunch of sadistic Nazis.

Their job qualification…zero compassion.

Their mission…bend your body in the most agonizing position imaginable.

I constantly hold up my middle finger begging them to stop. They stretch me more. Probably think I'm flipping them off.

When they wheel me back to my room, my cheeks are wet with tears.

Gargoyle says she'll "dope me good" to help me sleep.

She empties a syringe in my I.V. tube.

"Hey, Sova," some orderly yells. "When you're finished, you need to do your magic on the guy in room six. He's getting out of hand."

She dims the light and leaves.

I barely doze off when I feel someone tugging at my gown. My neck is in traction. I can't lift my head.

A cool draft wafts over my crotch as my diaper is peeled away.

It's probably Gargoyle.

I wait to be cleaned, but nothing happens.

If it were Joseph, he'd be done already.

As I lay exposed to the world, a cold hand touches my stomach. It slides over my pubic area. Bony fingers spread my labia and poke my vagina.

I jerk and moan, not with pleasure, but fear.

"Dammit, Sova. I thought you took care of her," a man whispers.

The I.V. stand rattles.

I pass out.

Joseph shakes my shoulder to wake me.

"Come on Roz, rise and shine. It's a new day."

It's 9:30 a.m.

I vaguely recall last night.

Was someone molesting me or was it another horrible nightmare about Gavin?

Chapter 30

Nona is only twelve. Her body isn't. Puberty hit early. Her mother dresses her in baggy clothes to hide her developed figure. In the slums of Cite Soleil there is no moral code. If a man sees a female he wants, he takes her, even if she's a child. Scrawny girls get no attention. Those with boobs and butts become targets of rape.

"Go straight to the well and come back," her mother sternly warns. "The storm is almost here."

Rumors throughout the shantytown have everyone afraid. Jenise has become the strongest hurricane in Haiti's history. She already devoured the eastern half of the island, rapidly approaching the slums of Cite Soleil.

Villagers are filling every container they can find with fresh water. Once Jenise hits, it may be days before potable water can be found.

Nona hurries to the community well with two plastic jugs. Dozens of women surround the cast iron pump. No one is in charge, but they work efficiently. Some pump water, others fill jugs.

The wind is calm, but a heavy rain is soaking everyone.

"Give me your jugs," a woman says.

Nona resists.

"I will not steal them…I'm Christian."

Nona believes her. Christians in Haiti are not well-received. Her confession of faith could get her killed.

The woman fills the jugs to the brim and gives them back.

"Hurry home, child. I pray Jesus keeps you safe."

Nona respectfully nods and rushes away. As she hurries home, the wind picks up. Stinging rain pelts her face.

"Give me a drink," a gruff voice demands.

Nona glances at a man standing outside his hut. She doesn't stop. At the next alley, she turns right. While zigzagging through a maze of dirt paths, a roar of thunder booms overhead. It scares her, but a strong hand on her shoulder scares her more.

"I said give me a drink," the man growls, spinning her around.

He rudely grabs a jug and guzzles the precious liquid. When he hands it back, his eyes drift down. Nona's rain-soaked shirt is clinging to her body revealing her ripe breasts.

He smiles at the sight.

She turns to run, but he catches her arm. He drags her into a vacant hut. She tries to scream, but he grabs her throat.

"Shut up, or I'll kill you!" he snarls with a Creole accent.

He knocks the jugs from her hands. They spill, merging with muddy puddles.

"Sit!"

She drops to the ground, her eyes wide with fear.

Outside, the conditions are tornadic. Angry winds are tearing through the village creating deadly flying debris.

Ignoring the weather, the man smiles as he slides his filthy shorts to his knees. Other than her little brother, Nona has never seen a man's penis—especially erect.

He kneels in front of her. She scoots away, but he grabs her ankles. He yanks her skirt to her waist. Her crotch is bare. She's not wearing underwear. She doesn't own any.

He shoves her back, forcing himself on her. She screams, but he smothers her mouth with his large hand.

Defiantly, she squeezes her knees to protect herself.

"Open your legs!" he snarls.

She refuses.

He slaps her several times, stunning her.

With savage strength, he pries her legs apart. Before he can steal her innocence, the roof tears free. A small section flies away, but a large piece of sheet metal drops in the hut. Like a giant guillotine, it slices into the man's back severing his spine below the kidneys.

Paralyzed and hemorrhaging, he dies on the spot.

Nona screams hysterically as warm blood gushes over her naked thighs. Wrestling to free herself, she rushes out the door. The wind knocks her to the ground. Before she can stand, someone grabs her arm. She thrashes and fights thinking the rapist has revived.

"Come with me!" a woman shouts.

It's the woman from the well—the woman who prayed for Nona's safety.

Turning from the wind, the tall slender woman drags Nona behind her. She takes several steps and falls. She yanks Nona to the ground with her. A large chunk of debris whizzes overhead.

The woman runs again. She takes about thirty paces and drops, pulling Nona close to protect her. More debris hurls by.

Sprinting and crawling, they make their way through the village avoiding deadly debris multiple times as if God himself were guiding the woman's footsteps.

When they reach the outskirts of town, she drags Nona into a drainage ditch. She falls next to her.

The trench is only a foot deep.

It's flowing with torrential rain.

There's no place else to hide.

Keeping their faces above water, they hold each other tight.

Amid the roaring storm, Nona hears the woman praying for God's mercy.

"Lord Jesus, please protect us. The storm is powerful, but nothing is too strong for you."

Nona has never heard of Jesus, but the woman's prayer is comforting.

Chapter 31

They rewired my jaw. I was conscious the entire time. Hurt like hell.

Gargoyle has upped my pain meds again. Doesn't matter. The pain is inescapable.

Around midnight, my door opens.

I'm afraid.

Is it the molester?

I don't hear footsteps, but Dr. Barry appears at my side...the same mysterious man who visited a few nights ago.

I feel defenseless.

He must have sensed it.

"Don't be afraid. I won't hurt you."

Why would he say that? He's a doctor.

"I just want to talk. You don't have to say anything."

Dr. Barry, you're a dumbass. My voice box is crushed. I can't talk.

He slides a tall stool next to my bed. Without any preamble, he starts chatting. Nothing specific. A movie he watched. A girl he liked in high school. The price of gasoline. When he brings up politics, I give him the middle finger. Surprisingly, he understands and changes the subject.

He talks a long time. His voice is soothing. Warm and deep like a late-night radio host.

"I have to go now," he says after nearly an hour. "I hope to see you again."

He gently touches my forehead, flesh to flesh, caressing my brow several times.

Waves of heat gush through me.

It's powerful.

When he removes his hand, the heat fades.

I want him to touch me again, but he's gone.

The only evidence of his visit is the tall stool next to my bed.

In the morning, Joseph questions me about it. I have no way to explain it was left there by Dr. Barry—the mysterious man with beautiful blue eyes whose visited me twice in the middle of the night.

Maybe he's an angel?

Chapter 32

"Yo! Mrs. Muer, I thought that was you."

Linden is a small town. Bev enjoys running into people she knows at the grocery store. Not this guy.

"Gavin, nice to see you," she says with a cold smile.
"How's Mr. M?"

"He's good."

Gavin's eyes are bloodshot. He's either high or coming down from a serious bender. Despite his slurred speech and smelly breath, he's slick. Bev knows he'll ask about Rozlyn. She needs to be on guard.

"Hey, I finally heard from Roz," he says excitedly. "Sounds like she's loving the weather down south. Enjoying that Louisiana sunshine."

Bev stiffens.

How does he know?

She has no idea Gavin broke into their house and found a rent-a-car brochure with a Louisiana address.

She plays dumb.

"Down south? What's she doing down there?"

"I have no idea, she didn't say."

Bev doesn't have a good poker face. She needs to end the conversation. She glances at her watch.

"Oh, wow, it's getting late. I gotta go."

They exchange a stiff hug.

Without looking back, she hurries down a canned food aisle into the produce section.

Far from Gavin, she calls her husband.

"Sam, I just ran into Gavin. He knows Roz is down south. No, I didn't tell him. Yeah, he specifically mentioned Louisiana. I have no idea. Okay. Bye"

Behind a tall display, a disheveled young man smiles.

He heard every word Bev said.

Chapter 33

Today's surgery was awful.

They inserted a synthetic plate under my right cheekbone. It feels like a metal spoon embedded in my face. Not just any spoon, a hot spoon off a fiery grill bathed in jalapeno sauce. There's no way to escape the burning pain.

Gargoyle is at my bedside jotting a note on my medical chart.

"A nee muudz," I gurgle, desperately trying to say "I need meds!"

She walks away not even trying to communicate.

You bitch!

The clock ticks slow.

Each minute feels like an hour—an hour like a day.

The reflection of the clock is straight-up.

It's midnight.

My pain is unbearable.

God, help me! I can't take this anymore.

He must have heard my prayer.

Within minutes, Dr. Barry appears at my side.

I weep with relief.

"A nee muudz," I gurgle.

He glances at the I.V. bag. The tube delivering morphine is pinched between the bedrail and frame. He unkinks it. A burst of morphine shoots into my arm bringing instant relief.

"That should help," he says.

He didn't tell me what was wrong but simply caresses my sweaty brow. His touch is comforting. I'm not sure what's relieving my pain—his magical touch or the morphine?

"Do you have time to talk?" he softly asks.

If I could roll my eyes I would. It's a stupid question.

Nope, can't talk. I'm playing tennis shortly, then taking my sky-diving lesson.

Of course I have time!

He must have read my mind.

"Sorry, that was a stupid question," he says with a bashful smile.

I love his smile. Boyish. Pure.

He leans close.

His breath smells good. Not minty or even clean, just good.

"What's your name?"

Damn! This guy is clueless.

I CAN'T TALK!

He waits for an answer.

Oh, I get it. He's testing my vocal skills.

"Roozln," I gurgle.

"Rozlyn. That's a beautiful name. How old are you, Rozlyn?"

"Twunnee ay."

"Twenty-eight."

I'm amazed he understands me—till I catch on to his game. There's a whiteboard above my bed. It has my name, age, and med schedule.

I thought he was connecting with me, but he's just pretending to understand my garbled nonsense.

"Who hurt you?" he asks, touching my swollen face.

I don't want to answer cuz I'm pissed.

I do anyway.

"Buuuzz."

"No, I'm not talking about the bus. *Who* hurt you?"

His question is deep...personal. This info is not on the whiteboard.

Through tears, I say "Gaubn."

"Gavin? He's the man who hurt you?"

I can't breathe. How does Dr. Barry know about the pain in my soul?

"Where does Gavin live?"

Oh, shit. He'll never understand 'Michigan?'

"Migiggon."

"Michigan? Well, at least he's far away."

I can't believe he understands me.

"Rozlyn, I gotta go, but I'll see you again soon."

He turns to leave.

I want to reach out and hug him—but can't.

He stops and glances back.

"I'll take a raincheck on that hug," he says with a playful wink.

WHAT?

Out of the blue, he kisses my forehead, the only place on my face not bandaged or bruised.

A tsunami of heat surges through me.

My body tingles.

My heart flutters.

I close my eye, enraptured by the sensation.

For some reason, my neck cracks multiple times. My cervical pain fades. I think my twisted vertebras just reset themselves.

Did his kiss heal me?

I open my eye. I want to tell him, but he's gone.

Is Dr. Barry real or is it the morphine?

Chapter 34

Nona and the woman crawl from the shallow canal. The hurricane has moved west.

Cite Soleil is a wasteland. Hundreds of shanties have vanished, many heavily damaged. A few stand unscathed.

An eerie calm surrounds them. No screaming. No crying. Just shell-shocked silence.

A few looters are collecting random clothes and dented cookware, but it's worthless. The smart ones are gathering stray containers partially filled with fresh water—a priceless commodity.

"Momma…" Nona tearfully mutters.

She knows her family is dead.

"Do not be afraid, child," the woman says. "Trust God."

Amid the rubble, they find the village water pump. It's undamaged.

"Thank you, Jesus, for sparing the water," the woman says.

Nona knows nothing about Jesus or Christian religion, but this woman's faith is unwavering.

"Show me where you live."

Nona scans the area. Every landmark is gone. Buildings and well-traveled streets are buried beneath wreckage or erased from the earth.

"Nothing looks familiar."

"I will take you where I found you. We'll start from there."

Weaving through a maze of destruction, they pass the hut where Nona was nearly raped. She glances inside. Her attacker is face down partially buried in mud. Next to him are her jugs of water. She rushes in and grabs them.

She takes a sip. The water is not tainted.

She offers some to the woman.

"No, child, save it for your family."

"Nona!" a woman screams.

Her mother is rushing toward her with her arms wide.

They embrace, sharing a million tears of relief.

"Where have you been?" she sobs.

"This woman saved me."

"Who saved you?"

Nona looks over her shoulder. No one is there.

"There was a woman—she saved me from the storm."

"Nona, you were the only one in the alley."

"Momma, I swear—"

"Look, child," she says, pointing at the ground. "There is only one set of footprints—yours."

Nona stares at the muddy earth. She's right. Only one set of prints.

Her mother takes the jugs and leads the way home. Miraculously, their hut survived.

Still confused, Nona looks over her shoulder. At the far end of the alley, she sees the woman watching.

"There she is!" she shrieks, grabbing her mother's arm.

Before she can turn, the woman vanishes into thin air.

Her mother frowns.

"Nona, stop this nonsense."

The girl smiles. She knows in her heart the woman was an angel sent by God to protect her.

Nona knows nothing about Jesus or Christianity…but she will.

Chapter 35

I wish Dr. Barry would visit.

I miss him.

I can't prove it, but I think he healed me when he kissed me. Not all of me, just some of me. My neck doesn't hurt as bad, and the pain in my face is tolerable.

He's amazing. Understands my gurgling words, even reads my mind. I wish Gargoyle had the same ability.

Speak of the devil—she just walked in.

I think I'm building a tolerance to the pain meds she gives me each night. Sometimes, I fall asleep. Mostly, I'm restless, racked with pain. Her sorcery is inconsistent.

"Time to go night-night," she says with her thick accent.

She pricks my arm. Hot chemical shoots through my vein.

It hurts.

She's never given me a shot before. It's usually an I.V. injection.

"Spakoynay nochee," she says in her Russian tongue.

Yeah…kiss my ass too.

I don't like her. There's something dark about her.

"Gavin, don't! You know I'm ticklish."

Our laughter is real as we wrestle on the living room floor.

"I'll stop under one condition."

I already know what he wants.

"No, we don't have extra money to go to Bruno's."

That's Gavin's favorite restaurant.

"Sounds good, but that's not what I'm thinking."

A crooked smile grows on his face.

"I'll stop tickling you if you do the wild monkey dance with me."

I belly laugh.

"That's sounds so stupid. Why don't you call it what it is…sex?"

"Wild monkey dance sounds more animalistic."

I want to please him, so I unzip my jeans. They're not even at my knees when he yanks at my panties, tearing at them like an aggressive Pitbull.

"I'd like a few minutes to get in the mood."

He doesn't listen.

He's on me and in me before I'm wet.

It hurts.

He pumps harder—faster.

"Babe, take it easy."

My suggestion enrages him. His face turns red, not with pleasure, but evil.

He pinches my nipple, grinning the whole time.

"Gavin, that hurts!"

I want to scream, but nothing comes out.

"Roz, wake up!"

Gavin's face evaporates.

I open my eye, panting.

Joseph is staring at me.

"I think you were having a bad dream."

I was.

The mind is a powerful thing. I frequently dream about Gavin attacking me. My nightmares somehow transcend into my physical world. I often wake up feeling violated—my sweet spot sore as if I'd been raped.

Chapter 36

Trident Major is a huge oil rig in the Gulf of Mexico.

She's stands four-hundred-feet above the waves.

Eighty people call her home.

Trident is a buoyant rig. She floats on massive pontoons. When the sea is calm, you feel nothing. When it's rough, you wish you lived on land.

"Time to pack up, Tom. We've got orders to evacuate. The hurricane is coming."

"It's too late," he grumbles.

"What do you mean?"

"I told the bigwigs we needed to evacuate days ago. They ignored me. Jenise is going to be here before we know it."

Tom Vorcy is the senior crew chief on Trident Major. He can read the sky better than any Doppler radar.

Hans Getz, the rig supervisor, can vouch for Vorcy's uncanny ability to forecast dangerous weather.

He's done it several times.

Most recently, a Chinook helicopter was delivering supplies to the rig. Vorcy was sipping coffee in the control room listening to Getz chat with the chopper.

"Bravo 63, what's your ETA?" Getz asked.

"I'm forty-six miles out. Should be there in eighteen minutes."

"Okay, let me know when you're close."

"Roger…see you shortly."

Vorcy finished his coffee and headed for the door.

"I hope they have some chocolate. I haven't had a sugar fix in two weeks," he said over his shoulder.

Clopping down a flight of stairs, he glanced over the placid water.

His heart sank.

Getz was literally twiddling his thumbs waiting for the chopper when Vorcy stormed into the room.

"Tell them to turn back!"

"Why?"

"They're heading into a micro-burst."

"What in the hell are you talking about? The weather is beautiful."

"If they don't turn back, they're dead."

Getz grabbed a pair of binoculars and stepped outside. He scanned the skies to the north. He saw a dot on the horizon. It was the chopper. The sky was hazy, but not threatening.

"What was in your coffee, Tom? I don't see anything."

"Hans, for God's sake, trust me. Tell them to turn back."

He reluctantly agreed.

"Bravo 63…abort and return to the mainland."

"Trident…please repeat."

"I said, abort…return to the mainland."

"Why?"

Getz looked at Vorcy for an explanation.

He grabbed the mic.

"There's a ghost wind shear moving through the area. It's gonna take you down."

Ghost shears are exactly what they sound like—they're invisible. They can generate a powerful downburst of wind over a hundred miles per hour. If it hits an aircraft, it's usually a death sentence.

"If I return loaded, someone has to pay for the fuel," the pilot said.

"I'll pay for it!" Vorcy screamed. "Just get the hell outta there."

"Roger…Bravo 63 aborting…over and out."

Two hours later, the U.S. Coast Guard sent a wire to the rig. A small airplane went down eight miles north of Trident Major. The pilot issued a 'Mayday' saying he was plummeting rapidly. His radio went dead as he screamed for help.

The Coast Guard found the wreckage the next morning. It hit the water so hard the biggest piece was no bigger than a cereal box.

Back to present.

Getz has no idea how Vorcy can predict dangerous weather, but he's always spot-on.

"Can't cry over spilled milk, Tom. Let's get the evacuation underway."

"We can't leave yet. Alpha-3 is not capped. She won't make it through the storm."

Getz scratches his head. Tom is right—as usual.

Alpha-3 is a new well. It will supply 2600 barrels of crude oil a day once it's pumping. If it's not capped before the hurricane hits it could pollute the Gulf with tons of sludge.

"How much time do you need?"

Vorcy glances at his watch.

"Give me a handpicked crew of five—I'll have it capped by 6 p.m. tomorrow."

"That's all I can give you. Jenise is supposed to hit in forty-eight hours."

"Twenty-six is my guess," Vorcy mutters.

Chapter 37

Dr. Barry just walked in.

I haven't seen him for two days.

Strange, I only see him at night.

No one on staff ever mentions him. No medical documents reflect his name. It's like he doesn't exist.

I'm sure he's a surgeon, but he never says a word about my condition. Every visit seems personal, like he's interested in me. I have no idea why. I'm a train wreck inside and out.

His bedside manner is awesome.

Soft-spoken.

Gentle touch.

Plus, he's eye-candy…so handsome. I'd love to run my fingers through his thick wavy hair.

"How are you doing, Rozlyn?" he quietly asks.

I don't answer. I'm tongue tied. Hypnotized by his piercing blue eyes. Even if I speak, it's a bunch of mumbo jumbo. Sounds like I've got a mouthful of marbles.

"How are you?" he asks again.

Breaking free from his hypnotic trance, I answer.

"I goo," (I'm good) I gurgle.

"I can tell. You look great. You're healing fast."

I have to take his word for it. I haven't seen my reflection since the accident.

He starts to make small-talk, but I steer the conversation in a different direction. I need to know something.

During his last visit, he asked some personal questions. Things only God would know. Specifically, who hurt me? He knew about my damaged soul, the result of Gavin's abuse. How could he know this?

Taking a deep breath, I blurt the question.

"Ha oo no sum mun hut me?" (How did you know someone hurt me?)

His eyes narrow with concentration. I don't know if he's lost in thought or trying to figure out what the hell I said.

I try again.

"Ha oo no sum mun hut me?"

My words are so garbled, I may as well speak Swahili. It would be easier to understand.

As frustration builds inside of me, I see something I didn't expect...his blue eyes glistening with tears.

He softly touches my cheek.

"I can't explain it, but I feel a connection to you...something deep. I just knew you were wounded in your heart."

I've never heard such intimate words.

It opens a flood gate of emotions.

I sob.

He leans close. His warm breath on my face is soothing. I want him to kiss me again...the same healing kiss he gave me two days ago.

Before I can ask, he says something that blows my mind.

"May I kiss you?"

With my head in a neck brace, I can't nod 'yes.'

Sobbing, I'm unable to speak.

I can't pucker with my wired jaw.

All I can do is close my eye, yearning for him to do it.

He kisses me. Not on the lips. On my cheek. A peck.

I cry harder.

He does it again, absorbing my tears with his lips.

With each kiss, my heart erupts. Waves of heat gush through me...a healing power.

Who is this man? How is he able to touch me so deeply?

Chapter 38

"You're Uber is waiting."

"Ahh! I hate to fly."

"You can't swim back, so get onboard."

Delany White is one of six women on Trident Major. She loves to rock climb, scuba-dive, and is fiercely independent. Her only weakness is not being in control. She can't fly the helicopter. She needs to rely on someone else. She hates that.

"If this thing crashes, I'm gonna haunt you the rest of your life."

Supervisor Getz laughs in her face.

"See you after the storm."

She tosses her duffel in the chopper and joins seven others.

Aircruze, a private aviation service is evacuating Trident members to the mainland.

"Aircruze 77...ready for lift-off," the pilot says.

"Roger 77...ETA to mainland 57 minutes."

The chopper rises and banks north. It's barely out of sight when the radio squawks.

"Aircruze 77...return to the rig. You've got some cargo they need."

The chopper banks hard-left and returns to the helipad.

Getz opens the door.

"Delany, grab your gear. Vorcy needs you in the mess hall."

She doesn't ask any questions. Just climbs out.

The oil rig is eight-stories tall, a maze of catwalks and stairs.

After four flights of stairs and three catwalks, she enters the mess hall.

Vorcy and four men watch her walk in.

"Hellooo, sweet cheeks," a young man sings out.

"Save it, Punk. The clock is ticking. We don't have time to watch her kick your ass."

"Yessir," the young man nods.

Vorcy is well-respected. No one gives him any lip.

Vorcy scans the room locking eyes with each crewmember.

He handpicked each of them.

Patrick Simms is in his late-thirties. His nickname is Crater because he's got a deep dimple in the middle of his chin. He's been on Trident Major for eight years as a welder and diver. He works a thousand feet underwater every day.

Patriot, whose real name is Mark Renald, loves God and country. He prays out loud all the time. He's strong as an ox—has to be. He handles the heavy stuff—pipes, collars, steel plates. He's big as a bear, but kind as a kitten.

Forrest Wood—that's his real name, is a crane operator. He's a master at rigging things. He can transform a toaster into a radio with just a diode and a paperclip.

Trevor Punkowski, "Punk," is the youngest member of the crew. He's a 3rd generation driller. Born to be on a rig. He's strong, handsome, arrogant as hell.

Delany is Trident's drilling engineer. She's young for the responsibility she carries—only thirty-three. She's tiny in stature, but mean as a hornet if you rub her wrong.

Vorcy grabs a data sheet from a clipboard.

"Okay, here's the deal. We have fourteen hours to cap Alpha-3 before the storm hits. There's no room for error."

"Fourteen hours?" Crater interjects. "How does that work?"

"We're gonna double up. You and Forrest are going to take care of the drop and stop, while Punk and Patriot do the heavy lifting."

"What about sweet cheeks?" Punk asks, nodding toward Delany.

She gives him a dirty look.

"*Sweet cheeks* will make sure you guys don't mess up. I'm the boss, but she's the brains. If you don't please her—"

"Oh, I can please her," Punk grins.

"Listen, asshole, one more smutty remark and I'm gonna punch you in the throat," she says with a cold stare.

Punk believes her. He apologizes with a nod.

"Focus people!" Vorcy barks. "I got a feeling Jenise is going to be here sooner than we think. Every minute counts."

The gravity of the mission is heavy in the air.

Everyone knows it's a race against time.

"Patriot, you need to pray to God we get Alpha-3 capped and evacuated before the hurricane hits."

The big guy removes his ballcap and bows his head.

"Not now! We don't have time."

"Excuse me, Sir, I disagree. I believe if we give the good Lord his time, he'll give us our time."

Vorcy can't argue with his logic.

Everyone respectfully bows their head.

"Dear Lord, help us git-r-done. Amen."

Everyone looks at Patriot with a blank stare.

He smiles ear-to-ear.

"The Bible says to be sincere when you pray, not long-winded."

Vorcy can't argue with his logic.

Chapter 39

"Glad you're here…thought you'd be out jogging."

Dr. Barry just walked in smiling ear to ear.

I love his smile.

Maybe I just love *him*.

I want to ask a huge favor, but not sure if he's willing. Knowing my luck, this will be the first time he's unable to understand my garbled words.

"Coo bing mur?"

He doesn't answer—just stares.

Maybe he didn't understand?

"Coo bing—"

"I heard you," he gently interrupts. "Are you sure?"

I give him a 'thumbs up.'

"Okay…I'll be right back."

His expression is unreadable as he heads out the door.

His absence lingers.

A moment ago, I felt confident. Now I'm scared…not sure if I'm ready.

Maybe I should wait.

Too late…he's back. It's in his hand.

"Is this your first time?"

I give him a thumbs-up.

"Okay, we'll take it slow."

My heart is pounding.

Fear?

Excitement?

He stands at the foot of my bed and holds it up.

"Coser."

He steps closer with the mirror. It's a cheap mirror made of Plexiglass. Maybe they don't allow real glass in case patients freak out and smash their reflection.

"Coser."

He steps again, stopping twelve inches from my face.

My first glimpse is startling. Fat nose, puffy cheeks, distorted features like a fun-house mirror.

I'm surprised my 'forked up' eye is not bandaged. The iris isn't brown, but cloudy and gray like a cataract. The white area is blood-red. Looks creepy—devilish. At least it moves in sync with my good eye.

My head is shaved—a shitty buzz cut. I had stitches on my scalp, but they're gone. Only red scars remain.

My left cheek looks normal. My right cheek is trashed. Sunken and deformed with a zipper-like incision running from my ear to my nose. The entire area is bruised adding to its ugliness.

The sight triggers a horrible memory. I've seen my face battered before thanks to Gavin's abuse.

I push the haunting image from my mind.

I focus on my mouth

Other than cracked dry lips everything looks normal…until I expose my teeth.

I almost scream.

My mouth is sewn together with heavy wire—a crisscross pattern between my upper and lower jaw. The wire is attached to two plates screwed into my gums. Looks like dental braces on steroids.

Thank God I still have teeth. They're scummy and dingy. I have no idea the last time they were brushed.

Overall, I look…awful.

A female Frankenstein.

Tears drip from my eyes.

Dr. Barry takes the mirror away. He replaces it with his handsome face.

"Don't cry, Roz. You're beautiful."

"Boosit," I hiss.

"It's not bullshit."

How in the hell can he call my shattered face beautiful? He must be half blind too.

I glare at him, enraged by his hypocrisy. He counters my dark mood with a kiss—a gentle kiss on my mouth.

He actually kissed my dingy-toothed, dry-lipped, wired-shut mouth.

I want to stay mad, but a wave of heat hits me like a bonfire.

"You're beautiful, Roz."

I cry harder.

"Again," I whisper.

"You're beautiful," he repeats.

"No…kiss me…again."

It's the first time since the accident my words are clear.

He doesn't hesitate. He kisses me with a lingering kiss. His lips are warm—soft and satisfying like a comfy pillow.

Another blast of heat hits me—a gush of healing love.

"Rozlyn, you're truly beautiful."

He's so sincere, I believe him.

89

Chapter 40

Midday turns to evening.

Evening fades to night.

My thoughts are consumed with Dr. Barry...specifically, his wonderful kiss.

I stare at the door, yearning for him to enter.

In the wee hours, a gentle touch stirs me awake.

It's him. He's smiling, but looks confused.

"I'll be right back," he says.

He darts out the door. He's gone a long time...almost five minutes.

Okay, not long, but it felt long.

He comes back with a mirror—the same mirror from yesterday.

"I'm not sure what the doctors are doing, but...WOW!"

He shows my reflection again. Initially, everything looks the same, until I study the details of my face more closely.

My right cheek is a little puffy, but not bad. The bruising has faded significantly.

The scars on my scalp are practically invisible.

I look at Dr. Barry, amazed, then back at my reflection.

My right eye is less cloudy—more brown. I close my left eye to test my vision. The room is blurry, but visible.

"Ah ca see!" I scream with all the volume I can muster.

"Really?"

"Ya!"

"How clearly?"

"Bury, bu na baa."

"Blurry, but not bad?"

I give him an enthusiastic 'thumbs up.'

I don't know if Dr. Barry is responsible for my miraculous recovery, but I thank him anyway.

"Tay coo, Doker Burree! Tay coo!" I gurgle, saying his name for the first time.

He cocks his head.

"What did you call me?"

"Doker Burree."

"How did you know I was a doctor? I never told you."

My eyes dart between his face and nametag.

He glances at his chest and laughs.

"Rozlyn, my nametag says, D.R. BARRY…D.R. are my initials. My name is David Randal Barry. I'm a veterinarian, not a people doctor."

He sees my confusion.

He leans close showing me the fine print beneath his name.

It says, 'Resident Service Program.'

"I'm a patient too…a psychiatric patient."

What?

"I tried to commit suicide a few weeks ago. I wanted to tell you, but was afraid you'd think less of me— think I'm crazy."

That's exactly what I think.

"My wife and baby died in this hospital. Four weeks ago, was the third anniversary of their death. Apparently, I tried to jump from the roof."

Shit! I've fallen for another crazy guy.

"I swear to God I have no memory of it. Please, believe me."

His eyes plead for my trust.

Yesterday, he told me I was beautiful.

I believed him.

Today, he's asking the same of me—to believe.

With all my soul, I make a decision.

"I blee oo."

"Thank you," he whispers, kissing my forehead with teary eyes.

Chapter 41

"RRRRRRRR"

An annoying wail hijacks my TV.

A robotic voice follows:

"The National Weather Service is tracking a severe hurricane sixty miles west of Haiti. Hurricane Jenise is moving north-northwest at 16 mph with sustained winds of 192 mph. Stay tuned for further updates."

"Don't worry, Roz. If things get nasty, we have an evacuation plan. You'll be outta here before the storm hits."

Joseph must have read my mind.

I'm scared.

The hospital is across the street from the Gulf of Mexico. This place would be a death trap.

He sits on my bed and stares thoughtfully out the window.

"I was living in New Orleans when Katrina hit in 2005. It was scary…killed my neighbor. A flying stick impaled his neck, stabbed him like an arrow."

Joseph, I don't want to hear these stories.

I flip him off, signaling 'no.'

He doesn't see my finger.

"Another guy was found in his car. The storm surge carried so much mud it buried him alive. When they found him, his throat was packed with mud like wet cement. Could you imagine dying like that?"

He glances at the clock.

"I could tell you more horror stories, but my shift is over. See you in the morning."

He smiles and leaves.

I close my eyes. All I see are dead people—a man speared with a stick, another strangled by mud.

Thanks, Joseph. I'll sleep like a baby with those images burned in my mind.

Chapter 42

Gargoyle just poked me again—the same shit she used a few nights ago. It burns in my vein with awful side effects.

Brain fog.

Paralysis.

Horrible nightmares…nightmares of Gavin raping me.

She just gave me the shot.

I already feel weird.

No focus. No physical strength.

"Rozlyn."

It takes every ounce of effort to open my eyes.

It's Dr. Barry…I mean David.

"How are you?" he whispers.

I give him a thumbs-up.

"No, tell me…how are you?"

Oh, yeah, we can talk.

"Gooin fin."

"You're doing fine?"

"Ya…bu willy sweepy."

"Really sleepy?"

"Umm hmmm."

My heart yearns to spend time with him, but I can't stay awake.

"Get some rest, Rozlyn. We'll talk tomorrow."

I don't know it, but he snuggles my blankets around me. He kisses my forehead. Though asleep, I moan. His kiss is magical. Even zoned-out, I'm aware of his beautiful soul.

When he leaves, his warmth goes with him.

It's immediately replaced by something cold and evil.

Another man is in my room.

He shakes my shoulder.

"Roz," he hisses.

I don't respond.

He pokes my wired jaw with a stiff finger. I groan with pain, but don't wake up.

He glances over his shoulder making sure the door is shut.

"Good job, Sova. I won't need this tonight."

He removes a small bottle and syringe from his pocket. He sets them on my food tray.

Using my bed controller, he adjusts the mattress until my feet slope downward like a child's slide. He untucks the blankets, flipping them to my waist. Grabbing my ankles, he drags my body toward him until his crotch is near mine.

He peels off my diaper and unzips his pants.

"Time to do the wild monkey dance," he whispers—the same creepy phrase Gavin's been saying in my nightmares.

Fumbling with his erection, he pats his pocket.

"Shit…forgot my condom."

He re-zips his pants.

"Hold that thought, honey. I gotta run to my car."

He hurries out the door.

Chapter 43

I just left Rozlyn.

I'm unsettled.

Something isn't right.

She seems drugged—dangerously drugged.

Maybe they gave her too much medication?

The elevator opens on the sixth-floor. It's not even midnight. Bart is gone—the stairway door propped open. I'm supposed to check-in at the end of my shift, but...

I hit the button to the fifth-floor. I want to check on Roz again.

When the elevator opens, I see a man running in the opposite direction. He looks like Bart. Skinny. Cropped haircut. Dark blue scrubs.

He disappears around a corner.

I don't think much of it till I see Roz's door gliding shut.

Was he in her room? Why is he running?

My gut tightens.

I rush to check on her.

"What the hell?"

Her blankets are bunched around her waist exposing her bare crotch. I quickly cover her. While straightening the blankets, I bump the food tray. A small bottle topples over.

The label says Ketamine.

I'm familiar with this drug. It's an anesthetic. I use it in my clinic to sedate animals before surgery.

The drug has a dark side.

On the street, Ketamine is called *special-K*.

Sexual predators use it as a date-rape drug—makes their victim unconscious with no memory of what happened.

"That son of a bitch!"

I rush out the door after Bart. When I near the corner where he disappeared, I hear voices. People arguing. Coming closer.

I glance at the bottle of Ketamine in my hand. Because of my suicide attempt, I was warned by the State Licensing Board not to touch any drugs for one year. If I violate the order, I'll lose my veterinarian license.

Fearing the ramification, I slip inside a janitorial closet and shut the door.

Two people, a man and woman, stop outside, whispering angrily.

"I wouldn't have taken the Ketamine from your stash if you would have done your job," the man hisses.

"I know what I'm doing," the woman snarls, her Russian accent adding to her anger.

"I'm paying you good money. I almost got caught the other night because you screwed up."

"Careful doorah (fool). Don't insult me. I once killed a pregnant woman for calling me a fucking gorilla. I wouldn't bat an eye killing you."

I almost scream at her words. She's talking about Angie. My wife didn't die from heart failure—she was murdered. Her killer is outside the door. It's the nurse who smiled at Angie as she struggled with labor pains.

"Don't threaten me, Sova. I'll go to the cops and expose your dirty little secrets…you've got a lot of them."

The service elevator 'dings' open.

Nothing more is said.

Footsteps walk away as the elevator glides shut.

I melt to the floor almost vomiting as I replays Sova's words.

"I once killed a pregnant woman for calling me a fucking gorilla."

She killed my wife and baby.

I struggle to stand.

I return to Rozlyn's room with a heavy heart.

With teary eyes, I tuck her blanket around her tiny frame.

I pull a stool close.

Weeping with anguish, I watch her sleep.

With a condom in hand, the rapist returns to finish his dirty deed.

He cracks Roz's door.

A man is sitting next to her on a tall stool.

Shit…probably a doctor, he frowns.

He slinks away unnoticed.

Chapter 44

5:45 a.m.

Roz is still asleep.

I kiss her cheek and head to the sixth floor.

I'm in trouble.

I've been gone all night. I needed to protect Roz.

The elevator opens.

"Where in the hell have you been?" Bart growls.

"I accidently fell asleep in the visitor's lounge after my shift."

His jaw tightens, but he nods with understanding.

"Don't let it happen again," he warns.

I'm surprised he's being so gracious.

I don't feel the same.

I swear Bart was the man running from Rozlyn's room.

It takes every ounce of self-control to walk by.

I want to beat his ass.

No, I want to beat him to death.

Tonight, I'm going to follow him.

I need to know.

Chapter 45

Bev has covid.

Two tests don't lie.

"Roz will understand," Sam says, throwing his suitcase in the car.

They were going to visit Rozlyn for the weekend.

Sam is going solo.

"I'll call when I get there."

He blows a kiss and drives away.

Bev is bummed. She doesn't feel bad, just a slight cough.

Still wearing her bathrobe, she plops on the couch and shuts her eyes. She barely dozes off when a loud crash startles her.

She rushes into the kitchen. Gavin is standing at the backdoor holding a carving knife. He forced his way in.

"Don't scream...don't even blink," he threatens. "I saw Sam leave. Now it's our turn. We're taking a little road trip to Louisiana."

Bev is terrified, but talks calm trying not to trigger Gavin's psychotic temper.

"Can I get dressed first?"

"Nope, your dressed fine. Grab your purse. Let's go."

They weave through the neighborhood to the main road. They're on I-75 southbound within twenty minutes. There's usually a lot of traffic. Not today.

"Set the cruise at 70 mph. I don't want any attention," Gavin snarls.

Bev obeys.

She tries to make small talk to ease the tension in the air.

"Have you ever been down south, Gavin?"

"Shut up and drive," he growls.

Leaning against the passenger door, he closes his eyes.

When they reach the Ohio border, Bev gradually picks up speed. She's hoping to get pulled over. She almost reaches 90 mph, when Gavin opens his eyes. He glances at the speedometer.

"Slow down!"

She takes her foot off the gas.

"Do that again, they'll find you dead in a ditch."

"Sorry, I need to find a restroom."

"Tough shit. Piss in your panties. I'll tell you when to stop."

Bev glances at the gas gauge. It's three-quarters full. It's the first time in her life she wishes she didn't own a Prius. With a full tank of gas, she can go nearly 600 miles before refueling.

Three tanks and they'll be in Louisiana.

Chapter 46

"I want my money back."

"What do you mean?"

"I didn't get my goods last night. A doctor was in her room."

"You're lying. There was no doctor on the floor all night."

"Maybe he wasn't a doctor, but some guy was with her. I didn't get what I paid for."

"Not my problem."

"You better work with me, Sova. I gave you $300 for nothing."

"I drugged her. I did my part."

He glares angrily, but she's unmoved.

"Tell you what, I'll eat the $300 if you arrange something special for me."

He looks over his shoulder and leans close.

"I want a boy...a young one."

Sova ponders his request.

"Let me see what I can do. Meet me outside the service elevator at midnight."

They part ways.

Pediatrics is on the second floor.

Lots of children.

Sova scouts the area searching for the perfect package.

She finds him in room 228.

Blonde hair, blue-eyes, seven-years-old.

He's getting his tonsils out.

He'll be groggy after surgery.

Sova will make sure he sleeps a little longer tonight.

Chapter 47

12:12 a.m.

"You're late," Sova growls.

"Got here as fast as I could."

"That's no excuse."

He ignores her rebuke and cuts to the chase.

"Did you find what I want?"

"Yes. It's gonna cost extra…$500."

"Why so much?"

"It wasn't easy to set up."

He digs in his pocket. Pulls out two condoms, a tube of chap-stick, and a wad of large bills.

He counts five $100s, shoving them in her hand.

"What room?"

"228."

A wicked grin grows on his face. He presses the call button for the elevator.

"Wait!" Sova says. "You need to wear a mask."

"I don't have one."

She gestures to 'wait a minute.'

Across from the elevator, she opens the janitorial closet. She pulls out a cleaning cart and grabs a N95 surgical mask.

Still grinning, he slips it on.

Sova steps beside him on the elevator.

"Are you going too?"

"Only to the third-floor…you're not my only client."

The elevator 'dings' shut.

Five minutes earlier.

Bart just strolled passed my room. He is about to disappear.

I hear the stairwell door click. I wait a few seconds and peek down the hall.

He's gone.

I hurry to the stairs. A flight below, a door clicks shut. I rush to the fifth floor.

Bart is half-way down the hall headed toward Roz's room. He is not wearing scrubs, but street clothes. I don't know how he changed so fast.

I start to yell his name, but he walks past her room disappearing around a corner.

I hurry to check on Roz.

She's awake. She gives me a happy thumbs-up.

"I can't stay tonight, Roz. I need to take care of something."

I give her a quick kiss and leave.

I jog to the corner where Bart disappeared.

Voices are talking around the corner. I wait in the adjacent hall not wanting to be seen.

The service elevator 'dings.' Their voices fade as the door glides shut.

I peek around the corner. No one is there—just an abandoned cleaning cart in the hall.

The floor indicator shows the elevator stopping at the third-floor.

I clench my fist. I'm determined to stop Bart.

I swear to God, he'll never touch Roz again.

Chapter 48

Crater's dive suit looks like a life-sized Buzz Lightyear costume. Clear bubble helmet atop a bulky armored suit. The outfit weighs about four-hundred pounds. It allows him to dive over a thousand-feet without decompressing when he resurfaces.

"Okay, Forrest, take me down," he says through a built-in radio.

Forrest nudges a joystick. It spools out a long cable connected to Crater's suit. This cable will lower him to the seabed and bring him up again.

Around 200 feet, Crater's world fades to an eerie gray.

At 350, twilight surrounds him.

Below 600, his world is pitch-black.

He settles on the seabed at 1040 feet.

His only source of light is a glow-bar attached to his chest. It's no brighter than a child's nightlight.

He taps a keypad on his wrist. It remotely activates two light stations staged on the ocean floor. They illuminate the area like a pair of miniature suns. Doesn't matter. There's nothing to see. The landscape is bleak like the surface of the moon.

"Okay, Forrest, drop the box."

Forrest hand-signals Punk and Patriot.

With thick gloves and lots of muscle they manhandle a cable bigger than a man's arm. They attach it to a contraption called a PLET. It looks like a windowless school bus.

This device will transfer oil from Alpha-3 to the main supply line once Crater joins them with a permanent weld.

With ten minutes to kill waiting for the PLET, Crater double-checks his welding equipment. It uses electricity, which seems weird considering he's underwater.

"The PLET is at 440," Forrest radios.

"Give me a shout when it's at a thousand. I'll watch for it."

Crater can only see about 60 feet in any direction, roughly the size of a tennis court. Beyond the lights there's nothing but hellish darkness.

Shuffling around the well-head, he positions the equipment. While humming to himself, one of the light stations dim to near darkness. He glances at the wrist controller thinking he bumped the brightness control.

It's full-on.

He turns to check the dulled spotlight.

His gut wrenches with fear.

A huge creature is passing by eclipsing the light. Looks like a pre-historic lizard, large and scaly.

"Forrest!" he pants.

"Yeah."

"Tell Vorcy to turn on the fish-finder. Something is down here…something big!"

"Crater, we're on a tight schedule. He's not going to waste time looking for a fish."

"This ain't no fish."

"Alright…if he chews my ass, you owe me a beer."

Forrest flips the radio to channel 4.

"Vorcy…do you copy?"

"Yeah...go ahead."

"Crater has a strange request. He wants you to pop on the fish-finder. He says something is swimming around down there...something big."

The fish-finder is not what you think. It's not used to locate schools of fish. It's a high-tech sonar providing real-time images of the ocean floor. They use it to stage equipment.

"We don't have time for this bullshit," Vorcy growls.

"He's not messing around...sounds scared."

Vorcy knows Crater. He's no sissy. If he's afraid, it's legit.

"Delany, power up the sonar."

She presses a few buttons. Her monitor illuminates. The display is like an ultra-sound, but clearer.

She focuses on Crater's location. They see him turning in a tight circle looking in every direction.

She widens the view. Dozens of fish are milling around. Nothing bigger than a few feet.

She expands the beam.

Just beyond the lights, a dark form is lurking in the shadows. She switches to infra-red to track its body heat.

"What in the hell is that?" she gasps.

Vorcy leans close.

"Clean up the resolution."

She clicks a few buttons. The image magnifies.

Vorcy has no idea what he's looking at. The creature looks like a mix between a crocodile and an eel. It's over forty-feet long, slithering away from Crater's location.

"Delany, keep your mouth shut. I'm going to tell him it was nothing. He needs to focus."

"That's a bad idea. He needs to watch his back."

Vorcy hates to admit it, but she's right.

"Forrest, patch me through to Crater."

His radio crackles with static.

"Crater...do you copy?"

"I hear ya,' Chief."

"Something was in the area, but moved away."

"What was it?"

"I have no idea. Just concentrate on your job."

"That's easy for you to say. You don't have T-Rex breathing down your neck."

"Crater, if I could trade places with you, I would."

"I know. Just keep your eyes peeled...please."

Chapter 49

A shrill scream echoes in the parking garage.

Not a scream of distress, but horror.

A mangled body is hanging from the service elevator. A man was crushed between the elevator carriage and concrete shaft—a space less than two-inches wide.

He wasn't cut in half, but close.

"How could this happen?" Detective Warnen of the State Police asks.

"I don't know. I need to look at the security footage," the maintenance supervisor says.

Tucked away in a small office, the two men review the film.

According to the time stamp, the man entered the elevator at 12:11 a.m.

At 12:18 a.m., the door opened.

The man, now wearing a surgical mask, teetered in the doorway. He dropped to his knees appearing to faint. When he fell, he grabbed the doorframe to steady himself. For some reason, the elevator surged upward with the door open. Caught in the pinch-point between the elevator shaft and carriage, he was fatally crushed by 8000 pounds of mechanical torque.

"I want to see the footage of every camera for this elevator," the detective says.

"There are no other cameras. It's a service elevator."

Warnen watches the film again.

"This doesn't look like an accident," he mutters.

Chapter 50

The glow of the welder is blinding.

Crater uses a dark visor to shield his eyes. When sparks are flying, his world is bright. When the welder stops, everything goes black—pitch black.

He keeps asking Vorcy about the sea monster. Vorcy saw it twice, but it never came close. He didn't tell Crater because he's already freaked out.

A PLET usually takes nine hours to connect if two men share the work. Crater has been underwater for ten.

He's cold and hungry.

At ten hours and fourteen minutes, he radios the rig.

"The PLET is secure. Give it a tug-test."

Forrest lightly bumps the control putting tension on the cable.

The PLET wriggles, but holds tight.

"The weld looks good. Let me disconnect the line."

The buoyancy in deep water makes the heavy cable easy to handle. Crater disconnects it himself.

"Take up the main."

The PLET cable ascends, disappearing in the dark water above him.

Scanning the area, he activates the glow-bar on his suit. He's reluctant to shut off the light stations. Once they're off, it'll be dark as Hades. He hopes T-Rex is not hiding in the shadows.

"I'm ready. Get me outta here."

Forrest nudges the joystick to take the slack out of Crater's cable. When his feet lift off the seabed, he taps the keypad on his wrist to kill the lights. He's never been afraid of the dark until now.

Delany and Vorcy sigh with relief. The mission is an hour ahead of schedule. While sharing a high-five, Delany sees movement on the sonar—a large object moving toward Crater.

"Shit! The monster is back."

Vorcy grabs the radio.

"Forrest, get Crater out of the water—now!"

He relays the message.

"Hang on, buddy, we're picking up the pace."

Before Crater can respond, his body jerks.

His rate of acceleration doubles.

So does the monster.

Spewing obscenities, Vorcy digs through his desk. He grabs something and runs out the door.

Delany is glued to her monitor.

The creature is at 484 feet.

Crater is at 370.

The small light on his suit is attracting the monster like a fishing lure.

Vorcy rushes down three flights of stairs to the main deck.

Crater is at 105.

The monster is at 117. It's closing in like a hot missile.

"Go full-throttle!" Vorcy shouts.

Forrest hammers the joystick.

Crater accelerates so fast he slightly vomits. He has no idea T-Rex is directly beneath him with its mouth gaped wide.

Like Iron Man soaring from the sea, he flies upward dragged by the cable. The creature erupts on his heels.

Releasing an angry bellow, it chomps down on Crater's legs below his knees. His titanium suit stops the creature from biting his legs off.

Dangling like a fish on a hook, the lizard thrashes and roars, refusing to give up its meal. Its weight is unbearable. Crater's body is about to snap in two.

Fighting for his life, he slaps the disconnect handles to release the lower-half of the suit. It separates at his waist, sliding off his legs like a bulky pair of pants.

As the creature falls away, canon fire fills the air. With dead-aim, Vorcy puts six rounds of hot lead in its skull with a .44 magnum.

Splashing into the sea, the monster sinks from sight, leaving a pool of blood on the surface.

Punk and Patriot rush to help Crater. They pull off the upper-half of his suit.

Shaking with adrenaline, he slaps his legs.

"Thank God, they're still there!" he pants.

They help him stand.

Vorcy elbows through the crowd. He scans Crater head to toe.

"You alright?"

"Yeah, but effective immediately, my dive pay is doubled."

"Hell no...it's tripled."

The two men laugh and hug as Patriot does what he does best.

"Dear Lord, thank you for keeping Crater safe, and thanks for blessing Vorcy with good aim. I'm sure that monster ain't gonna bug us again."

"AMEN!" they all shout.

Chapter 51

Sam is freaking out.

He's called Bev a million times. She's not answering her phone. In a panic, he calls his oldest daughter.

Darleen hurries to the house.

"Mom's car is gone! The back door is kicked open!"

"Darleen, don't go in…call the cops."

They arrive within minutes. With guns drawn, they cautiously enter through the shattered doorway. Other than the broken door, nothing looks disturbed.

Darleen rushes to her parent's bedroom. Mom always keeps her purse tucked behind the bed stand.

It's gone.

With few clues to work with the police issue an APB. They circulate Bev's picture and license plate to every law enforcement agency in the Tri-State area.

Chapter 52

An old Ford pickup rolls into the parking garage. It's in pristine condition—a trophy vehicle.

An old man wearing faded coveralls steps out. He retrieves an equally old toolbox from the bed of the truck.

"Do you know anything about elevators?" Detective Warnen asks.

The old-timer laughs.

"Sure do."

Bo Shemmer is black.

He's quiet and wise.

He's a maintenance man at the hospital. Not just any maintenance man. He's the guy who can fix anything.

"Elevators are like good whiskey," the old sage says. "Smooth going down...hell-fire comin' up."

"What does that mean?"

"Good whiskey slides down your throat like sweet butter. Burns like hell if you barf it up."

"I still don't understand what that has to do with elevators?"

"Elevators never fail going down...it's all gravity...smooth like butter. Going up, that's when all the gizmos get stupid. In the old days, it was just counter-weights and pulleys. Now-a-days, these things have more electronics than a spaceship."

"Do you have any idea why this elevator would ascend with the door open?"

Bo scratches his head.

"That's not supposed to happen. They have sensors."

"Well, you need to solve a mystery. This thing killed a man."

Bo opens his toolbox and grabs a flashlight. He shines the beam between the door panel and wall where the man was crushed. Organic goo is stuck to the frame. It's impossible to clean without taking the elevator apart.

"What are you looking for?" Warnen asks.

Bo doesn't answer.

He presses the 'door close' button. The panel glides shut. He stops it with his foot.

He shines the light on the opposite side of the door.

Nothing there except a quarter-sized optic disc.

He presses the button again. The door starts to close, but he stops it.

Digging in his toolbox, he pulls out a weird looking screwdriver.

"This control panel uses torx screws. Can't be opened without the right tool."

He jimmies the driver into the screw head.

"Righty tighty...lefty loosey," he mumbles.

His weathered knuckles turn white as he firmly grips the tool.

"Damn! That's tight."

Warnen steps into the elevator to watch.

Bo tries again. The screw doesn't budge.

Determined to win, he leans his weight against the tool. It slips. Falling forward, he rams his shoulder into the control panel. Without warning, the elevator jerks and accelerates upward with the door open.

"WHOA!" he shouts as several floors flash by.

The carriage jerks to a stop at the roof-level garden.

The two men rush out not knowing what the demon-possessed lift will do next.

"What in the hell did you do?" Warnen pants.

"Nothing...just fell against the—"

Bo stops mid-sentence.

"Wait a minute..." he mutters.

Without stepping inside, he slaps the control panel.

Nothing happens.

Peeking inside, he presses the 'garage' button.

The door slowly closes.

"Let's take the stairs."

Back in the parking garage, he presses the call button.

The elevator glides open.

"Wanna take another ride?"

Warnen reluctantly steps in.

"You might want to sit down," Bo suggests.

Warnen drops to his butt and grabs the rail.

"Get ready...you may shit your pants again."

Spreading his hand, he presses several buttons simultaneously. The elevator jerks and rockets to the roof-level again with the door open.

"I think I found your murder weapon. This thing has a bad circuit board."

The man's death wasn't foul play, just a freak accident.

Chapter 53

"RRRRRR"
My eyes shift to the idiot box.
A robotic voice drones.

"The National Weather Service has issued a hurricane warning for the entire Gulf region. Hurricane Jenise is currently five-hundred miles south of New Orleans moving north at 22 mph. Stay tuned for further updates."

The evening news continues.
I'm not paying attention.
I'm scared.
I've never been in a hurricane.
What if they don't evacuate me? I'm helpless.
As images of drowning haunt my mind, the news anchor says something that catches my ear.

"…the case is still on-going as police investigate Mersk's death. Mersk was a long-time employee at First Mercy Hospital. Details of his funeral have not been released."

I can't breathe.
Are they talking about my Joseph? My bundle of joy?
Gargoyle marches in.
She writes a big #16 with a red marker on my whiteboard.
"That is your exit number if we evacuate."

"Es Jof dead?" I pant.

She gives me a cold stare—I think she understood.

She leaves without a word. I don't know if she's heartbroken or heartless. She never shows emotion.

Shortly after midnight, David slips into my room.

He doesn't say anything, just forces a smile. He seems distant.

"Oo kay?"

"Yeah, I'm okay—just a lot on my mind."

He glances at the whiteboard.

"Number 16, huh? All the psych-patients are being shipped out on buses. I don't know if we'll be sent to the same facility."

Maybe that's why he's melancholy. We might be separated.

"I heard they're starting the evacuation tomorrow."

A tear dribbles from my eye. I don't want to be separated from David.

He read my mind.

"Don't worry, Roz. I'll find you."

God, I love this man!

"Was Joseph Mersk your nurse?" he bluntly asks.

More tears spill from my eyes.

He kisses my wet cheek, sharing my sorrow.

I cry harder.

His sympathy is heartwarming...so I think.

I know Roz is heartbroken about Mersk's death.

I couldn't be happier.

Justice was done.

She has no idea he was a sexual predator. He paid Sova several times to drug her so he could rape her.

122

I'll never tell.

Honestly, I feel bad about Bart. I was certain he was the rapists based on his looks until I saw Mersk's picture on the news. The two were doppelgangers. From a distance, they looked identical.

Mersk is gone, but another evil resides in the hospital—Sova, the monster who murdered my wife. I would have Angie's body exhumed to prove it, but she was cremated. At this point, it's just my word against Sova's.

Who would believe a psych patient over a reputable nurse?

Chapter 54

Bev rolls into La Rogue at 4 a.m.

She's been driving for twenty hours. They only stopped twice for gas and food.

"Over there," Gavin grunts, pointing toward a secluded parking lot.

She U-turns in the empty street and parks behind a dilapidated building.

"Get in back," he orders.

She squeezes over the center console into the backseat. Gavin follows. He throws his legs across her lap so she can't move. Within minutes, he's snoring. Bev never felt herself fall asleep.

"This ain't no campground," Marta grumbles.

A vehicle is parked behind her restaurant.

Strutting with attitude, she approaches the car. When she gets close the license plate catches her eye…Michigan.

In the thirty-eight-years she's owned the Crusty Crab, only one other car was parked behind her restaurant. It belonged to a troubled young woman named Rozlyn Muer.

Marta peeks inside the car.

Two people are sleeping in the backseat—a middle-aged woman wearing a bathrobe and a disheveled young man sprawled out like he owns the place.

Marta lightly taps the window near Bev's head. It startles her awake.

Gavin doesn't move.

Marta mouths, "Are you okay?"

Bev shakes her head 'no.'

Marta gives her an all-knowing nod and walks away.

"What the fuck you looking at," Gavin groans, stretching and yawning.

She was watching Marta go inside the restaurant.

"Nothing…I'm just hungry."

"Well, it's your lucky day. We're parked at a restaurant. The sign says *open*."

"I'm not dressed," she says, tightening the robe across her chest.

"We're in fuckin' Hicksville. They dress like that to get married."

Gavin shoves her purse in her hand.

"Get out…you're buying."

Walking in single file, he presses a knife against her back.

"Play nice or I'll kill ya."

A little bell tinkles above the door when it opens. The place is empty except for a burly woman wiping a counter.

"Mornin," she says with a bayou twang.

"Mornin," Gavin twangs back, mocking her.

The two women make eye contact.

"Sit where you like," Marta politely says.

"You got waffles?" Gavin grunts.

"Yep…strawberry, blueberry, or plain?"

"I'll take blueberry with coffee. The old lady will have the same."

They walk to the rear taking a corner booth. Gavin faces out so he can see everything. Bev sees nothing but his gaunt face and the wall behind him.

Marta walks with a limp carrying a pot of coffee and two cups.

"The waffles are cookin'…be about ten minutes."

She sets the cups and pours Bev first.

"Would you like some cream?"

Before she can answer, Gavin shoots off his mouth.

"She'll drink it black. Just get our damn food."

"No need to be rude, young man."

"Save the speech, Miss Manners. I'm hungry."

Marta smiles at Bev.

"Here in Louisiana, we call this Cajun hospitality."

Without looking, she dumps the entire pot of scalding coffee on Gavin's lap.

"You crazy bitch!" he screams, jumping to his feet.

As the word "bitch" leaves his mouth, Marta rams a baseball bat in his gut. He doubles over. She cracks his head, knocking him out.

She wasn't limping with an ailment. She had the bat tucked under her apron hiding it behind her leg.

"Oh my God! Thank you," Bev pants. "He kidnapped me two days ago—forced me to drive from Michigan."

When she mentions Rozlyn, Marta jerks with surprise.

"You know Roz?"

"She is my daughter. This is her ex-boyfriend."

Marta glances at Gavin's crumpled body. Roz told her all about this abusive asshole. She raises the bat. She wants to whack him again but knows she won't stop if she gets started.

"He's trying to find Roz. He wants to hurt her. Please call the police."

"Honey, this boy ain't worth callin' the po-leese. I'll deliver him myself."

Marta locks the front door and turns off the 'open' sign. She grabs a pair of rusty handcuffs hanging on a nail near the kitchen door. She fastens Gavin's wrists.

"My daddy escaped from Orleans Prison wearing these cuffs back in 1972. I knew they'd come in handy someday."

Without any help, she drags Gavin outside and piles him in the bed of her old pickup. Using a chain, she padlocks him to the roll bar.

"Those waffles should be done. Help yourself."

"Where are you taking him?"

"He's going to the courthouse. Enjoy your breakfast."

Chapter 55

Bev digs through her purse.

Her cellphone is almost dead.

She speed-dials Sam.

"Bev!" he pants.

"Sam…" is all she can say before tears choke out her words.

"Where are you?"

"I'm in La Rogue. Gavin kidnapped me."

She glances at the sign outside.

"I'm at a restaurant called the Crust—"

Her phone goes dead.

Sam screams her name, but gets dead-air.

He has no idea what's happening.

Shaking with fear, he calls 911.

"Please, help! My wife has been kidnapped. She just called from a restaurant in La Rogue called Crust."

"Sir, there are no restaurants in La Rogue by that name. The only similar listing is the Crusty Crab."

"All she said was 'Crust' and her phone went dead."

"I'll send a unit to check it out."

Within minutes, two police cars race into the parking lot.

Bev runs out to meet them.

"Are you Bev Muer?" an officer asks with his gun drawn.

She says nothing. Just drops to her knees, weeping.

He assumes the answer is 'yes.'

"Dispatch said you were kidnapped? Where's the kidnapper?"

Bev shakes her head, confused.

"He was taken to the courthouse."

"What courthouse?"

"I don't know. The woman said she was taking him to the courthouse."

"What woman?"

"An older heavy-set lady."

The two officers look at each other.

"Marta…" the older cop says.

"Where did she take the kidnapper?" the younger officer asks again.

"Some courthouse," Bev mumbles.

The two men look at each other and shrug.

They have no idea what she's talking about.

Chapter 56

"Delany, we ready?"

"Yup! Alpha-3 is snug as a bug. Let's get outta here."

The crew joke and chitchat while Vorcy calls Aircruze.

"Hello, this is Trident. We're ready to be picked up. What? You're kidding. What do you mean, *ride it out*? That's bullshit!"

Click.

Vorcy shakes his head.

"We got a problem. Aircruze won't send a chopper. They said Jenise is too close—they won't risk it."

The room is silent, except for Patriot.

"Dear Lord, please protect us."

"Amen," one or two mutter.

Rex Goodall has worked at Aircruze for eighteen months. He doesn't need the job...he's retired...he just loves to fly. Chiseled and fit, he's a phenomenal pilot. Over forty-years-experience, including two-hundred missions during the Iraqi war.

He overheard the conversation between Vorcy and Aircruze's owner Martin Sota. Sota is young, arrogant, and spoiled. Living off daddy's dime.

"Mr. Sota, have you ever been on an oil rig during a severe storm?"

"No."

"Have you ever been in a hurricane?"

"Nope."

"They're both scary."

"Yeah...so what?"

"We've got over an hour before the nasty weather hits. Why would you leave that crew stranded?"

"My choppers are valuable."

"More than a man's life?"

"Rex, I appreciate your concern, but we're not going."

"If you let me go, I could—"

"We're NOT going!" Sota snaps.

He rudely escorts Goodall to the door, locking it behind them.

"Stay safe, old man," Sota grins, shouldering passed him.

Goodall says nothing as they go their separate ways.

The weather over the Gulf is ominous.

Dark skies.

No wind.

Glassy water.

"It's the calm before the storm," Goodall mutters as he climbs into his SUV.

He starts the engine, but doesn't move. The approaching storm reminds him of another storm years ago...Desert Storm...the coalition war against Iraq in the early 1990s.

Something happened during the war that changed Goodall's life. An event seared in his mind. He remembers every detail as if it happened yesterday.

Staring at the black sky, he drifts away in deep thought.

I was twenty-nine. A chopper pilot in the U.S. Army—a medevac unit. Tony Trist, my partner, was the PIC (pilot in command). He was twelve weeks from retirement.

Tony laughed a lot. Swore a lot. A gutsy pilot. He'd fly into Hell without batting an eye to save a wounded soldier.

He was a hoot to work with. Never said anything straight, always colorful riddles. For example, if he wanted a shot of whiskey, he'd say, "I'll take a short shit with a big hit." Bartenders would laugh as they set him up with a stiff drink.

It took about four months before I could quickly translate Tony's cryptic nonsense.

The war in Iraq was raging.

We flew dozens of missions together.

August 12th, 1990 was the day that changed my life.

As we flew over the hot sand of the Al-Hajarah desert, Tony was filling my ears with a string of brainteasers.

"We got two clients forty clicks inside the oven," he said over the headset.

Translation…we needed to fly forty miles behind enemy lines to retrieve two wounded soldiers.

He always called injured soldiers "clients."

It was a sign of respect.

"RECON says we got lots of mosquitos. They'll be biting our ass before we hit pay-dirt."

There would be a lot of enemy gunfire between us and our destination.

"We'll ride the camel's ass into the fort then find a good radio station."

Translation: We'll fly low to avoid enemy radar. When we reach the city of Fallujah, we'll locate the injured soldiers using a homing transmitter. It'll take us right to them.

The first thirty miles were quiet. When Fallujah appeared on the horizon, all hell broke loose. Gunfire slammed the underside of our armor-plated Black Hawk as we passed over enemy bunkers. Some hit so hard it jarred our teeth.

Tony always called me, "Good-Boy."

"Good-Boy, if I had a few burritos in my gut, I'd fart all over those sand fleas," he growled.

He wished he had some bombs in the cargo bay to drop on the insurgents.

"These bastards look hungry. Let's give them a sand-witch."

We were already flying low when Tony tilted the chopper forward. The rotors nearly scraped the earth creating a blinding sand storm. A few stray bullets hit the chopper, but it was blind luck...no pun intended.

When we reached Fallujah, bullets ricocheted off the chopper's windshield. Snipers nested on rooftops were trying to put bullets in our head. Thank God the glass was bullet-proof.

"Find our clients," Tony said.

I activated the homing system. A beacon locked on to a location a quarter-mile east.

"Straight ahead," I pointed.

Tony nearly clipped several buildings as he dodged and weaved to avoid gunfire.

On a small isolated roof a squad of soldiers were hunkered down. Tony hovered, scanned the landing zone, and dropped fast.

"Go get em', Hercules," he said to the medic.

A muscular young man with massive arms bolted from the chopper. He manhandled not two, but four clients onboard.

"Shit! I didn't expect this much company."

Tony wasn't prepared to transport the extra soldiers. The added weight was an issue.

"We gotta tickle the clouds to get out of here."

We needed to fly high. The chopper was too sluggish to maneuver at low altitude.

The medic jumped in and slammed the door.

"Go! Go! Go!" he shouted.

Tony hammered the throttle, climbing straight up.

Gunfire pelted us from every direction.

We banked west and accelerated.

"Tony! We got another beacon a half-mile north."

More soldiers needed help.

He glanced over his shoulder, calculating the weight of the four clients, plus the chopper's fuel.

"We'll be dragging ass, but I'll make it work."

He turned north. As we raced low over the city, the window near Tony's shoulder shattered. Bullets peppered the dashboard, destroying the radar and radio.

We flew blind looking for the clients.

We spotted them pinned down on a narrow street between two bombed-out buildings. Tony never flinched as he dropped into the tight opening, sliding between the buildings like a letter in an envelope.

It was a three-for-three situation. Three soldiers, all wounded…no one to provide cover-fire against the enemy.

The medic jumped out.

He was immediately cut down by a spray of bullets.

"You sand sucking bastards!" Tony screamed as he hurried from the chopper.

He dragged the medic inside.

Zigzagging, he ran toward the injured soldiers. He helped two get aboard. When he turned to help the third, an explosion shook the ground. A mortar hit twenty feet away. It blew Tony's right arm off.

Swearing at the top of his lungs, he assisted the remaining soldier, forcing him to sit up front in the pilot's seat.

"Get em' home, Good-Boy…get em' home!"

Those were Tony's last words before he dropped dead.

Our medic was severely wounded, but jumped out. He slung Tony over his shoulder as bullets whizzed by. Covered with blood, he dumped Tony's body inside the chopper. He wasn't gentle, but refused to leave him behind.

"Get us outta here!" he screamed, clinging to the door.

I froze, staring at the controls. I was scared. The lives of these men were in my hands.

Tony's spirit must have been lingering in the cockpit because I heard something very 'Tony-esque.'

"Peter Pan ain't no man if you take his Peter away."

That was Tony's way of saying, "MAN UP!"

A gush of adrenaline shot through me.

I became hyper-focused. Every sight and sound was amplified.

I lifted-off as bullets rattled the chopper.

I had no radio. No radar. Just a simple compass.

West was the way home.

Facing the sun, I flew dead-reckoning toward the blazing orange ball as it sank in the desert sand.

Artillery exploded all around.

By the grace of God, we stayed airborne.

With no ability to communicate with ground control I had to rely on my instincts to get us out of the city. As I beelined over rooftops, a weird phrase echoed in my head…Tony's lingo.

"You better dance like you need to piss your pants…you're an easy target."

In other words, don't fly straight. I needed to bob-n-weave to avoid anti-aircraft weapons.

Just as I veered from my intended path, a rocket sizzled past the chopper. It missed by inches.

"Thanks Tony!"

I landed at a combat support hospital an hour later.

It was the longest flight of my life.

Medics hauled everyone away.

I didn't leave the chopper for a long time. Just sat there staring at Tony's empty seat. As I hung my head still shaking, I heard his voice one more time. No riddle. No cryptic nonsense.

"Goodall, as long as you can fly, don't let anyone die."

His words pierced my heart.

They became my mantra.

I flew 116 missions after Tony's death. I was shot down twice, wounded four times, but saved 477 soldiers.

A flash of lightning followed by an angry roar of thunder disrupts Goodall's thoughts.

He shakes his head, returning to the present.

Jenise is getting close.

The water is choppy.

The wind stiff.

The sky darkening to an eerie shade of gray.

The crew trapped on the oil rig is heavy on Goodall's mind.

"As long as you can fly, don't let anyone die," Tony whispers.

"Yes, Sir."

Chapter 57

Sota squeals from the parking lot. He heads north on Highway 55. There's no traffic. With the hurricane looming two-hundred miles away, everyone evacuated hours ago.

Setting his cruise control at 90 mph, he cranks up the stereo of his 700 Series Mercedes. With the radio blaring, he can't hear his cell phone buzzing on the passenger seat.

Drumming his fingers to some nasty rap band, he pulls a fat joint from the breast pocket of his Armani suit.

One hit and he's floating. It's good stuff.

He glances in the rear-view mirror.

"You handsome son-of-a-bitch," he grins.

He grabs his phone to take a selfie.

The screen is cluttered with text messages from a security app.

ALERT...2:06pm—Aircruze office door ajar.

ALERT...2:24pm—Aircruze hanger accessed.

ALERT...2:28pm—Aircruze vehicle in motion.

Sota calls the cops.

The door at Aircruze was solid, but Goodall's foot was stronger. The wall safe was locked, but poorly built. He pounded off the hinges with a fire extinguisher.

He grabbed the keys to Aircruze 77—the chopper he regularly flies.

The airport is empty. Most of the planes have flown north. Those that remain are locked in hangers.

Goodall enters the passcode to Aircruze's hanger.

Heavy double doors roll open.

He fires up a sleek Bell 429.

The fuel tank is topped out.

He hovers from the hanger and rises. Turning south, he heads into the black sky.

As he accelerates over the Gulf, a stream of police cars race onto the runway.

"Goodall, get your ass back here or you're fired!" Sota screams over the radio.

Goodall chuckles as he turns it off.

"Fired? I'm probably going to prison. Breaking and entering. Stealing an aircraft. Not to mention I'm parked in a handicap zone."

He doesn't care. He knows God will forgive his misdemeanors. He couldn't live with himself if he left the Trident crew behind.

"As long as you can fly, don't let anyone die," he whispers.

Chapter 58

Vorcy and his team are in his office sharing an unauthorized bottle of Scotch. Liquor is prohibited on the rig.

"You were right, Vorcy. Jenise is ahead of schedule," Forrest says, knowing the hurricane is less than an hour away.

"I've seen some nasty storms...this one will top them all."

"How do you know?"

Vorcy takes a swig of Scotch and tilts his chair.

"When Crater was yanked from the sea, I noticed the water currents were flowing south toward Jenise."

"Yeah, so what?"

"The wind is blowing west."

"And?"

"Jenise is so strong she's sucking the sea into her lungs. She's gonna hit us with some big waves. Might flip the rig."

Everyone is silent as they digest his words.

"Trident...this is Aircruze 77...anyone home?"

Vorcy cocks his head and grabs the radio.

"This is Trident...did you change your mind?"

"No, Sota is back on shore shitting his pants. I borrowed one of his birds without permission."

"What's your name, Sir?"

"Rex...Rex Goodall."

"Mr. Goodall, you've got half-a-dozen people ready to buy you a drink."

"Sounds great, but let's get home first. My radar shows a wall of destruction fifty miles south. I'm still thirty miles north fighting a stiff headwind. It's gonna be a race to see who gets there first."

Chapter 59

Marta stops her truck on a lonely two track. She's surrounded by endless miles of swamp.

"Your ass is going to prison," Gavin snarls. "This is kidnapping."

Marta belly laughs.

"You got that ass-backward…you're the criminal, not me."

She grabs the chain to unlock it. He spits in her face, calling her every name in the book. Without a word, she wipes drool off her cheek and grabs her bat. Cussing and cowering, Gavin shields his head. She waylays him several times, knocking him cold.

Dragging his limp body from the truck, she dumps him in the bow of an old row boat. She climbs in and starts the outboard. The motor coughs and sputters as she pushes from shore.

She checks the gas tank.

It's half-full.

"That'll work," she mutters.

Humming an old Cajun tune, she weaves through a labyrinth of haunting mangroves decorated with tendrils of Cyprus moss. A lingering mist over the water adds to the eeriness.

Gavin jerks awake with his hands still cuffed.

"I'll set you free. Do something stupid, I'll knock you out and throw you overboard," Marta says with no emotion.

He scowls, but keeps his mouth shut.

She removes the cuffs, slipping them in her shirt pocket.

They travel for miles, meandering deep into the swamp.

Around midday, she grounds the boat on a lonely mound of dirt in the middle of nowhere. It's surrounded by twisted roots and murky water.

"Get out."

Gavin cusses, but obeys.

"The water is not deep. You can wade back in the morning. Maybe you'll have a better attitude by then."

"You lard ass, you're gonna pay for this."

Marta shakes her head.

"One day you're gonna meet someone with a bigger mouth than yours. You ain't gonna like it."

"You have no idea who you're fucking with lady."

"Push me out," she demands, ignoring his threat.

She drifts about ten feet.

"On second thought, here's a lantern in case you start back today. You won't make it far before dark."

She tosses an old dime store flashlight. It splashes in the water just off shore. Gavin steps in to pick it up, but plunges over his head. Clawing to the surface, he gasps for air.

"You lying bitch! This water is deep."

By the time he crawls onto the mound, Marta is gone.

Chapter 60

"We enhanced the resolution—got lots of detail."

Warnen takes a seat in the forensic lab.

The technician loads a video on her computer.

It's enhanced footage of the elevator accident.

It's graphic.

It shows a man being crushed in slow motion. It's amazing how solid, yet soft the human body is. When the elevator ascended, it momentarily stalled as the man became trapped at the pinch-point. When his body started to compress, he slid into the two-inch gap like he was made of butter.

Splintered bones, blood, guts splattered everywhere.

"Where are his personal belongings?" Warnen asks, unfazed by the video.

"In number seven."

He slips on a pair of rubber gloves and pulls a tote from locker 7. Poking through the clothes, he examines the garments. Dried chunks of internal organs are embedded in the fabric. If he had a weak stomach he'd puke.

Inside the tote is a tray of miscellaneous items. A tube of Chap-stick. Two condoms. A wad of cash.

Lying next to them is a surgical mask sealed in a zip-lock bag.

He takes it out.

"Don't touch that, we haven't analyzed it yet," the tech says.

He ignores her.

There's a powdery residue on the mask. It sticks to his rubber glove.

Curious, he slips on his reading glasses to get a better look.

"When will you analyz—"

Before he finishes his sentence, he withers to the floor.

The tech rushes over.

"Detective Warnen, what's wrong?"

He doesn't answer.

His eyes are glazed over. He's not breathing.

She calls for help, afraid he's having a heart attack.

An off-duty officer rushes in.

"What happened?"

"He was looking through the victim's belongings and collapsed."

The officer checks his pulse. It's weak.

His pupils are fixed and dilated.

He sees a powdery substance on Warnen's glove.

"He overdosed!"

The officer hurries from the room. He returns with Narcan…medicine to reverse an opioid overdose.

He shoves the applicator up Warnen's nose, pumping several blasts.

"He should come around in a minute."

The tech holds her breath.

Moments later, Warnen stirs and opens his eyes.

"What happened?" he mumbles.

"You OD'd."

"I told you to leave the mask alone!" the tech scolds.

"Sorry, I was curious."

Warnen is taken to the hospital.

He's released within the hour.

According to the lab report, he ingested fentanyl. A few particles can kill a man.

Warnen now knows why the victim fainted in the elevator. He was poisoned.

His killer knows something about drugs and how to use them.

Chapter 61

Jenise is evil.

Raging winds have created monstrous waves— some higher than Trident's main deck.

Flying low, Goodall uses the valleys between the waves as wind-breaks. Through a rain-soaked windshield, he sees Trident bouncing on the horizon.

"Trident, I'm here, but got a problem. I can't land on the helipad. It's too windy."

Flying around the rig, he searches for another option. On the west side between decks 2 and 3 he sees a tight opening. He can land, but he'll have to come straight in like parking in a garage.

"Trident, go to the west side—level 2."

"We're on our way," Vorcy shouts over a walkie-talkie.

Struggling against the wind, they move down four flights of stairs.

Goodall sees them coming.

Punk and Delany are leading the pack.

"Stay back. I'm coming in to land."

Vorcy says something. It's all static.

"Trident, I repeat…stay back."

Vorcy shakes his head '*no*,' signaling for Goodall to stop.

Something is wrong.

Vorcy points into the water.

Goodall backs away and tilts the chopper.

Two bodies are bobbing in the sea. It's Punk and Delany. They were washed overboard when a huge wave rocked the rig.

The situation looks bad, but Goodall sees a blessing. The waves are pushing them away from the rig. If he hovers low, they could grab the skids beneath the chopper.

"I'll drop down and get them," he radios.

Vorcy says something, but the wind snuffs out his words.

Goodall starts to descend.

The crew frantically wave, motioning to be picked up first. Goodall doesn't want to lose sight of the bodies in the water, but yields.

He tries several times to land, but it's impossible. The rig is pitching and jerking in every direction.

Turning sideways, he hovers close. Patriot grabs the door. It slides open like a mini-van.

Like trained commandos the men dive aboard.

Patriot hops on last.

"Hold tight, we're going down!" Goodall shouts.

With the door still open, he drops low.

The power of the sea is punishing. Delany is struggling to keep her head above water. Huge swells are tossing her like a tiny human cork. Fear and fatigue are zapping her strength.

She thinks she's alone until a strong arm grabs her waist.

"I gotcha, sweet cheeks!" Punk shouts over the roaring waves.

She's in disbelief. Even in their dire situation he's an arrogant ass. Despite his condescending attitude, she is amazed by his strength. He's holding her tightly against his chest with one arm—keeping them afloat with the other. Above all, he's remarkably calm. His confidence is comforting.

She throws her arms around his neck holding him tight.

Patriot shouts instructions to Goodall.

"Go left…more...down…more…more…STOP!"

Leaning out the door, he snatches Punk's arm. With the strength of a grizzly, he manhandles both aboard at the same time. They collapse side-by-side on a bench next to the bulkhead.

Forrest removes his jacket and drapes it over Delany's shoulders. Soaked and shivering, she looks at Punk with gratitude.

"Thanks for the hug, sweet cheeks. Maybe next time we can cuddle a bit longer," he says with a sexy grin.

She can't help but smile. His flirty nature is charming.

"We're all set!" Patriot shouts, slamming the door shut.

Even with the door closed it's impossible to hear. The wind is deafening.

Goodall banks north.

He doesn't go far before turning back.

"The storm is too strong. We'll never make it."

He tries several times to land between decks 2 and 3 but Trident is bucking like a rodeo bull.

147

"The helipad is my only option."

He can land on rough seas using a device called a bear-trap. There's only one problem…

"The trap isn't set," Patriot yells. "Do you have any rope?"

"Got some tie-downs under the seat."

He opens a utility box and removes two straps, each about forty-feet long.

"If you hover over the pad, I'll climb out and set the trap."

"No, I'll go," Punk insists.

He's the best choice. Patriot is stronger, but Punk is more agile.

Goodall hovers at twenty-feet. He can't get any closer. The rig is oscillating too much.

"This is the best I can do."

Patriot secures the strap around Punk's chest. He knots the other end around his own waist acting as an anchor.

When he opens the door, Jenise assaults the crew with a blast of angry wind and rain.

Punk scoots toward the exit. He winks at Delany as he wriggles by.

"A kiss for luck?" he teases.

Surprisingly, she plants a big one on his lips.

He slides out the door smiling.

Patriot slowly lowers him. Instead of dropping straight down the wind blows him sideways like a shirt flapping on a clothes line. Patriot gives more slack, but Punk continues to drift away from the bear trap.

"You gotta get lower," he shouts.

Goodall has flown in a lot of nasty weather—thunderstorms, blizzards, even heavy gunfire in war, but he's scared. He's afraid Punk will be crushed between the chopper and the helipad if the rig bounces in the wrong direction.

Pushing fear from his mind, he stares straight ahead. He focuses on the framework of the rig. Seemingly hypnotized, he moves the chopper side to side mirroring the rhythm of the raging sea. Within a minute, the chopper and rig are moving in unison.

He inches down.

Down.

Down.

"He's on the deck!" Patriot shouts.

Goodall nods, but continues to stare straight ahead maintaining his focus.

Unable to stand in the driving wind, Punk belly-crawls beneath the chopper. He needs to do three things to set the bear trap.

-Remove the safety bar.

-Spread the jaws.

-And get the hell out of there.

If the chopper sets down before he's clear, the trap will cut him in half.

He removes the safety bar. A gust of wind tears it from his hand. It disappears in the sea.

He crawls over the trap and grabs the jaws. Straining and swearing, he spreads the metal clamps. With a heavy *click* they lock in place. He's surprised by his strength. It usually takes two men with crowbars to set the trap.

"Adrenaline is amazing," he mutters.

He crawls from beneath the chopper.

He reaches for Patriot's hand. Before their fingers touch, the mother of all waves hits.

It tilts Trident nearly 40°.

She'll capsize at 45°.

Punk tumbles across the deck. He falls over the edge. The strap around Patriot's waist draws taut. He locks his arms against the door struggling not to get yanked out.

Forrest and Crater jump to help. As they reach for Patriot, the chopper lurches. It throws them toward the door.

Vorcy grabs their ankles to keep them from falling out.

"God, help!" Patriot screams.

Goodall glances over his shoulder. The crew is a tangled mess dangling out the door.

With lightning reflexes, he steers over the trap. Trimming the rotors, he kills the engine. The chopper drops like a rock. It slams hard on the pad. The trap snaps shut with an aggressive 'bang.'

"Thank you, God-all!" Patriot shouts, tongue-tied trying to say 'Thank you, God,' and 'Thank you, Goodall.'

"I'm not God, but glad to help," Goodall grins.

Chapter 62

The afternoon passes slowly.

With nothing to do but wait, Gavin's thoughts are consumed with revenge.

That bitch is going to regret the day she met me.

He wants to torture Marta.

I'm gonna chain her to the bumper of her truck—drag her for miles—let asphalt and gravel peel about forty pounds of flesh off her fat ass.

A boom of thunder disrupts his evil vision.

The sky is dark and angry like his mind.

The humidity is suffocating.

Hot and thirsty, Gavin kneels at the water's edge. He scoops a handful of swamp water. He sees sediment, but no bugs. He samples it with his tongue. It tastes earthy, but tolerable. Crouching like a dog, he sucks several mouthfuls to quench his thirst. He has no idea he ingested thousands of parasites. Within twenty-four hours, diarrhea will be his worst enemy.

The sun was never visible, but obvious when it set. The veil of night turns the swamp into a house of horrors. Shrill screams. Moaning beasts. Billions of biting insects.

Afraid of unseen demons, Gavin turns on the flashlight. It's pitifully dim.

"Piece of shit," he mutters.

Pissed off, he hurls it in the water. It makes a small splash, but unleashes a chain reaction of reckless motion like he startled several creatures hiding in the water.

Startled by the commotion, he nervously backs away from the water's edge. He can't go far. The mound is no bigger than the rooftop of a tiny house.

It's not raining, but lightning is strobing like a rock concert. Each time it flashes, he sees a momentary burst of the landscape.

The mangroves look scary. Their twisted limbs look like bony creatures lurking in the water. Amid the flashes, he sees long ropes hanging from their branches. With the outdoor skills of a city-slicker, Gavin has no idea the dangling ropes are water moccasins. They're not big. Four feet at best, but their bite is deadly.

He also sees reflective dots scattered across the water—hundreds of them. Most are small. Nickel-sized. A few are larger. Golf ball-sized. During one prolonged flash, he sees a set of dots bigger than baseballs. When the lightning strobes again, the huge dots are gone.

The dots are alligator eyes. Gavin never saw any during the day. Nighttime is when they hunt the swamp.

Droning like a symphony of netherworld demons, the gators growl and groan. One growl sounds frighteningly deep like Godzilla purring.

When the sky illuminates, Gavin looks in every direction trying to locate the monster. He sees nothing, just hundreds of reflective dots surrounding the tiny island.

Godzilla growls again. He sounds close.

Gavin turns toward the source and waits. When angry shards light up the sky, he nearly shits his pants.

A huge gator has joined him on the mound. Its craggy body is weathered and scarred—over sixteen-feet long—it's head nearly three-feet wide.

Terrified, Gavin backs away until his foot squishes in the mud. One more step and he'll be in the water.

Something hisses near his head. He swings his arm. A dangling snake tangles around his wrist. It bites him several times. Thrashing to escape the viper, he slips. Before his butt hits the ground, Godzilla charges.

Strobing lightning illuminates the attack.

With its jaws spread wide, the giant reptile chomps down on Gavin's torso. Without slowing down, it lunges into the swamp. Diving deep, the thousand-pound killing machine tumbles in a death roll.

Marta's prophecy came true…Gavin met someone with a bigger mouth than his.

As nighttime creatures croon their haunting dirge, Godzilla lumbers onto the mound. He releases Gavin's body. Grabbing a single leg, he viciously tears the limb from the corpse. Rearing his head, he swallows the chunk in one gulp.

Dozens of gators gather to feast.

The alpha refuses to share.

Ignoring the angry sky, he digests Gavin's body piece by piece till nothing is left.

Bloated with flesh, he slides into the murky water. Gliding past a community of hungry spectators, Godzilla sinks from sight. At that moment, angry claps of thunder shake the ground like a giant gavel.

The Cajun court found Gavin Butler guilty of crimes against humanity. His sentence…death.

Thunder pounds again.

Court is adjourned.

Chapter 63

Southern hospitality is like no other.

The two officers sit with Bev for hours waiting for Sam to arrive.

He finally arrives in an Uber. When they reunite, the policemen share their joy. Nine times out of ten, kidnappings don't have happy endings.

After chatting with Sam, the officers wrap things up.

"It's getting late. We'll come back later to interview Marta," the older policeman says.

As they head for the door, Marta drives up in her old pickup.

Bev rushes to greet her.

"Thank God you're here. I told the police you took Gavin to the courthouse, but didn't know which one."

Marta, with bat in hand, smiles at the older cop.

"Wayne, want some pie before you hit the road?"

"I'd never say no."

The older policeman is Wayne Pettit. He grew up with Marta in a sleepy hollow east of La Rogue. They've been friends their entire life…over sixty years.

Everyone follows Marta inside.

She places the bat on a shelf like a prized trophy.

Digging in her pocket, she hangs the rusty handcuffs on a nail near the kitchen door.

The policemen take a seat at the counter bar. Bev and Sam join them. Chatting about the weather, Marta cuts a full pie in equal pieces. She gives a generous slice to everyone with a cup of hot coffee.

"Can I go *à la mode?*" the younger cop asks.

Wayne slaps the back of his head like a grumpy dad.

"Hell no! You ain't gonna ruin this pie."

"Thanks, Wayne. I was gonna smack him myself if you didn't," Marta says.

Everyone chuckles.

"So, where did you take Gavin?" Sam asks.

"He went to the Cajun courthouse," Marta says, slurping her coffee.

Wayne swallows hard, forcing a chunk of pie down his throat.

"You didn't?" he says with wide eyes.

"Sure did."

Wayne knows all about the Cajun courthouse. Some of Louisiana's most notorious criminals have gone there.

"Marta, I ought to arrest you for murder."

Everyone stops mid-bite and stares at Wayne.

"This pie is a killer," he grins, shoving another forkful in his mouth.

Marta gives him a playful wink.

Felix, the newbie on the police force is still confused about the courthouse.

"Where's the Cajun courthouse? I've never heard of it."

"It's in Terrebonne," Wayne says.

"Isn't Terrebonne a swamp?"

"Yeah, but it's got a nice courthouse. The judge is tough. What's his name, Marta? Judge…Croc-jaw?" he asks.

Marta snickers.

"No, I think it's Al…the Honorable Al Gator," she counters.

156

Wayne nearly spits his coffee, laughing.

"He'll eat ya' up if you make him mad," Marta adds.

Wayne nearly falls off his stool, cackling.

"I'm not sure what's so funny, but will they contact us about Gavin's trial?" Bev asks.

"I don't know. Some guys get swallowed up in the system—never make it to trial," Marta says with a dead-pan expression.

Wayne, beet-red with laughter, begs her to stop.

Chapter 64

The rig is pitching and jerking like a rollercoaster. The helipad is on the top deck, magnifying the violent motion.

Unable to talk over the roaring wind, everyone is lost in their own head.

Crater is thinking about the sea monster that tried to eat him.

Vorcy is still pissed at the bigwigs for waiting to evacuate.

Patriot is reading his pocket Bible, while Forrest and Goodall take a nap.

Delany is staring straight ahead, her eyes locked on Punk. He's seated across from her with his eyes closed. She knows he's not asleep. He occasionally opens his eyes and looks around.

Ten hours ago, she thought he was an egotistical jerk.

She feels different now.

She has no doubt he saved her life when they were washed overboard. The moment he grabbed her waist and pulled her close she felt safe. Honestly, the event is seared in her mind. His embrace was powerful. His body rock-solid like a Greek statue. As she clung to his neck it felt…erotic.

She still feels weird about that.

Their lives were in jeopardy, but she was getting aroused like something sexual was happening between them. Maybe it was the raw power of nature? Maybe it was Punk's dangerous good looks. Whatever it was, she wants to experience it again.

Every time I open my eyes, Delany is staring at me. I feel uncomfortable. I started out on the wrong foot this morning. Came across as an arrogant ass calling her 'sweet cheeks.'

A poor first impression.

I was nervous. I've been watching Delany for months—a secret crush. Rig grunts typically don't rub shoulders with tech-people. It's like a brain surgeon mingling with a ditch digger—not a lot in common.

I remember the first time I saw her. We rode on the same transport chopper to the rig. She had her nose glued to her laptop the entire time. I tried to make small-talk, but she was cold. Until today, I don't think she knew I existed.

I admit, getting washed overboard was…awesome! When she held onto me it felt right, like she belonged in my arms.

I'd like to cuddle her again.

Chapter 65

At 3:26 p.m., the angry weather abruptly stops.

Sunlight beams through the windows.

The rig continues to sway from the energy of the waves, but everything is calm.

"Welcome to the eye of Jenise," Goodall says.

It's an amazing sight. A giant stadium built by towering wall-clouds. It's capped with a clear blue sky. Even seagulls are soaring in the placid haven.

"This is our ticket home. We'll fly inside the eye to the mainland."

"That's a great idea," Forrest says.

"Don't breathe easy yet. Deadly weather can spawn inside the eye. We need to watch for tornados and wind-shear."

"That's not a problem...we got Vorcy. He can read the sky better than any weather satellite."

"Hop up front," Goodall says. "I could use a set of keen eyes."

Vorcy slides into the co-pilot seat and buckles up.

"The storm is moving at 26 mph. That's our speed."

Goodall fires up the chopper.

Patriot opens the door. Punk jumps out and releases the bear-trap. He's back onboard in less than a minute. He plops down in Vorcy's empty seat next to Delany. He shares a flirty smile. She grins...actually blushes.

There's no doubt, there's chemistry between them.

Goodall lifts off and heads north.

Chapter 66

Marta turns on the TV.
Nothing but hurricane updates.

"Jenise is currently one-hundred-twenty-six miles south of Louisiana. She's projected to come ashore within six hours. The Governor has issued a mandatory evacuation for everyone in the Gulf region," a news anchor says.

"Bev, we need to check on Roz before they make us leave."

"Too late," Wayne says. "All traffic into La Rogue was cut off an hour ago."

Bev cries.

Sam is unable to console her.

Marta glares at Wayne.

"Can't you do something?" her eyes scold.

Overcome with guilt, he caves in.

"Alright…I'll take them in my patrol car," he mumbles.

"I want to see Roz, too!" Marta blurts.

"Sure, the taxi is leaving in two minutes," Wayne grumbles, visibly annoyed.

Marta leans over the counter and kisses his cheek.

"You're my hero."

He scowls at her compliment.

With lights and sirens blaring, they race to the hospital. When they arrive, emergency vehicles are parked everywhere.

"You gotta make this quick. They're evacuating."

"We'll be back in fifteen minutes."

The trio hurry into the hospital. They take the elevator to the fifth floor. Bev leads the way into Roz's room. When Roz sees her mother, she bursts into tears.

Sam was with Roz when Bev's kidnapping came to light. Roz has been praying non-stop for her mother's safety. She knows Gavin is a violent man.

"I'm okay, baby," Bev says, embracing Roz with a tight hug.

Sam steps close. He gives his girls a 'group hug.'

Roz glances at the door. Marta is smiling ear-to-ear.

"Gamma!" she squeaks.

Three months ago, these two were strangers. Roz now calls her "Grandma."

Bev and Sam step aside.

Marta devours Roz's tiny frame in a momma-bear hug. She briefly saw her after the accident. She was still in ICU, unconscious, a broken bloody mess.

"You look great!" Marta says, marveling at her progress.

"Tak oo, Gamma."

Marta glances over her shoulder. Bev and Sam are talking in the corner. She leans close and whispers in Roz's ear.

"Just between you and me, your ex-boyfriend is gone. He'll never hurt you again."

A confused look distorts Roz's face. She doesn't understand.

"I took care of him, honey. That's all you need to know."

Roz closes her eyes and quietly weeps.

A cruel chapter in her life is over.

Chapter 67

Marta's cell phone rings.

"Hello? Yeah. We're on our way."

"Honey, we gotta go. Our ride is getting antsy."

She kisses Roz's cheek.

"See ya' after the storm."

Sam is next.

"Have your doctor call us when you get relocated."

He kisses her forehead.

Bev has no words. Her lingering hug says it all...I love you.

Wayne is drumming his fingers on the steering wheel.

"Hurry up! Dispatch is chewing my ear off."

Sam hops in front.

Bev gets in back with Marta.

Wayne squeals from the parking lot.

"You folks need to head north as soon as we get back."

"That's our plan," Sam nods.

"How about you, Marta? Where are you going?" Bev asks.

"I ain't goin' nowhere. God knows I've been through a million storms."

"That's dumb!" Wayne growls. "You're a half-mile from the coast. The storm surge could be deadly."

"Deadly-shmedly," she mocks. "Every time we get a little rain, people turn into a pack of sissies. I'll be fine."

Wayne pulls into the parking lot of the restaurant.

"You folks have a safe trip."

Sam shakes his hand and jumps out.

He opens the back door for Bev. They only open from the outside.

Bev hugs Marta, thanking her for everything.

They wave goodbye.

Without a word, Wayne speeds away.

"Hey, let me out!" Marta shouts.

He glances in the rearview mirror.

"I'll let you out when we get to Baton Rouge."

"What?"

"Ain't no way in hell you're staying. Dispatched ordered everyone to head north…that includes you."

Spewing obscenities, she hammers the protective cage between the seats with her fist.

Wayne turns a deaf ear. He's going to keep Marta safe if it kills him.

Chapter 68

I'm waiting to board a bus.

Most of the psych patients are gone.

They're taking us to a low-security correctional facility near Baton Rouge. It's the only place available for patients who require supervision.

My blue scrubs with my nametag attached are draped over a chair. They belong to the hospital. Everything I own is in a plastic bag on the bed.

I'm ready to go, but want to check on Roz.

In the chaos to get everyone ready, no one sees me sneak away.

I take the stairs—Bart's favorite escape route.

Every night after 8 p.m. the hospital turns into a ghost town. It's only 4 p.m. but has the same feel.

Roz's door is open.

I've never seen her during the day—always at night.

She's seated in a wheelchair facing the window. She has a great view of the Gulf of Mexico across the street. Actually, a scary view. The horizon is near-black with shards of lightning heating up the sky. Massive waves are pounding the shore.

"Ready for a swim?"

"Dabid!" she squeals, struggling to turn her head.

I give her a hug. She can't reciprocate. Her arms are entombed in heavy casts.

"Are you packed?"

"Doe got non."

"You don't have anything?"

She shakes her head 'no.'

Poor thing. I feel sorry for her. No family in town. No flowers. Not even a greeting card.

"Wait a minute! I'll be right back."

She does have something.

I rush down the hall and up the stairs. In my room, I dig in the pocket of my scrubs. I pull out the heavy necklace I found in ER. I totally forgot about it. I'm sure it's hers. Her initials are engraved on the back.

RRM...Rozlyn Renay Muer

I hurry toward the stairs. Before I reach the door, a male nurse built like an NFL linebacker cuts me off.

"All patients need to go to the elevator," he growls.

Shit.

Shit!

SHIT!

I screwed up. I can't get back to Roz.

They escort me and six others into the elevator. Us crazy folks are wearing white jumpsuits. It's easy to tell who's who.

We descend to the first floor.

An idling charter bus is waiting outside the door.

The staff surround us as we walk through the lobby. We look like rock stars needing protection.

I consider bolting, but where? They'd probably put me in shackles.

I dawdle at the curb.

Eventually, I'm the only patient left.

"Hop on," the NFL nurse says.

I climb aboard. The bus is packed.

I head to the rear looking for an empty seat. There's one left next to the restroom. I drop heavy into the 'never been cleaned' upholstered seat.

I glance at the necklace in my hand. I don't have a pocket. I slip it around my neck.

Crap! I forgot my belongings. They're still in my room.

I rush to the front.

"I forgot my stuff."

The linebacker nurse glances at his watch.

"Too late. We're leaving."

I start to protest, but his eyes say *"don't give me any shit."*

It steals my thunder.

I mope back to my seat.

My mood further darkens when someone exits the restroom. A burly guy brushes passed me. A rank odor follows. A nasty blast of out-house air assaults my nostrils.

Really? You couldn't take a shit before we left?

Now I sound like my dad. He'd always bitch and moan during road trips when someone took a dump in the family RV.

Not only did shit-man pollute the air, he left the restroom door open. Frowning with disgust, I reach across the aisle to close it. Before I slam it shut, I notice a window above the toilet...it's partially open.

"Alright, listen up. We need to take roll," the linebacker says.

"Armstrong, Jim?"

"Here," a voice drones near the front.

"Ashford, William?"

"Yeah," another drones.

"Barry, David?"

"Here," I shout from the back.

"Draper, John?"

"Here."

I slip into the restroom. Voices fade as I shut the door. I throw the lock to 'OCCUPIED.'

The window opens about six inches and stops. I struggle to squeeze my head through. Grunting and squirming, I wriggle out the tight opening like a cat through a keyhole. I tumble to the ground and bang my head. A huge welt immediately forms on my forehead.

How in the hell does Tom Cruise make it look so easy?

Rubbing my head, I peek beneath the bus. A dozen feet are on the opposite side—staff members.

The bus starts to roll. With nowhere to hide, I dive behind a row of shrubs.

The space is immediately replaced by several ambulances filling the void where the bus was parked.

The staff members disappear inside the hospital.

I sprint to the east side of the building.

I enter at the emergency room.

It looks creepy.

Dozens of scattered gurneys and empty wheelchairs. Not a soul in sight.

A perfect setting for a zombie apocalypse.

I run to the elevator and press the button.

This is a bad idea. I might get caught.

I hurry to the stairs.

Voices echo in the stairwell.

"Make sure you're the last one down," a man says.

Dammit! I'm out of options.

I wander the halls trying to find a way up.

At the end of an inconspicuous corridor, I find the service elevator. It's cordoned off with yellow tape.

'POLICE LINE DO NOT CROSS' the banner reads. It's a crime scene. They're still investigating Joseph Mersk's death.

I don't care.

I tear off the tape and ride to the fifth floor.

Chapter 69

The door 'dings' open on Roz's floor.

Directly ahead is the janitorial closet where I was hiding when Sova confessed to killing my wife. That's also where I learned Joseph Mersk was a serial rapist. Mersk is no longer a problem—Sova is. That murderous bitch is still roaming free.

I push the thought from my mind.

Two steps to my left, I peek around the corner.

A mob of confusion surrounds the main elevator.

"Somebody screwed up!" a nurse shouts. "We've got nine patients and four ambulances. Six of these people are bedridden. They can't pile into four vehicles."

"Hey, don't bitch at me. I've been working around the clock evacuating other facilities," an EMT hollers back.

I see Roz. They've pushed her wheelchair to the rear giving critical patients top priority.

One by one, the gurneys disappear in the elevator.

Within ten minutes, 'Roz is the only person left. I'd love to join her, but my white jumpsuit is a dead give-away. If anyone sees me, they'll know I'm an escaped psych patient.

I wait five minutes.

Then ten.

The interior of the hospital is usually library-quiet. Not today. The hurricane is roaring like an angry giant. Booms of thunder add to its wrath.

I know Roz is scared.

'Ding.'

The elevator door glides shut.

Someone else is ignoring the police banner.

The floor indicator descends to the garage-level. A moment later, it ascends, passing several floors.

I duck inside the janitorial closet and hide behind the door as the elevator 'dings' open.

I hear Sova's heavy accent. She's on her phone.

"Yes, the pharmacy is next. I'll have it cleaned out in twenty minutes. Meet me in the garage."

A cleaning cart bumps the door.

I hold my breath and peek between the hinge gap.

Sova is covering several boxes with a heap of dirty towels.

Stepping into the elevator, she descends to the third floor. I'm guessing that's where the pharmacy is located.

Curious, I dig beneath the towels. The trash bin is loaded with boxes of narcotics worth a fortune on the street.

Not only is Sova a murderous sex-trafficking monster, she's also a drug dealer. How can so much evil exist in one person?

I peek around the corner to check on Roz.

She's still there—abandoned.

I shout her name. She looks in my direction. As I run toward her the lights blink and go out.

A backup system immediately kicks on illuminating a few auxiliary lights.

"You okay?"

"Ya."

"Don't worry, I'll get us out of here."

I steer the wheelchair to the elevator.

The control panel is dark.

"No power. We need to take the stairs."

"K, lay go," (let's go), she gurgles.

I love her.

She's such a trooper.

I bump the door open with my butt. The stairwell is dark except for scattered exit signs. It's scary for both of us. My shoes are slippery. She needs to trust me as I clunk down countless stairs in near-darkness.

Clunk. Clunk. Clunk.

Twelve clunks.

We've reached the landing between the fourth and fifth floors.

As I start down the next flight, Roz does something I've never heard. She screams—a blood-curdling scream.

Did I run over her foot? Pinch her hand?

"What's wrong?!" I gasp.

She points her casted arm down the stairwell.

"Jof ghos!" she shrieks.

In the dim light, I see him too—Joseph Mersk's ghost. He's standing on the next landing staring at us.

Terrified, I yank the wheelchair backward, retreating up the stairs.

Without a sound, the ghost follows.

I open the door to the fifth-floor. Popping a wheelie, I charge down the corridor on two wheels. Before I reach the first corner a strong hand grabs my jumpsuit. It pulls me to a halt.

I swing my arm to fight, but it's impossible to hit the sinister spirit.

"Stop! Stop it!" the ghost shouts.

171

Panting with fear, I turn toward the disembodied soul.

Bart is staring at me.

"What in the hell are you doing?"

I sigh with relief.

I forgot, Bart and Joseph were doppelgangers.

Roz never met Bart. Her fear was legit.

"Sorry, I thought you were someone else."

How could I explain I thought he was a rapist returned from the dead?

"Why are you still here?" he asks.

"I forgot something in my room. When I got off the bus, they left without me."

I flip the question.

"Why are you here? Aren't you supposed to be on the bus too?"

Bart glances down the hall. He peeks around the nearest corner.

"I need to tell you something...you gotta keep it a secret."

He double-checks over his shoulder.

"I don't work here," he whispers.

I knew it! I knew he was a psych patient pretending to be a supervisor.

"I'm with the FBI."

Okay, not a psych patient...but close.

"I've been working undercover for months trying to bust a drug ring. The ring-leader works in the hospital."

"Is that why you kept disappearing every night?"

He jerks with surprise.

"You knew about that?"

"You're not the only snoopy person in the building."

"Thanks for not reporting me."

"Who are you looking for?"

"An old Russian, Sova Garbishnova."

"Gargoyle," Roz mutters.

"She's stealing drugs. I don't know where they're stashed."

"I do...follow me."

Chapter 70

I lead Bart to the janitorial closet. I drag the cart into the hall, revealing the bin filled with drugs.

"How did you know about this?"

"I was hiding in the closet when she hid the boxes. She said something about the pharmacy."

"That's on the third-floor."

The power flickers.

The lights come on.

"I need to catch her before she gets away," Bart pants.

"She told someone over the phone to meet her in the garage in twenty minutes."

"Okay, I gotta go!"

Bart pushes the call button.

The elevator opens.

He pulls the cart inside.

"Hop in...I'll take you to the first-floor."

I push Roz beside the cart and squeeze next to Bart.

He hits the 'lobby' button.

We drop two floors and stop.

The door glides open.

Sova greets us with surprised eyes. We're startled too. It's a 'deer in headlight' moment for everyone.

She has two boxes tucked under her arm.

Before we can react, she pulls a .38 revolver from her smock.

"Thank you for bringing my merchandise," she says, eyeing the cart.

"Turn around...face the wall," she snarls.

I do. So does Bart.

Roz can't.

She dumps the boxes in the cart and presses the 'garage' button.

She looks at Roz, frightened in her wheelchair.

"Too bad about Joseph," she sneers. "He really enjoyed you."

My jaw tightens with anger.

I know what she means...Roz doesn't...thank God.

It's amazing how slow an elevator moves when a gun is pointed at the back of your head.

The door finally 'dings' open.

I hear the cart roll away followed by the distinct *click* of the .38 being cocked.

She's either shooting me first or Bart.

I don't wait to find out. Spinning, I lunge. She was aiming at Bart. Before I can reach her, the barrel shifts. I see a flash but hear nothing. I grab the gun and shove it away.

It flashes again. I hear it this time. It's deafening, exploding inches from my ear.

Fighting for my life, I slug Sova in the face. She recoils, but quickly recovers. Tough bitch!

Like a Mafia hitman, she pistol-whips the side of my head.

174

I'm not James Bond. Instead of absorbing the blow, I stumble backward falling into the bin filled with drugs.

I look stupid.

My butt is sunk low with my feet poking in the air. I look like a toddler who slid in the toilet potty-training.

It gets more embarrassing.

Bart and Sova start playing tug-o-war with the cart. She yanks it from the elevator, he drags it in. I'm stuck in the middle jostled between them like a wild carnival ride.

As they jerk me back-n-forth, two men exit a dark sedan parked in the garage. They sprint toward us with guns drawn. Before they get close, several shots ring out.

They drop dead.

"Police! Don't move!"

Detective Warnen steps from the shadows, his gun aimed at Sova. She glances at the two dead men, then at Warnen. With nerves of steel, she casually aims her gun at my face.

"Come any closer, I'll kill him."

Warnen freezes.

"I'm taking my goods and leaving."

Her voice is so calm, it's scary.

"Put your gun down and back up," she growls.

He reluctantly complies.

She turns and glares at me.

"Get your ass off my drugs."

I struggle, but can't get out.

"I'm stuck."

"You have five seconds…one…two…"

I wriggle and squirm.

Bart tries to help, but I'm wedged tight.

"…three…four…"

Before she says "five,'" Roz swings her arm. She misses the gun, but her heavy cast slams against the control panel. The elevator jerks and rapidly ascends with Sova hanging out the door. Before she can react, her upper body gets caught between the elevator shaft and rising carriage.

She tries to scream.

Nothing comes out but blood.

With the elevator crushing her torso, her eyes bulge. Before they burst, she looks at me. The last thing she sees is me mouthing, "*Goodbye, fucking gorilla.*"

Compressed by 8000 pounds of mechanical torque, she disappears between the narrow gap like a slice of bread in a toaster.

She just experienced the same death as Joseph Mersk.

Without slowing down the elevator races to the roof. It jerks to a stop at the garden level. The door starts to open, but the power dies. Roaring wind howls through the small opening. It shakes the elevator like an angry monster.

"Bart, I'm stuck."

He tries to help, but it's futile. With no choice, he dumps the cart spilling me onto the floor. I stand, surrounded by boxes. There's blood everywhere. I thought it was Sova's till I see bright red oozing through my jumpsuit.

I open the zipper. There's a bullet wound in my chest.

The sight makes me woozy. I sink to the floor trying not to faint. Bart catches me. He props me against the wall. Grabbing a handful of dirty towels, he presses them over the wound.

"Keep pressure on it," he demands.

I mindlessly obey.

I glance at Roz.

She's crying.

"Pee doe die!" she begs.

"I won't...I promise."

With every breath, I feel weaker.

My vision is fading.

I hope I can keep my promise.

Chapter 71

David is slumped against the wall, blood seeping between his fingers.

"Pee doe die!" I plead.

He promises he won't, but his eyes betray him. They look dim.

"I'm going onto the roof. I'll take the stairs to the lobby and get help," Bart shouts.

He creeps me out. It's not him—it's his looks. He looks just like Joseph—just a little taller.

I nod.

He pries the door open and wriggles out. He slides it shut, leaving me alone with David.

I feel helpless.

The hurricane is frightening, but I'm more afraid for David.

His eyes are closed. His breathing shallow. I need to be near him.

"Dabid!"

He struggles to open his eyes.

Drawing a deep breath, I shout as loud as I can.

"Don't die! I love you!"

My words are strong and clear. They came from my heart.

"I love you," he mouths.

He closes his eyes. His chest heaves a few times, then...nothing. His hand slowly slides from his bloody wound onto his lap.

I lunge from my chair.

The toppled cart between us seems like Mt. Everest, but I'm determined to climb it. My casted arms and neck brace make every move clumsy.

"I comin,' Dabid!" I scream, encouraging him to live.

I tumble over the cart onto his lap.

"I here, Dabid...I here!"

He doesn't answer. Doesn't move.

When I was broken and dead inside, he loved me back to life.

Now it's my turn.

Lifting my bulky arms, I touch his face. My casts are heavy, but I force myself to be gentle.

"I luv oo, Dabid," I whisper, caressing his cheeks with my fingertips.

I stretch my neck to kiss his mouth. My wired jaw makes it painful to pucker. I don't care. I want him to feel my kiss—the same healing kiss he gave to me.

I press my lips against his. I linger until the pain in my neck is unbearable.

Yielding to the agony, I rest my head on his shoulder.

The elevator shudders, shaken by the wind. I imagine it's David stirring, coming back to life from the warmth of my kiss.

Trembling with pain and emotion, I press my mouth against his. I'm not trying to be passionate—I'm trying to resuscitate him. With my jaw wired shut, I can't form a seal over his mouth. All I can do is puff burst of air into his lifeless body.

I puff and puff till I'm dizzy, then puff some more.

He suddenly jerks.

I thought it was the elevator, till I feel his chest rise.

His eyes flutter open. He struggles to focus on my face inches away.

"Roz, did you fall? Are you hurt?" he gasps, realizing I'm not in my wheelchair.

I burst into tears.

He just came back from the dead and all he cares about is me.

Chapter 72

Bart is on his knees more than his feet.

Wind keeps knocking him to the ground. It doesn't help he's on the roof exposed to the full wrath of Jenise.

Belly-crawling, he reaches the stairwell on the opposite side of the roof—the same place where David tried to commit suicide six weeks ago.

He yanks the doorknob.

"Dammit!" he screams.

It's locked.

Scooting on his butt, he backs away and stands. With the wind pushing him, he charges at the door with his shoulder.

It's rock-solid.

The impact sends a shockwave through his arm.

Cussing like a sailor, he tries again. This time, he goes feet-first. The doorframe fractures at the handle, busting open.

Cradling his injured arm, he scurries down dozens of stairs to the lobby.

Not a soul in sight.

He heads for the basement parking garage.

Detective Warnen is taking pictures with his cell phone. He's snapping images of the two dead men. He already has several shots of Sova's mangled body.

"I need help!" Bart shouts.

Instinctively, Warnen draws his gun, spinning on his heels.

Bart holds up his hands, wincing from his injury.

"I'm with the FBI."

Warnen eyes him up and down.

"Why are you wearing scrubs?"

"I've been working undercover to catch a drug dealer. The elevator got her before I did."

Warnen holsters his weapon. He reaches to shake Bart's hand.

"I'm Bruce Warnen with the State Police."

Bart nods, but doesn't shake his hand.

"Not trying to be rude—I hurt my arm."

"What happened?"

"I had to bust a door open. There's a young couple trapped on the roof. One's been shot, the other is in a wheelchair. They need help."

"Why don't you use the elevator?"

"No power."

Warnen glances at the lights. Only auxiliary lamps are lit.

"You said they're on the roof?"

"Yeah, we gotta take the stairs."

"Shit! I'm too fat to run up a thousand stairs."

"Come as far as you can. I'll bring them to you."

They rush to the stairwell. Before they reach the first floor, an explosion shakes the building. The glass atrium in the lobby was holding back a wall of water.

Not anymore.

Gushing through the lobby, a roaring river spills into the stairwell. It washes Bart and Warnen down to the parking garage.

"We gotta go!" Warnen yells. "The basement is flooding."

Bart doesn't want to quit, but knows the first rule of rescue—a dead man can't save a soul.

They run to Warnen's SUV.

Water is rapidly rising above the front bumper.

Warnen accelerates up the sloping driveway onto the street. He has one option—head north. Behind him, floodwater is smothering everything.

"God, I hope those two survive," Bart pants.

Chapter 73

Wayne is the last vehicle heading north on Highway 55.

Jenise rides his bumper for forty miles before he outruns her.

Just after 6 p.m., he pulls into a mom-n-pop diner ten miles east of Baton Rouge.

"Dinners on me," he says, opening Marta's door.

She wriggles out, scowling.

"I have a notion to kick your ass and hitchhike back to La Rogue."

"Good luck, no one is going south."

She marches into the restaurant and takes the first booth.

"Get me a coke," she grumbles.

Without a word, he heads to the counter.

He returns with two large sodas and a heaping platter of food—enough fried food to clog the arteries of a football team.

Marta digs in before he's seated.

After inhaling several mouthfuls, her mood lightens.

"Sorry, Wayne…I was just hangry."

"No apology necessary, young lady."

Chapter 74

"Where's Bart?"

"Wen foe hep."

I must have passed out. I never saw him leave.

"We'll be okay, Roz. Don't be afraid."

"I not fade...I wif oo"

Her trust makes me tear up.

She said, "I'm not afraid...I'm with you."

I don't know how to protect her. I'd never tell her I'm scared.

She leans against my chest. The weight of her head is painful against my wound. I don't say anything. I need her comfort just as much as she needs mine.

It doesn't seem possible, but Jenise grows stronger. Her fury shakes the building. I hope it doesn't collapse.

Every few minutes, Roz lifts her head and looks at me.

"Oo kay?"

"Yeah, I'm okay."

I'm lying.

I'm fading in and out.

As I try to distract my mind from the pain, a horrendous crash scares the shit out of us. I jump with fright. It sounded like an airplane hit the building. I sniff for smoke. Nothing, just salty sea air.

Maybe I'm hallucinating, but the wall behind me is moving...it's bumping in and out like someone pressing their knees against your seat at a movie theatre.

The sensation is getting stronger.

Oh shit!

"Roz, we gotta move! The wall is collapsing."

Like two beached whales, we galumph toward the opposite wall. Before we reach it, a powerful gust hits the building. The elevator shudders, jarring the door open.

Jenise attacks with stinging wind and rain.

I hold Roz close.

"Don't be afraid, I've got ya!"

She says something, but her words are stolen by the wind.

It's funny. You never think about the quality of your life till you're about to die.

Did I love enough?

Did I share enough?

Could I have made this world a better place?

"You have!" she shouts.

I thought I was saying those words in my head. I was saying them out loud.

I embrace her tighter, loving her more.

Maybe I should pray.

What?

Hey God, it's me...the guy who ignores you 24/7 till I desperately need help.

I don't know if he'll hear. I pray anyway.

"God, help us!" I scream into the roaring wind.

BANG!

The elevator drops a few feet, cocking sideways.

"Roz, we gotta get out! The cable is breaking."

It hurts to move. Nauseating to stand.

How am I going to do this? The elevator floor is two feet below the roofline.

I can step out.

Roz can't.

I crawl onto the roof.

Specks of debris pelt my skin. It feels like I'm being sand-blasted.

I reach for Roz. She can't get off the floor. The two feet of height may as well be a mile.

I crawl back inside. Wobbly and weak, she's able to stand with my help.

I crawl out again. Like a small child, she reaches beckoning for help. I can't pull her arms. Her bones are still broken.

Grabbing beneath her armpits, I pull. Thank God my face is rain-soaked. She can't see my tears of pain as my wound throbs.

Just as her waist clears the doorframe, the elevator drops. It jerks to a stop leaving a narrow eight-inch gap. If it drops again, she'll be cut in half like Joseph and Sova.

I know Roz is self-conscious of her skinny body, but if she had junk in the trunk she'd be screwed. She'd never fit through the tight opening.

Screaming with agony, I pull with my remaining strength. She barely clears the frame when the elevator breaks loose. Clanging and banging, it ends its journey eighty-feet below with a heavy 'thud.'

I squeeze Roz tight. I almost lost her.

She looks at me with adoring eyes like a knight in shining armor. I hate to disappoint her, but this knight is losing the battle against many dragons.

We're trapped on the roof.

I'm bleeding to death.

We desperately need shelter.

Chapter 75

The visitor's garden looks like a war-zone. Benches and mangled tables are strewn everywhere. Every plant stripped of its leaves.

Sixty feet away, a bus-sized air conditioning unit is toppled. That's what crashed...not a plane. If I can drag Roz behind the unit, it'll provide some protection from the wind.

I yell and point, explaining what I need to do. Our faces are inches apart, but she can't hear me. The storm is deafening.

Playing charades, I motion to sit on my lap. She straddles my waist, but can't hug my neck. Her rain-soaked casts are like blocks of cement. I grab each limb, flopping them over my shoulders.

Scooting on my butt, I inch toward the AC unit. I only go a few feet and collapse onto my back.

I've lost too much blood.

My jumpsuit is more red than white.

Roz's clothes are equally messy.

It's impossible to tell who's bleeding.

She crawls on top of me to shield me from the driving rain...chest to chest, groin to groin. If we were naked on a comfy bed, it would be a perfect 'baby making' position.

With rain dripping off her face, she gazes into my eyes. She doesn't kiss me. Doesn't speak. Just rests her forehead against mine.

The rain abruptly stops.

Sunlight breaks through the clouds.

For a moment, I thought I died, seeing the light of heaven.

I struggle to focus.

"We're in the eye," I mumble.

I don't know how we'll survive once the eye of Jenise passes.

Chapter 76

Vorcy saw a few tornados. Nothing threatening. The ride to the mainland has been smooth.

"When Jenise moves inland, the eye will collapse. It's gonna get bumpy," Goodall says.

No one says a word, just tightens their seatbelts.

Through scattered clouds, the shoreline comes into view. The leading edge of Jenise has pushed water a mile inland. Hundreds of homes are underwater. Taller structures are severely damaged—some collapsed.

Goodall sees a familiar landmark. Directly ahead is First Mercy Hospital, the highest building in La Rogue.

Every window on the ocean side is broken. Large sections of the exterior are missing. It looks like a bomb hit it.

As they pass over the city, the crew is hypnotized by the damage. Staring out the window, Vorcy jerks his head straining to look behind the chopper.

"Someone is on that building!"

"No way…" Goodall groans in disbelief.

"I'm serious. Someone's down there."

Goodall doesn't bank left or right—just hovers backward until he's over the hospital. Next to a toppled AC unit, a man and woman are lying together.

Patriot slides the side door open to get a better view.

That was a mistake.

An angry blast of wind floods the cockpit. It pushes the chopper sideways. Goodall nearly collides with a cell phone tower before gaining control.

"Hey, big guy, I need a 'heads-up' before you do that."

"Sorry, I didn't know," he frowns.

"It's all good—we're still alive."

Goodall is so chill you could slap his face and he'd still be your friend.

Steering back over the roof, he assesses the situation.

"There's no place to land."

"Get low…I'll play Tarzan again," Punk says.

Without a word, Patriot secures the strap around Punk's chest then around his own waist. It's the same technique they used to set the bear-trap.

"It's like déjà vu all over again," Punk says.

He glances at Delany.

"Hey, sweet cheeks, as long as we're reliving the past, how about another kiss for luck?"

She smiles ear-to-ear. This charming S.O.B. is winning her heart.

She kisses him twice, lingering the second time.

"Have fun, Tarzan," she says, pushing him away.

He drops out the door and repels to the roof.

He kneels next to Roz and David.

"Who's most critical?" he asks, seeing blood everywhere.

They point at each other.

Punk doesn't wait for a debate. He grabs Roz. Holding her tight, he gives Patriot a nod. Growling with stress, the gentle giant pulls them hand over hand. When they reach the door, Crater and Forrest haul them aboard.

Punk releases Roz and drops again.

David moans when he picks him up. He's in so much pain, he wants to puke.

Punk signals to Patriot.

Just as their feet leave the roof a blinding flash illuminates the area. An explosion of thunder drowns out the roar of the chopper. The sky unleashes a torrent of rain like Niagara Falls.

Pounded by water, the chopper jerks and sways. Before Goodall can gain control, nature attacks with a deadly downdraft of wind. It spins the chopper 360° sending Punk and David in a whirling motion. Rotating in a large loop, it looks like a swing ride at a carnival.

"Hang on!" Punk screams, struggling to hold David.

He doesn't answer. He's unconscious.

Goodall tries to counteract the spin by reversing the chopper's direction. It doesn't work. Punk and David are whirling faster.

Patriot is struggling too. The strap around his waist is pulling him out the door.

"I need to accelerate and gain altitude," Goodall shouts. "Get a grip on Patriot."

Forrest snuggles close to Patriot's back. He wraps his legs around his waist like an MMA fighter using a body lock. Crater does the same around Forrest then grabs the chair frame with his arms.

They look like a human chain.

"Do it!" Crater shouts.

Goodall goes full-throttle.

He climbs over eight-hundred-feet in four seconds.

Patriot is a God-fearing man, but he's swearing, feeling torn in half at the waist.

Punk has no idea why the chopper is gaining altitude, but it's killing him. The muscles in his back and arms are screaming for relief.

At 830 feet, they stop spinning.

Goodall rapidly descends—and not a moment too soon. As soon as Punk's feet touch the roof, David slips from his arms. They crumple in a heap.

Panting with adrenaline and pain, Punk grabs David's collar. He jerks him upright.

"You're not a wuss! Get your ass up!"

He's not screaming at David. He's screaming at himself...a Punk pep talk.

Roaring with stress, he throws David over his shoulder.

"Take us up!"

Working in tandem, Crater, Forrest, and Patriot use a tug-o-war method.

"One...two...three...PULL!"

Punk rises a few feet.

"One...two...three...PULL!"

He's six feet up.

After a dozen tugs, the two men are hauled aboard.

Punk dumps David on the floor.

He collapses on the seat next to Delany.

No smile.

No flirty comment.

He's spent.

With everyone focused on David, no one pays attention as Punk peels off his blood-stained shirt...no one except Delany.

Peeking sideways, she can't help but notice his muscular chest as he pants with exhaustion. His arms are so pumped with blood they're bigger than her thighs. And his abs...a washboard of lean meat.

Damn! This guy is Captain America's cousin.

Delany prides herself on self-control. It takes every ounce of effort not to stare.

Punk tries to clean his arms with his rain-soaked shirt. It's useless. There's too much blood.

Frowning with disgust, he drops the shirt on the floor between his feet. His neck and chest are still grossly smeared.

Without a word, Delany removes the jacket Forrest draped over her shoulders when she was pulled from the sea. She lays it across her lap.

Unbuttoning her blouse, she takes it off. No one notices except Punk—everyone is focused on David.

He's not discreet about looking.

Delany is wearing a bra, but it's wet…see-thru.

She doesn't care. She's not lacking in that area.

She tries to wipe Punk's chest with her shirt, but he stops her. He grabs the jacket—makes her put it on.

He zips it to her neck.

"I'm already out of breath. Don't give me a heart attack," he sighs.

Smiling at his compliment, she gently cleans his chest.

She's in no hurry to complete the task.

Chapter 77

David looks dead.

Roz is cradling his head.

Patriot sees her lips moving, praying.

He joins her.

"Jesus, we need a miracle."

His prayer doesn't sound desperate, but intimate, like a beloved child asking his father for a favor.

In the next instant, something weird happens.

A ball of light streaks passed the helicopter moving in a northwesterly direction. It literally melts a hole in the clouds forming a tunnel. The tunnel begins to swirl, rotating like a horizontal tornado. Before Goodall can react, the chopper gets sucked into the vortex.

They accelerate.

The chopper's speedometer only reaches 180 mph, but it's pegged out.

Everyone stares at Patriot with wide eyes. They have no doubt the big guy has a direct line to the Almighty.

The weirdness continues.

An LED screen on the dashboard illuminates. It scrolls past several displays, stopping on a navigation screen like Google Maps.

There's a destination locked in.

Ochsner LSU Hospital in Shreveport.

It's three-hundred-miles away. The vortex is pulling them in that direction.

On a normal day, it's a two-hour flight from La Rogue to Shreveport.

They reach the medical center in twelve minutes as if carried on angel's wings.

When they near Shreveport, the vortex dissolves.

Goodall radios the hospital alerting them of his arrival.

He lands hard and fast on the front lawn.

A trauma team rushes to greet them.

They transfer David onto a gurney and hurry away.

Battered and numb, Vorcy and his crew climb from the chopper. They watch the medical team disappear into the hospital.

Without a word, everyone joins hands as Patriot prays.

"Heavenly Father, thank you for everything. We're only here because of your mercy. Please put your healing hand on that young man, and…and…" he chokes up.

After several moments, he regains his composure.

"…and thank you for Mr. Goodall. I believe he's an angel. May his kindness be greatly rewarded. Amen."

"Ah mun," a voice gurgles from the chopper.

Everyone turns to the source.

Roz crawled to the door, but couldn't get out.

Patriot walks over and scoops her up. He holds her gently in his arms like a small child.

"God bless you too, young lady. You've been through a lot."

There's not a dry eye in the bunch.

Chapter 78

"Look, Mom!"

Cal is only eight, but has the energy of a race horse as he drags his mother by the hand. He's awestruck by the sleek helicopter sitting on the hospital lawn.

"Is this yours?" he excitedly asks, sprinting toward Goodall.

Goodall glances at his mother and smiles.

"It's not mine. I'm just the pilot."

"I'm so sorry," Cal's mother says. "He loves anything that flies."

"I understand…that's why I'm a pilot."

"Can I touch it?" Cal asks.

"Honey, don't bug him."

"It's okay."

"Are you sure?"

"Yeah, he can look inside if that's okay with you."

The boy squeals with excitement.

Every adult smiles, wishing they had the same enthusiasm.

Cal's mother pulls out her cell phone to record the moment.

Goodall opens the pilot's door. He hoists the little guy inside. While pointing at all the cool stuff, Delany steps next to the mother.

"I think you're going to have a pilot in the family."

She agrees.

"Why is this helicopter here?"

"It's a long story—an amazing story."

Without thinking, the mother turns, accidently filming Delany as she shares the details of their harrowing adventure.

"Six of us were trapped on an oil rig in the Gulf of Mexico. Mr. Goodall risked his life to save us. We got off the rig in the middle of hurricane Jenise…flew inside the eye. When we were flying over La Rogue, we saw a man and woman trapped on a roof. Mr. Goodall saved them too. One was badly injured. This was the closest hospital from the evacuation zone."

"You flew through a hurricane?!"

"We didn't…Mr. Goodall did. He's the bravest man I've ever met."

With wide eyes, Cal's mother gets a close-up shot of Goodall with her son.

After a few minutes, he helps the little boy from the cockpit.

He runs to his mother.

"I'm gonna be a pilot just like him when I grow up," he shouts.

Saying a million 'thank-you's,' the mother leads Cal away.

When she gets to her car, she uploads the video to her social media. It's not every day your kid gets to sit in a helicopter.

Within hours, her video has been shared hundreds of times with twice as many 'likes.'

Chapter 79

The x-ray tech places several slides on a light box.

The surgeon leans close and cocks his head. He sees a bullet in David's chest—but something else.

"What is that?"

"I have no idea," the tech says. "Looks like a bunch of junk."

"Dr. Bryant, the patient is ready," the pre-op nurse says.

Bryant scrubs down and goes into the operating room. A staff of four surround David. Bryant nods to his team and starts talking. He's recording the procedure.

"We have a male patient approximately thirty-three-years-old with a bullet wound to the chest. The wound is six-centimeters inferior to the left clavicle. Severe powder burns mark the point of entry. The wound is atypical. It appears something else has penetrated the patient's chest. I'll do an exploratory once he's open...scalpel."

An assistant hands him a razor-sharp implement.

He makes a deep cut across David's sternum.

The aid clamps the incision open.

"The bullet penetrated between the third and fourth rib," the surgeon says into the microphone.

Using a small rotary saw, he detaches two ribs from the sternum. With a large clamp, he holds the bones away.

Flipping down his magnifying visor, he peers into David's chest.

"Long forceps."

The assistant sets a large tweezer-like implement in his hand. He probes deep and pulls out a bullet. It's pancaked flat like a fat dime. With a distinct *clink*, he drops the nugget in a surgical pan.

He hands off the forceps and flips up his visor.

He studies the x-rays again trying to get his bearings on the location of the mysterious debris.

"It's next to his heart—medial side."

Reaching into the incision, he explores with his fingers.

David's beating heart makes it difficult to find the object. Every time the surgeon gets close, David's heart bumps his fingers away.

"Clamp him wider."

An assistant widens the opening.

With forceps in one hand and a spoon-like implement in the other, the surgeon pushes David's heart aside.

"What the hell?" he mutters.

He flips down his magnifying visor to get a better look. With a steady hand, he carefully extracts a quarter-sized medallion with a chain attached. There's a noticeable dent in the medallion.

"This guy is lucky. I think the medallion stopped the bullet from penetrating his heart."

He drops the bloody artifact in the surgical pan next to the bullet.

"Get another x-ray. I don't want to close him up until I know he's clean."

The x-ray tech wheels-in a bulky contraption.

He takes a few more images.

The results are clean—no more debris.

The surgeon nods with approval and leaves.

An assistant takes over, resetting David's ribs, sewing him shut.

Chapter 80

Roz is in ER.

A young doctor steps into the cubicle. His eyes grow wide, scanning her head to toe.

"What the hell happened to you?"

Roz understands his reaction.

Her clothes are stained with blood—David's blood. The casts on her arms are soaking wet, sagging like wet bags of cement. Her face is marred with stitches and bruises. Her jaw wired shut.

"Hee by buzzz," she gurgles.

"What?"

She repeats herself.

He can't understand her garbled words.

He grabs a pen and paper.

"Shit," he sighs, realizing she can't hold the pen.

She tries anyway, scribbling 'hit by bus.'

Her handwriting looks like a three-year-old.

"Hit by bus? When?"

She scribbles, '5 weeks.'

"Why are you all bloody?"

'David shot.'

He has no idea what that means.

A nurse enters to assist. She heard rumors of Roz's rescue.

"This woman has impaired speech. Do you know what's going on?" the doctor asks.

"She was brought here on a helicopter from La Rogue—rescued from a roof in the middle of a hurricane."

"Why is she all bloody?"

"Dr. Bryant is in surgery removing a bullet from a man's chest. Apparently, she was on the roof with the man when they were rescued."

The doctor looks at Roz in awe.

"Sweetheart, sounds like you had a rough day. I'll take good care of you."

He instructs the nurse to get her bathed.

"After you're cleaned up, I'll reapply your casts."

The doctor goes above and beyond to care for Roz. After he applies fresh casts, he re-stitches the surgical incision on her right cheek. The old stitches ripped during all the chaos. He even gets her a cute pink ballcap to cover her shaved head.

Chapter 81

Every hotel, motel, and evacuation shelter are full.

Vorcy and his crew are trying to sleep in the visitor's lounge at the hospital.

It's noisy and crowded.

Around 10 p.m., Dr. Bryant, David's surgeon, walks in.

"Is the family of David Barry here?"

Patriot stands up. He doesn't say he's family, the doctor assumes he is.

"David's surgery went well. He's in ICU."

"Thank the Lord," Patriot sighs.

"I'm not sure how it happened, but I pulled this out of his chest."

The surgeon hands Patriot a necklace with a dented medallion attached.

"I think it saved his life...stopped the bullet from penetrating his heart."

Patriot swallows hard, trying not to cry.

"Another miracle," he whispers.

He shakes the doctor's hand, thanking him for the update.

The doctor turns to leave, but stops.

"How many people are here for David?"

Patriot does a quick head-count.

"Seven."

The doctor motions for Patriot to follow him into the hall.

"Around the corner is the surgeon's suite. I use it occasionally to get some rest when I have a long day. It's empty. You and the others are welcome to use it...you look exhausted."

Patriot's eyes glisten with tears.

Another blessing.

"Thank you. I appreciate your kindness."

Patriot waves to the group. They join him in the hall.

Dr. Bryant leads the way.

He unlocks the door and leaves.

"It's not the Hilton, but it's quiet," he says over his shoulder.

The room is small. Two hospital beds. One couch. One recliner.

Vorcy gives Goodall first dibs.

"I'll take the recliner."

"Delany, the couch is yours," Vorcy says.

The five remaining men look at each other. Playing 'rock-paper-scissors,' they vie for the two beds.

Vorcy and Crater get eliminated first.

Patriot is next.

They head for the door, returning to the visitor's lounge.

Punk feels bad.

Vorcy is no spring-chicken. Patriot is so big no lounge chair is comfortable.

"Vorcy, you can have my bed," Punk says. "I'll take the floor."

He doesn't argue as Punk drops on the floor beside the couch.

Overcome with guilt, Forrest caves in too.

"Hey, Patriot, take my bed. Those lounge chairs are too small."

"You sure?"

"Yeah."

"Thanks, bro," he says, giving him a hug.

Forrest plops next to Punk.

"Crater, you may as well stay too. There's plenty of room on the floor."

There's not, but he joins them anyway.

As everyone gets situated, the scene looks comical...like a frat-house party. Bodies everywhere.

Punk has the worst spot. If he turns right, Forrest is panting in his face. If he rolls left, the couch is forming a barricade.

Goodall flips the light switch near the door. The room is momentarily dark until a small nightlight activates over the coffee bar. It's just bright enough to see shadows.

Within minutes, a cacophony of loud snores shakes the walls. You'd think Patriot would be the worst, but he's quiet as a church mouse. Forrest sounds like a bellowing sow, followed by Vorcy, Goodall, then Crater. Between the four of them, they could wake the dead.

Punk is still awake. He's debating whether to smother Forrest in his sleep.

Damn! No wonder he's single. He snores like a great ape.

Unable to move, he stares at the ceiling. A moment later, a cute little face peeks over the edge of the couch. It's Delany. She thought Punk was asleep, but got caught spying.

They make eye contact.

Giving her a wink, he reaches up and playfully boops her nose.

She smiles, gesturing with her finger to 'come close.'

He raises in a sit-up position.

She palms his cheeks.

A two-inch gap separates their faces.

"You're so sweet giving Vorcy your bed," she whispers.

He gives her a mischievous grin.

"Ya' know, if we spoon, we could share the couch."

She leans closer, almost kissing him.

"I don't want to make Forrest jealous. You look cozy snuggled together," she says with a teasing smile.

"You're cruel."

She doesn't answer. Just releases him.

He drops to his back, still staring at the ceiling.

A moment later, Delany dangles her arm off the couch purposely resting it on Punk's chest. He grabs her hand, gently massaging her palm. His touch is pleasing. She never dreamed a hand rub could feel so sensual.

Scowling with disappointment, she regrets turning down his offer to share the couch.

In the morning, everyone looks rested except Punk and Delany. Neither slept. They were too busy fantasizing what could have happened if they were alone.

Chapter 82

"In the midst of death and destruction, an amazing story of courage has come to light," a news anchor says. "Apparently, a helicopter pilot rescued a crew trapped on an oil rig during hurricane Jenise. The following video was uploaded on social media by a woman who encounter this brave man."

The program cuts to a simple cell phone video. It shows a little boy sitting in a helicopter talking to an older gentleman. The interaction between them is heartwarming. But the video becomes more interesting when a bystander shares an amazing story. It's Delany, talking about Goodall's courage.

Within twenty-four hours, every network airs the story.

The phone at Aircruze is going crazy.

Everyone wants an interview.

Martin Sota, the owner, is basking in the limelight. He's telling everyone he was "very instrumental during the rescue." He wasn't the pilot, but "guided Goodall during the rescue operation."

In the visitor's lounge at the hospital, several TVs flash Sota's arrogant face as he spews his deceitful comments.

"That guy is a piece of work," Vorcy growls. "He's telling the world he saved us."

Goodall grins.

He has no comment.

Chapter 83

"I'm sorry, only family is allowed."

The nurse's faint words draw me into consciousness.

Roz is at the door. A big brawny man is trying to push her wheelchair into ICU. The nurse is not being cooperative.

It takes every ounce of energy to speak.

"She's my wife," I blurt, my words muffled behind my oxygen mask.

The nurse turns. She's surprised I'm awake.

Roz is surprised too, caught off guard by my "wife" comment.

"Okay, you can visit a few minutes."

She steps aside.

The big man pushes Rozlyn close.

I reach for her hand. All she can offer are fingertips sticking out of newly applied casts. I squeeze them, grateful to touch her again.

"I won kiz," she gurgles.

The big man helps her stand.

She pushes my mask aside. Wobbly and weak, she falls across my chest. She's scrawny, but her weight is painful against my incision.

I wince.

The big man holds her upright, helping her balance. She tries again.

Our kiss is clumsy. My mask is blocking half my mouth. Her wired jaw makes it difficult to pucker.

We don't care. We bump lips.

"luv oo," she whispers.

I say nothing…just cry. Words can't express my love for her.

Unable to stand, she drops into her wheelchair. The big man helps her get settled then steps close.

"Hi, my name is Mark Renald. Everyone calls me Patriot."

I nod hello.

"The surgeon gave me something—says it belongs to you."

He pulls a heavy necklace from his shirt pocket. It's scarred with a deep dent in the medallion.

"The doctor said this saved your life…deflected the bullet away from your heart."

When he hands it to me, Roz gasps.

"My neckus!" she pants.

Patriot looks confused. He's not sure who to give it to.

"It's hers," I nod.

He drapes it across her fingertips.

She weeps, holding it against her chest.

I want to ask why she's upset, but the nurse interrupts.

"I'm sorry. He needs rest. You can come back after 5 p.m."

It's only 11 a.m.

I shake the big man's hand. It's like shaking the paw of a grizzly bear—it's huge.

I blow a kiss to Roz through my mask. She tries to reciprocate, but bumps her mouth with her heavy cast.

Poor thing. I'm sure it hurt.

Patriot wheels her away.

After they disappear, my mind drifts to the ER cubicle where I found the necklace a month ago. It was my mission to find its owner…to return the token of hope. Little did I know that trinket would change my life. It brought me to Roz and ultimately saved my life.

God, you work in mysterious ways.

Chapter 84

I must have needed sleep.

I'm awaken by a gentle touch—fingers caressing my face.

It's Roz.

It's already after 5 p.m.

"Hi Babe."

"Hi Dabid."

I pull the oxygen mask off my face, wanting a kiss. She leans close. Our lips bump. Not really a smooch, more like a soft collision.

"I luv oo."

"I love you more."

I glance over her shoulder looking for the big guy.

It's just us.

Roz's empty wheelchair is beside my bed. I realize she's lying next me, cuddling close. I have no idea how she climbed in.

"Don't get frisky," I tease.

She giggles…a cute giggle. Makes me laugh, something I haven't done in a long time.

"I'm glad you got your necklace back."

Her eyes brim with tears.

Something about the necklace touches her deeply.

I gotta know.

"Honey, are you okay?"

She doesn't answer.

David thinks I'm upset.

I'm not.

I'm blown away.

This necklace belonged to my grandmother, Rosemary Rae Muer.

We have the same initials.

It's an heirloom. She gave it to me on her deathbed.

The trinket itself has little value...cheap, made of brass. The story behind it makes it priceless.

Grandma got this necklace on her nineteenth birthday. A gift from Grandpa Muer before he was shipped overseas during World War II. Grandma insisted he wear it until he returned. He reluctantly agreed.

He was sent to the Pacific theatre. Battles with the Japanese were horrific. Thousands died on each side.

On October 14, 1945, three years after going to war, Grandpa disembarked from a ship in San Francisco. Weathered and aged by war, he tightly embraced my grandmother on the dock.

They didn't speak for a long time, just held each other, crying.

When he finally loosened his grip, he reached inside his shirt. He slipped a chain off his neck. It was the necklace he gave Grandma three years earlier. It was tarnished and scarred.

He told Grandma the necklace saved his life.

She couldn't breathe as he shared his story.

He told it once…never again.

With fixed bayonets, he and his squad were attacked by Japanese soldiers. Skewered bodies fell left and right. In the heat of hand-to-hand combat, an enemy soldier plunged a knife in Grandpa's chest. Instead of killing him, the blade snapped, leaving a harmless nub in the enemy's hand.

Both men froze, not understanding what happened. In an act of respect, the Japanese soldier bowed. He yelled something in his native tongue. The mob retreated into the jungle leaving the American soldiers alone on the battlefield.

When Grandpa returned to camp, he took off his shirt. Dead-center in the medallion was a deep gouge. It stopped the enemy's blade from piercing his heart.

"I'm sorry I ruined your necklace," he said to Grandma as they stood on the pier.

"Ruined it! It saved your life," she said through tears.

In an attempt to make it right, Grandpa had Grandma's birthstone, a ruby, added to the medallion to conceal the deep scar.

Now, eighty-years later, this necklace saved the man I love…my David.

Thank you, God. You work in mysterious ways.

Chapter 85

Violent storms rage all night as Jenise sweeps over Louisiana.

By daybreak, she's putters out to steady rain.

Wayne is heading back to La Rogue.

The traffic is light—mostly utility trucks and Red Cross.

He exits four miles north of La Rogue. Taking backroads, he and Marta sit in silence as they absorb the devastation from the storm.

Downed trees.

Damaged buildings.

Huge ponds of standing water everywhere.

Marta fidgets in her seat. She has her head down as they pull into the parking lot of the restaurant. She doesn't know what to expect.

Taking a deep breath, she slowly lifts her eyes.

The building has a few broken windows and missing shingles, but the Crusty Crab is standing strong. Even has electricity.

Marta sighs with relief.

"I could've stayed," she mutters.

"Yup, you could have, but I'd been worried sick about ya," Wayne says.

The two friends lock eyes and smile, knowing their love runs deep.

"Swing by in a day or two. I'll have a fresh pie waiting for you."

"Sounds good."

Wriggling from the car, she hikes up her pant legs. Without looking back, she wades through several puddles to the front door. She steps in and turns on the 'open' sign.

Taking a seat at the counter bar, she rubs her hand over the smooth surface, stroking it lovingly like a family pet.

"Well, old girl, you survived another storm," she says to the four walls.

No one answers, but she smiles like she heard something no one else could hear.

Chapter 86

"Attention passengers…we're ready to begin boarding. Those who need assistance or traveling with small children may board at this time."

Five days ago, I was in surgery getting a bullet removed from my chest. Being shot was painful, but nothing like the pain I feel now.

Roz is leaving.

Jenise destroyed First Mercy Hospital. Roz is returning to Michigan for medical care.

"Doe wanna lee," she mumbles, crying in my arms.

"I don't want you to leave either, but the sooner you recover, the sooner we can be together."

My words sound cliché. I'm trying to be positive.

"Come wiff me," she begs.

"I can't."

I'm locked into Louisiana's healthcare system. I've got a long road of recovery too.

"Ms. Muer, I'll take you aboard now," a flight attendant says.

She turns the wheelchair toward the gate.

Roz holds out her casted arms begging to be hugged.

I hold her tight.

"I love you."

She has no words, just heaving sobs.

The 125-mile bus ride from Shreveport to Alexandria is a lonely trip. The Red Cross is shuttling people place to place to accommodate displaced residents. My case is unique. I still need medical care. Alexandria is the closest facility to my home.

With the Gulf region wiped out by the hurricane, I have no place to go. I'm sure my house is destroyed. It's painful to think about, but being separated from Roz hurts more. We have no ability to communicate. I don't have a cell phone. No email. No permanent address.

I have no idea when I'll hear from her again.

Chapter 87

Two weeks later.

My hands are shaking.
I shouldn't be afraid, but I am.
I haven't been to my old apartment in months.
I don't know what Gavin was doing, but he obviously didn't pay rent and got in trouble with the law. The front door is decorated with eviction notices and court summonses.
I fumble with the key trying to slip it in the lock. My casted arms and trembling hands make it difficult.
Dad helps.
He flips the lock and opens the door.
A rank smell makes us nauseous.
The apartment looks like a garbage dump. It's littered with liquor bottles and empty boxes of microwaved food.
Gavin's clothes are strewn everywhere.
There's a blanket draped over the couch stained with semen and sweat. I'm sure my cable bill is racked up with pay-per-view porn.
I wander into the kitchen.
Flies are buzzing, feeding on rotted food and scattered trash.
Apparently, all Gavin did was eat, drink, and play with himself.
I go to the bedroom—the last place he beat me before I escaped.

The bed is bare. No sheets. No blankets. Just a tired mattress.

Every dresser drawer is pulled out.

My clothes are piled in a corner.

Curious, I check to see if anything is salvageable. I pick up a pair of familiar jeans, but almost puke. Gavin was so vengeful he literally pissed and shit on my clothes.

I can't believe I spent two years being tortured by him.

"Honey, let's pay the fee and get the hell out of here," Dad says.

The apartment is letting me break my lease if I pay a hefty fine. $5400. Thank God for Dad. I don't have any money.

I head for the door.

In the back of my mind, I wonder if Gavin will show up someday. Marta said he'll never hurt me again. I have no idea what happened to him—don't want to know.

I follow Dad outside.

Without looking back, I close the door.

When it clicks shut, the sound triggers something. Closure.

The knot in my stomach fades.

I stop shaking.

The demons release me.

"Goodbye, Gavin. I'm moving on...my heart, my mind, my life."

Chapter 88

The water receded slowly.

The National Guard would not allow anyone into the flood zone of La Rogue for two weeks.

Today, I'm returning to my house.

My neighborhood used to be nice, dotted with half-million-dollar homes. Now, it looks like a war-zone. Gutted buildings with no roofs. Toppled cars. Destroyed landscape.

My house survived, but the interior is a mess. There's a visible waterline three feet up the wall. Most of the furniture is dammed near the patio door that shattered from the flood.

Wading through a layer of mud, I see something precious buried in the debris…a wedding picture of Angie.

We'd be celebrating seven years in October if she were alive.

I pull the frame from the mire and wipe it clean.

Angie looks beautiful. Her gown perfectly complementing her tall slender frame.

"I miss you." I whisper, kissing the glass covering her face.

Wandering outside, I upright a patio chair and take a seat. I gaze at the sky, wondering where to begin.

"Life has been crazy, Angie. A hurricane hit a few weeks ago. Destroyed the house and my clinic. It's gonna take a while to rebuild."

Sighing deeply, I hold the 8x10 frame close to my chest.

"Angie, I need to tell you something. You're not going to like it."

Choking back tears, I tell her what happened three years ago.

"You didn't die from heart failure. You were murdered. Remember the nurse you called a 'fucking gorilla'...the chick with the Russian accent. She poisoned you. She was a drug-dealing, sex-trafficking monster. Tried to kill me too...shot me in the chest."

I open my shirt, showing Angie the scar.

"The bullet just missed my heart."

Out of the blue, a strong wind shakes the trees. It makes me smile. I faintly hear Angie spewing obscenities, calling Sova every name in the book.

"Calm down, Honey. Let me finish."

Angie was always hot-headed.

"I'm not saying it was God's justice, but the nurse experienced a gruesome death...got crushed by an elevator."

I chuckle.

"I know you're laughing. The story sounds crazy like a Road-Runner cartoon, but she really did get crushed by an elevator."

I barely finish my sentence when I roar with laughter, the kind of laughter that relieves stress.

When I settle down, I look at Angie with twinkling tear-filled eyes.

My grin evaporates.

"There's something else I need to tell you."

I hesitate.

I feel awkward...unfaithful.

"I met someone. Her name is Rozlyn. We met at the hospital after I tried to commit suicide. No, she's not a nurse. She got hit by a bus. I know, sounds ridiculous, another cartoon story, but it's true. Broke both arms. Shattered her face. You'd like her. She's nice."

I go silent, giving Angie a chance to respond.

Her voice echoes in my heart.

"I'm happy for you, David. You need to let me go and live your life."

"Thanks, Angie. I'll always love you."

"I know," the wind whispers, carrying her voice away.

Chapter 89

New York City

"We're on the air in…three…two…one."

Across America, TVs flash with dazzling motion graphics accompanied by fanfare music.

A studio camera pans wide displaying a pair of talk-show hosts with smiles pasted on their faces.

"Good morning," the lead host says. "We have a special treat for our viewing audience. Two months ago, a story circulated on social media that captured the hearts of millions. A courageous man flew a helicopter into hurricane Jenise to rescue a half dozen people trapped on an oil rig in the Gulf of Mexico."

The program plays the cell phone video of Goodall and the little boy.

Delany's narrative takes the spotlight.

When the video ends, the camera cuts back to the host.

"Please welcome to our show, the owner of Aircruze Aviation, Martin Sota, and the heroic pilot who risked his life, Mr. Rex Goodall."

The camera pans right, showing Sota and Goodall sitting next to the co-host.

"Before we get started," the host says. "We have a surprise. Please welcome the people Mr. Goodall rescued."

Vorcy and his crew excitedly rush on stage. Sharing a blur of hugs and handshakes, everyone takes a seat behind Goodall making a perfect backdrop of smiling faces.

Goodall hasn't seen these guys since he left them in Shreveport eight weeks ago.

"Mr. Goodall, this group wouldn't be complete if we didn't include the man you rescued from a roof in La Rogue. David Barry, come on out."

David hurries on stage. He vigorously shakes Goodall's hand. It's the first time they've met. David was unconscious, fighting for his life when he was rescued.

He takes a seat with the others.

The camera pans to the co-host, but there's still one more surprise.

"Hold on," the main host says. "We're still missing someone."

A backstage camera shows the silhouette of a woman standing in the wing.

"Ms. Muer, come on out," the host says.

Rozlyn steps from the shadows...walking.

No neck brace. No heavy casts. No wired jaw.

She looks great!

Everyone smiles, except David.

He's crying.

He had no idea she was coming. He hasn't seen or heard from her in six weeks.

Everyone gives Rozlyn a friendly hug, except David. He holds her tight for a long time. The host needs to break them up.

"It's obvious, these people care for each other," he says about the group.

He has no idea of David and Roz's backstory—the love they share.

After a brief commercial break, the interview begins.

"So, Mr. Goodall, how did this amazing rescue unfold?" the co-host asks.

Before he can respond, Sota butts in.

"Not many people know this, but Aircruze has supported the Trident team for quite some time. These people are like family. If they need us, we'll be there—even in a hurricane."

The camera zooms close to Sota's face so viewers can't see Vorcy and his team rolling their eyes. If one could read lips, they'd know Crater is saying words inappropriate for young viewers.

The co-host redirects the limelight back to Goodall.

"So, Mr. Goodall, we understand you were a highly decorated combat pilot. Did that help you overcome your fear of flying into the storm?"

"Well…"

"I'm glad you mentioned that—" Sota blurts. "At Aircruze, we hire only the *best of the best*. You can rest assured customer safety is our top priority."

"Yeah…safety is important," the co-host mumbles, trying to regain control of the interview.

"Anyway…Mr. Goodall…what was going through your mind as you raced over the Gulf of Mexico into a raging hurricane? Were you afraid the helicopter would crash?"

He doesn't answer—just looks at Sota waiting for him to interrupt.

"As you know, Rex was flying one of the best aircraft on the planet. The Bell 429 is so reliable even a hurricane can't take it down," Sota grins.

229

The camera pans wide as someone on Vorcy's team stands.

It's Delany.

Walking in front of the crowd, she faces Goodall.

"I know you'd never do this...so I will."

Drawing back her fist, she punches Sota in the throat.

"Shut your fucking mouth," she hisses.

The program immediately cuts to a commercial.

Coughing and gagging, Sota staggers off stage.

A few people off camera, including Vorcy's crew, applaud. Even the co-host gives Delany a high-five.

She returns to her seat next to Punk.

He leans close.

"I am so attracted to you right now," he whispers.

She says nothing, just offers a mischievous twitch of her eyebrow.

The remainder of the interview is gripping. The show's social media is blowing up with comments of Goodall's bravery and Delany's vicious right-hook.

After the show, everyone gathers in the lobby with luggage in hand.

They're headed to the airport.

"Mr. Goodall, it was a pleasure to meet you. Thank you for saving my life," David says with a warm handshake. "I don't know how you rescued us, but I'm forever grateful."

"Your wife told me you're pretty amazing too," Goodall says, nodding toward Roz. "She said you were shot fighting off an armed drug dealer."

Roz blushes at Goodall's "wife" comment. She didn't tell him that. Patriot did.

"Yeah, my *wife* is pretty amazing too," David says, smiling at Roz. "She was in a terrible accident a few months ago. Her recovery has been miraculous."

A concierge disrupts their conversation.

"Excuse me, Mr. Goodall, the shuttle is here to take you and the others to the airport."

David and Roz say their 'farewells.' They're taking a cab to the airport later. David's flight to Louisiana doesn't leave till late afternoon. Roz's flight to Detroit leaves shortly after. She plans to move to Louisiana, but needs to wrap up a few things in Michigan.

Vorcy and his crew pile into a van. They disappear in city traffic.

Chapter 90

David is still shocked by Roz's amazing recovery. "Want some breakfast?" he asks.

"Sure."

Her voice is just above a whisper, but her speech is perfect.

They step outside to hail a cab. Instead of an iconic yellow taxi, a flashy white limo pulls up. A well-dressed driver steps out and greets them.

"Mr. Barry, will you and your companion please come with me."

He takes their luggage and opens the door. David shrugs at Roz as they climb in. Without any explanation, the driver navigates through heavy traffic.

Twenty minutes later, he stops in front of the St. Regis Hotel...the most prestigious hotel in New York City.

He opens the door, grabs their luggage, and escorts them into the lobby.

There's no check-in.

No conversation.

He leads them to a private elevator. They step in.

The driver nods, but doesn't join them.

They ride to the top.

The door opens to luxury—the Presidential Suite. $35,000 a night.

Chilled champagne with exquisite finger food is staged on a glass table.

Fine art compliments every wall.

There's enough Victorian furniture to make a queen jealous.

They step inside, but don't go anywhere.

They're bewildered.

"Mr. Barry, will you please join us in the living room," a voice calls.

He takes Roz's hand. They weave through a maze of halls into a majestic room with towering ceilings.

"BART!" David shouts.

Bart Edmond is standing in the room with a woman and two teenage boys.

"Mr. Barry, I'd like you to meet my family. This is my wife Julia, and my two sons Rick and Chris."

He shakes hands with the boys, but Julia hugs him tight.

"Thank you, thank you," she whispers through tears.

David is baffled.

When she finally releases him, he introduces Roz.

"Bart, I don't understand...what's this about?"

"After the storm, several agents (FBI) went back to the hospital to clean up the loose ends of my investigation. They found a lot more drugs stashed throughout the building. They also reviewed the security footage in the elevator when Sova was killed. What they saw made them cry."

David cocks his head. He has no idea where this story is going.

"Sova was going to shoot me in the back of the head. You stopped her. You took a bullet for me."

Bart's wife burst into tears.

His boys are teary-eyed too.

"I can never repay you for saving my life, but the bureau and my family want to thank you. Please, enjoy a long weekend in New York City on us."

David has no words. He's humbled.

Chapter 91

After sharing a gourmet breakfast, Bart, and his family leave.

Alone in the sprawling suite, David smirks at Roz.

"Do you wanna jump on the beds or play hide-n-seek or something?"

She giggles.

"I'd love to. Let me call my parents first. They need to know I won't be flying back till Monday."

Her words prick his heart. He doesn't want her to leave. He wants her in Louisiana with him.

She steps into the foyer to make the call.

It's brief.

When she returns, David is reading the champagne label.

"Would you like some bubbly?" he says with an awful British accent.

She smiles and nods.

He unwraps the foil neck and stares at the wire mesh holding the cork.

"Okay...I feel stupid. I've never opened champagne before."

Roz rears her head and laughs. David has never seen her so joyous. Her countenance is glowing.

He sets the bottle on ice and grabs her waist. He pulls her close, scanning the details of her face.

She's healed amazingly well.

Her brown hair has grown into a cute pixie.

Her right eye is a little bloodshot, but her vision is perfect.

A few scars remain on her right cheek. They'll fade with time.

Her lips—they're perfect. No lipstick. No gloss. Just moist lips.

He leans in.

They share their first sensual kiss.

No wired jaw. No peck on the mouth.

It feels right, a perfect fit as their tongues dance and parry.

When they un-vacuum their mouths, Roz takes his hand. She leads him down a hall into a regal-looking den.

She U-turns and takes another.

The dining room is beautiful, but not what she's looking for.

Next hall—some frickin' exercise room.

"Is there a bedroom in this place?" she huffs.

David belly laughs.

Taking the lead, he beelines to the master suite.

The room is ginormous.

The bed looks like it was built for Goliath—makes a king-sized look like a daybed.

They hop aboard and crawl to the middle.

David lays on his back letting Roz nestle on top of him.

He doesn't pull at her clothes.

Doesn't play touchy-feely.

Doesn't do anything ungentlemanly—just holds her.

They lay in silence for a long time.

I can feel his love as he holds me.

She's so tiny—so frail. I'm afraid I'll hurt her.

I want him to undress me, but I'm no centerfold model. Maybe he'll be disgusted by my bony body.

I want her—badly. Maybe she's not ready. I know she was abused by her ex-boyfriend. I don't want to trigger any painful memories.

Should I ask him to make love to me? If he says *no*, I'll be so embarrassed.

I should give her some space. Take the pressure off.

David gently rolls Roz onto her side. He lays beside her propped on his elbow. He starts to say something, but she interrupts.

"Please, want me," she whispers.

"Oh, Roz...I want you."

They passionately kiss and undress.

It's midday. The room is bright. I wish it was dark. I don't want to see his expression when he looks at my body. I'll just close my eyes.

Her eyes are tightly shut. Maybe she's uncomfortable. I hope not.

I kiss her neck and gently explore her body.

Her skin is soft. Her features dainty.

Her arms are thin, atrophied from lack of use.

She's flat-chested, but noticeably aroused.

Her ribcage and hips protrude, but her stomach is flat complimenting the dimple of her bellybutton.

I'm torn. I want to yield to David, but I'm scared. He's kissing me, caressing me, expressing desire, but what if...

"Roz, I love you…all of you…inside and out."
He read my mind.
His words dissolve my fear.
I open up.
We merge.
We don't rock the world. Don't bump and grind.
Just melt into each other becoming one.

Chapter 92

A sleek helicopter sets down on Trident's helipad. The pilot shuts down the engine and climbs out.

Vorcy and his crew bail out the passenger doors.

With the rotors gliding to a stop, everyone gathers in a circle.

"Thanks for the gift," Goodall says, nodding toward the chopper.

Trident's parent company, Huron Energy, bought it for him. Henceforth, he's the only air service Trident will use.

"I'll be back in a few days with supplies."

"We look forward to it," Vorcy says.

These people are forever bonded.

Goodall climbs into his chopper and fires it up. Hovering for a moment, he turns north and flies into the evening sky.

Vorcy and his crew grab their gear.

Punk snatches Delany's duffel before she can grab it.

"I'll carry it for you," he offers.

She starts to protest, but stops. She likes the attention Punk is giving her. He's been super sweet ever since they survived the hurricane...not one 'sweet cheek' remark. She misses that, not to mention the sexy grin he'd give each time he'd say it.

Everyone clops up the stairs to the third deck—the living quarters. There are ninety cubicle apartments with all the comforts of home. Bed. Bath. Closet.

Atop the stairs the men turn right. Delany turns left.

"Excuse me," she says.

Punk turns.

"Aren't you forgetting something?"

"Oops."

He still has her duffel draped over his shoulder.

She reaches to take it.

"I'll deliver it to your door."

She walks past four apartments, stopping at unit 12.

Punk sets the duffel at her feet.

"Have a nice evening, Ms. White."

He turns to leave.

"Excuse me."

He turns back again.

"My co-workers call me Ms. White. My friends call me Delany."

He smiles.

"Have a nice evening...Delany."

He turns to walk away.

"Excuse me."

He turns back a third time.

"Would you like your thank-you gift?"

"What gift?"

"Your gift for saving my life when we were washed off the rig."

"Oh, it was nothing. I appreciated the little cuddle," he grins.

He starts to walk away.

Frustrated, Delany stands with her hands on her hips.

"What do I have to do, throw myself overboard to get another hug?"

Punk is rarely speechless, but he is.

240

Dropping his duffel, he steps close. He locks his arms around her waist making it impossible to escape. She has no desire to get away.

After a lingering hug, he loosens his grip.

"Not so fast, Tarzan…sweet cheeks isn't finished."

Grabbing his collar, she pulls him close. She kisses him hard on the mouth. Abandoning their duffels, she leads him into her apartment. With a frisky kick, she shuts the door with her foot.

Fires are dangerous on oil rigs, but there's no way to quench the flame between Punk and Delany.

Chapter 93

It sounds more like a bellow than a cry.

Roz hurries into the living room.

"What's wrong, Dee Dee?"

The toddler looks at her finger, pouting.

"The door bit me," she whines.

Roz examines the injury. She's sees nothing, but kisses Dee Dee's finger anyway.

"All better?"

"No...I want Daddy."

Roz rolls her eyes.

"Honey, will you come here, please."

David comes out of the bathroom, his face splotched with shaving cream.

"What's up?"

"Dee Dee has a booboo. Only Daddy can fix it."

He takes his three-year-old in his arms.

"Where's your booboo, honey?"

She pokes her pinky in his face. He grabs her tiny hand and kisses it several times, leaving shaving cream gooped on her fingers.

It makes her giggle.

"All better?"

"Yeah," she smiles.

He hands Dee Dee back to Roz, stealing a kiss during the exchange. His smooch leaves a glob of shaving cream on her face.

Dee Dee laughs at Mommy's Santa beard.

Grinning, David heads to the bathroom.

Dee Dee wriggles free, racing after him.

Roz smiles at the sight as she wipes goo off her chin.

She goes into the kitchen, but eavesdrops on David and Dee Dee's conversation.

"What's that stuff?"

"Shaving cream."

"Does it taste good?"

"No...it's yucky."

"Can I wear some?"

David must have smudged her face cuz she squeals with laughter.

Out of the blue, she sings an impromptu song.

"I love Daddy, yes I do...he makes my booboos go away," she sings with no rhyme or rhythm."

Roz chuckles.

"Yup, Daddy's kisses make your booboos go away," she whispers.

She clearly remembers five years ago when Dr. Barry kissed her battered face.

It was a wonderful kiss.

A healing kiss.

Barry's kiss.

Made in the USA
Columbia, SC
15 August 2024

40041421R00150

Bear, acting dumb, said, "Now what question would that be?"

Henry laughed. "They sorta like each other. There may be bells ringing in the future."

Bear asked, "Who is this Henry Harrison?"

Henry told them, "He is a true Patriot. His brother Benjamin Harrison has signed important documents up in Boston to make this a free country, independent from the British. Henry was wounded in the war with Spain. A good, good man."

Keeton looked at Thomas. "So you are going back north in the direction of Harrison's place?"

"Reckon so," he replied. "Now that we know letters are being carried by that route. We did pass this information on to Cousin Robbie Fretwell in Hopewell so that he can

245

send it on to Williamsburg and for other Patriot eyes."

Henry replied, "Good, good, we need to keep WAP in the loop so people at the farm will know too."

They laid around for a week until Henry and Keeton got restless.

Henry told the Hornets after supper, "I think Keeton and I will go back toward Leasburg. We can go north and just follow the North Carolina-Virginia line as best we can and see what is going on there."

Bear replied, "Guess we will just hang around. We'll try to let things be peaceful for a few days to calm down until we hit them again. We will wait for word on that new place. We can be ready to move out after the next raid."

Nathan said, "Yeah, we are getting tired of eating fish and oysters. We need some beef, so we will look for that on our next trip. We try to borrow food from the Red Coats every chance we get. Last time, we 'found' two large boxes of good beef jerky."

Henry laughed, "Yeah, tis neat to just 'find' things they have thrown away."

Keeton said, "We will pack up tomorrow and head out. Still much to do out there, and besides, we don't get news here."

Bear replied, "Be nice to have a daily newspaper."

Nathan laughed. "Now you are dreaming, and if we did get the paper, would the news be the truth or just what someone would write?"

Henry said, "You got a point there, depending if the reporter is for or against independence."

They had much discussion late into the night.

By mid-morning the next day, they were all packed.

Keeton asked them, "Have any clue what day it is?"

Nathan replied, "I think it is mid-March 1778. Of course, we don't have a calendar, so guess this is about right. Why?"

Keeton laughed. "You know it is hard to keep track of things being kinda isolated out here by the swamp."

Bear replied, "Yeah, be a good time to move to a new place, away from the swamp. The mosquitoes should be coming for fresh blood when it warms up."

Henry and Keeton said their goodbyes. "Be safe and do no harm. Well, that is, to the patriot side of this war."

Chapter 10

They rode two days northwest to the little place called Palmyra and stopped for the night. Few houses lined the old roadway. As they were camping, a couple of men came with rifles in hand to investigate.

Henry asked one of the men, "May we camp here tonight?"

The man replied, "Maybe. Who are you?"

Keeton replied, "We are just travelers, going up past Scotland Neck and on into Virginia."

The older man asked, "You boys for or against the King?"

Henry immediately replied, "We are true Patriots, for independence, to run our own country."

The men whispered to each other and again, the older man said, "We are family here and most of us just want peace."

Henry looked at both, "We can just move on. We mean no problems for Patriots. We are looking for land to rent or buy back along the Roanoke, if you know of any?"

The younger man asked, "And what would you be growing?"

Keeton laughed. "We might just raise cane."

The man said, "We heard of some men who can take care of troublemakers. Helped my aunt way up in Wilson a time back."

Henry asked, "Do you have any dogs?"

The man replied, "Just one ugly old dog."

Keeton asked, "What color is the ugly dog?"

The man replied, "Red. Why?"

Keeton held out his hand. "Did your aunt get any more ducks?"

The older man replied, "Sorry mister. We have to be careful," as he shook hands with Keeton and Henry. "Yes, we took her some ducks. So, you are the boys she talked about that found her and kept her alive?"

Henry said, "Yes. Does she still have the red and blue scarf?"

The older man replied, "Yeah. I'm John Wilson. This is my boy, Johnny. We shore are glad to meet you boys."

Keeton said, "Word sure gets around fast. And how is she doing now?"

"She is fine. One of my boys went there to live with her and take care of the trade horses. OK, serious. What can we do to help the cause?"

"We have some friends who are looking for a place to camp. Do you need to know more?"

Johnny replied, "Nope, we don't. That way if someone asks, we know nothing."

Henry told them, "The place needs a house, land for horses to graze, and to not be close to any other houses."

The two men talked, and one finally said, "I know a large place on the Roanoke River, just in the bend. A family tried to build a plantation there but could not get it off the ground. They finally gave up and moved back into Virginia. We kinda look after it for them. No one wants it. Buzzards roost there by the dozens. Do you want to buy it?"

Keeton replied, "No, just rent for a year if that is OK, and we do have money."

Johnny told them, "Have your friends come see us. We will take care of this, and no one else needs to know. Go 'bout a mile up this road. There are two small creeks almost running side by side. Turn and follow the right creek for a mile or so till you come to the Roanoke. There is good pasture for cattle or horses and a large house. Check it out. If you like it, we can rent it for the owner, and he don't need to know the details."

Henry and Keeton shook their hands, thanking them. Henry said, "Nathan Wright will come see you soon. We need to send a note back down to Plymouth to contact you two."

Johnny replied, "We will send the note."

Keeton said, "If you don't mind, we will go there this evening and stay a couple days?"

"Sure, make yourself at home there, and thank you."

They followed the simple directions and turned down the creek until it went into the Roanoke River. There on the rolling hill was a large house, once a well-kept place with plenty of room near the barn.

Both rode around the house, to the barn, and checked the small pasture between the house and barn.

Henry said, "Looks good to me. Kinda grown up. Needs some TLC."

Keeton replied, "We are not in the TLC business, guess Bear and Nathan can do that."

Henry said, "I better check the fencing. Don't want our horses to wander off."

They unloaded all three horses, turning them in the pasture. Tanner disappeared in the barn and returned in a few minutes with a groundhog.

Henry walked the fence line, from one end to the other. Most bordered Roanoke River, which made a natural fence. A couple places, he had to find a sapling to fill in the broken fence. He returned to the barn as Keeton was checking it out and had placed the saddles on a saddle pole inside to keep them dry.

"The fence is OK, and they can drink out of the Roanoke River."

Keeton asked, "Is it fresh or salty?"

"Fresh, the tide does not come up this far. But I did wonder and had to do the taste test. There is a good spring to the right, just outside the fence, near the house too. The little creek from the spring has plenty of watercress."

Keeton replied, "Yum, I do like the fresh watercress with any meat, just adds to the flavor." Keeton patted the large dog. "Now enjoy. We will be here a couple of days." The huge dog dropped the groundhog and just sat looking at Keeton. He laughed. "Now, are you trying to read my mind?" The dog just wagged his tail, picked up his supper, and walked toward the house.

The house was huge, with a large front porch and a breezeway from the house to a kitchen.

Keeton said, "Wow, they musta had lots of money at one time."

"Guess so," Henry replied. "But could not get good help to run it. Too bad for them, but good for us. This is a neat place, a mile off the beaten paths with plenty of grass and big enough for our friends."

They explored the house with three large upstairs rooms and four down plus the kitchen. All the furniture had been taken. Everything was bare except the kitchen, which had a huge wood-burning stove. Henry looked the stove over. "Guess this is why they did not take it?

"What?" Keeton asked.

"It must weight a ton. All cast iron and sets back into the rock wall. So where do we want to put our things?"

Keeton said, "Why not bed down in the kitchen. I see no need to try to heat the house with only two of us. That is a lot of firewood. There is a woodshed out back. I'm going to see if there's any wood there for the stove." He returned in a few minutes with an armful of wood, enough to cook a few meals, as he dumped it in a large box used to store wood.

Henry said, "I'll go get us some water and some 'cress too. We got jerky and cornmeal. We can make grits with the jerky?"

"Sure, sounds like a meal to me."

Soon they had a fire going in the old stove and water on for coffee and the grits.

They explored the house more as the water was getting hot. Henry looked around, "Now, how in the world could they keep four fireplaces fed at the same time?"

Keeton replied, "Takes lots of wood. Maybe that is one reason they left. Just not enough help?"

They put their bed rolls on the floor, away from the wood stove, and relaxed, sitting on the floor.

"This sure beats our little tent," Keeton said.

Henry replied, "Yeah, we could get used to this." They relaxed as the sun set in the west, with Tanner lying at Keeton's feet.

Keeton asked, "Think we stink that bad?

"What?" Henry asked.

"Those buzzards, lots keep circling to the north, up on the ridge. And Tanner got up and moved."

Henry laughed. "We can take a bath in the river tomorrow. Sure it's warm now."

Keeton replied, "Go right ahead. Gotta be icy coming from the mountains."

Henry replied, "Maybe tomorrow. Gosh, there must be fifty buzzards there, must be a roosting area."

The night went fast as they slept well. The next morning, Henry said, "Think we need to get in some firewood. I saw a couple dead trees down from the barn." A few minutes later, he came back in and got his bow and arrows. "There are some deer

259

feeding under the big white oak. Think I'll get us one."

"Good," Keeton replied. "Be nice to have a fresh deer steak. I'll keep Tanner here."

"Be back shortly," and off Henry went, sneaking toward the barn and beyond the deer feeding.

Half an hour later, he returned, dragging a small buck. "Now that was easy. They were distracted with a flock of turkeys trying to steal their acorns."

They skinned out the deer, giving Tanner his share of the guts, heart, and other parts. He was happily chewing on a deer leg as they hung the deer up to cool out.

Keeton told him, "We do need to do something until the others arrive. It may be a week before they get the word and get here."

The week went fast. They kept busy with cutting firewood and making a couple trips to the Roanoke River to fish. Tanner seemed bored with nothing to do. He kept sniffing around and a couple times completely disappeared for half a day at a time.

Henry said, "Think your dog is gone for good now?"

Keeton replied, "He has his own mind. He may be out looking for a lil' love."

Henry laughed. "Had not thought of that."

On day seven, Nathan and Bear arrived, bringing a couple of loaded packhorses.

Henry went out to meet them. "Where are the others?"

Nathan told them, "They are on the way. We brought most of the extra guns. Some we traded for corn and cornmeal down the road."

Keeton told him, "This is a good place. Why not put the corn and cornmeal in one of the rooms to keep dry and to keep mice away?" They carried the four bags inside.

Nathan asked, "Same room for the guns too?"

Keeton replied, "Yes, we can make one of the rooms our storeroom." They took two bags of long guns inside.

"No gunpowder?"

"Nope," he replied. "Elmer and Delmer is bringing that later today."

They turned the horses loose in the pasture as Star came to check them out. He turned and ran down toward the river.

Bear said, "He showing out or just glad to be free to run?"

Keeton replied, "Maybe a little of both."

Soon all four were on the porch, relaxing.

Nathan asked, "Where are the chairs?"

Henry replied, "Only thing left was the huge wood cookstove out back in the kitchen. Pick your sleeping area anywhere you want."

Bear said, "If it's OK with you folks, I'll get one room upstairs, so I can look and listen."

"Your choice," Keeton replied. "We will be leaving in the morning, going back north."

They ate well on the fresh deer meat with watercress and relaxed as the sun went down. By morning, Tanner had returned, apparently dead tired, and had slept on the porch.

Chapter 11

Three days out, they were near Norlina and camped in an old friend's barn. Being under roof, even in a barn, was nice during a spring thunderstorm.

Two days later, they were in another wide place in the road. Henry said, "See that old farmer? Think I'll ask him which state we are in."

The old farmer was cutting briars.

Henry asked, "What is the name of this place?"

The man replied, "We air on the state line. Reckon we call this Virgilina. Got to have a name, me wife says."

Keeton laughed. "Guess this is good as most names. What is north of there?"

The man asked, "What air ye a'lookin' for?"

Henry told the man, "We are just looking around for the enemy."

The man stopped cutting briars and replied, "Guess it depends on which side ye air on. Proud to tell you boys, I'm fur independence."

Henry smiled. "As we are. Maybe go up north get on the Trader's Road to the west?"

The farmer told them, "This a'road here is a trader's road a'goin' that way," pointing north, "and the other way," pointing south.

Keeton inquired, "Is it used much?"

The farmer replied, "Reckon so, up that a'way." He pointed north and continued, "Is where the Tories and Red Coats camp round a cluster of springs. Always good water and shelter to hide under the big old spruce trees."

Henry replied, "Thank you, sir. Have a good day."

He replied, "Try to have every day good, just too old to j'in the militia. You boys be safe. Hey, wait a minute. I got some taters to sell, if you got money?"

Henry said, "Yes, sir. We do have money and be glad to buy some."

The old farmer almost ran to a shed beside his house and brought back a sack of potatoes. "Reckon this air 'bout ten pounds. Is that enough? Got you fellers some eggs too, if you want?"

Keeton told the old man, "Thank you, sir," as Henry handed him some money. "Is that enough?"

The old man smiled, "Yes, yes. Not had money in me hand in so long.

Now can buy some coffee and sugar tomorrey."

Onward they rode, going north a few miles. Keeton remarked, "Maybe we should be careful. Might be a bunch of the enemy there now."

Henry replied, "Yeah, guess we better."

Slowly, they approached a large camp, with several freshwater springs as the old farmer had told them and the huge spruce trees to the north and west. Tanner, nose to the ground, sniffed the area and looked around, for something, anything, but all was bare ground.

Keeton said, "Wow, this has been used lots. Look at the horse crap piled up back of the trees."

Henry laughed. "They did pile it downstream from the springs. Least someone is using their brain."

Slowly, cautiously, they circled the area, finding firewood stacked under one ole spruce tree with drooping limbs to help keep the wood dry. One firepit still had smoke rising from the ashes.

"What do you think, Henry?"

"Why don't we move away for a mile or so, and if anyone comes close, we will hear them."

"Good idea."

They found a good, secluded camping area a half a mile north and off the road. It was right in the middle of several large spruce trees with good grass for their horses. They unpacked the packhorse and put up the tent, found firewood, and set up camp. The horses were staked in the tall, dry grass to eat. In a short time, Tanner returned with a large rabbit in his mouth.

Keeton patted him on the head. "Good for you, fresh rabbit."

Henry said, "We better just make a small fire. Don't want to stir up smoke."

Keeton replied, "Yeah, should anyone smell smoke, might think it came from the firepit at the campsite."

Soon they had coffee on the fire.

Henry said, "Put on the skillet. We gonna have some fried taters." He took several potatoes down to the little creek and washed them. There he found fresh watercress growing and got a huge handful, pulled off the roots, and washed them in the fresh, cold water.

When he got back to camp, the skillet was hot.

Keeton said, "You washed them, I'll cut them up." So he cut

them up, put them in the hot skillet, and added some wild onions.

Henry said, "That sure smells good, very good."

Tanner had eaten the entire rabbit and now stretched out beside the fire.

"Don't take much to make him happy," Keeton said.

"Nope, he is good to have around. He looks like he is passed out, but I know his ears are always listening."

The meal was excellent with plenty of fried potatoes and the fresh watercress added to the meal.

As dark closed in, they got the horses, brought them in close, and gave them some corn to eat.

The winds were whispering through the spruce trees. Keeton said, "I'm gonna turn in. Think that will put me to sleep." He patted Tanner.

"You have guard duty tonight." The big black dog wagged his tail and did not move. All was quiet as both sacked out in the tent.

Much later, Keeton whispered, "Wonder what time it is?"

Henry mumbled, "Still dark. Don't really care. Go back to sleep."

Keeton said, "Nope, mother nature calling. Gotta go pee." He got up, opened the flap on the tent, and saw Tanner sitting up, looking to the north, ears pointed, nose high in the air.

Keeton whispered, "What do you smell, boy?" The dog just sat, not moving. Keeton quickly peed and went back in the tent. "Better get up, Henry. Tanner has alerted to something."

Henry did not ask, just quickly got up, put his boots on, and grabbed his weapons. He whispered to Keeton,

"Wonder who could be out this early. Not really light yet."

They both just stopped to listen. Nothing, not even the sound of the wind or birds yet.

Keeton whispered, "I don't like it. Something is out there. Be it man or beast, I don't know."

Henry said, "Let's wait till good daylight. If Tanner is still alerted, we will find the answer."

"Think we can make coffee?"

"Yeah," Henry replied. "A small fire."

Keeton said, "We still got some taters from last night, and we better eat the eggs or they will get broke."

In thirty minutes, they had coffee, the fried taters from the night before, and the remainder of the eggs ready.

Henry took the skillet and tin plates down to the creek and washed

272

them as Keeton started taking down the tent.

By the time the sun was in the eastern skies, they were packed and ready for the road again.

Tanner was still alerted, now looking back toward the cluster of springs.

"Someone is there," Keeton said.

Henry said, "Yeah, and I'm gonna find out who." He got his small bow and arrows from the pack. He tied his boots to the saddle horn and put on his soft moccasins. "Just hang tight. If you hear me whistle, come on and bring the horses."

Henry slowly, silently, crept through the woods, back toward the springs and camp spot.

He could smell smoke and hear two men talking but not what they were saying. Closer he came until he

273

could see the men near the pile of wood. One was lying on the ground, the other sitting on the wood. He stopped, looked, checked, and checked again. He did not see any weapons, and there were no horses close by.

He went back to Keeton and told him, "Take the horses, and ride right in like you own the place. Give me a few minutes to circle behind the trees."

"OK," Keeton said, and waited for a few minutes, got on his horse, Star, leading the other two horses, rode near the camp, and yelled, "Comin' in friendly."

One of the men replied, "Ride on in. We are friendly too."

By that time, Henry was behind the wood pile, to the men's backs, watching. One did not get off the ground. The other held a long, sharp

274

stick in hand. They waited until Keeton approached.

The one standing, holding the stick, said, "We need help. My friend done been shot last night. We barely got away."

Keeton asked, "Where are your horses?"

"They got them too, just 'scaped with our lives."

Keeton dismounted, gun in right hand, Tanner by his left side, and walked nearer the man. He instantly noticed both had almost new boots, the kind the Red Coats wore.

The man sad, "I'm Oliver Worth. My buddy is Kenny. Can you help him?"

Keeton replied, "Where was he shot?"

"Way up the road. We got bushwhacked. It was dark, and we

just started a'walkin' south down this way."

Henry had overheard and came from behind the trees. He knelt to examine the wounded man. "Did you try to help him?"

Oliver replied, "Just to stop the bleeding. I don't know medicine."

Henry noted one bullet hole almost middle of his chest. "Did it go through?"

"Don't know."

Henry asked Kenny, "Can I roll you over?"

The wounded man nodded, opened his eyes just a little, breathed heavily, and moaned when Henry tried to roll him over to see if the bullet came out the back. While rolling him over, he saw a small leather pouch and started to take it off the man.

Oliver shouted, "Don't touch that!"

Henry asked, "Why not? I need to examine his back."

Oliver told them, "That was the reason we got shot. Them Red Coats wanted the message inside the bag. I sure hope you all are not loyalists. We have nothing left to fight with."

Keeton looked around, not seeing any other weapons, and told the man, "We are on your side. Do you know what is in the pouch?"

The man replied, "No, but it is for Colonel Easton down at Leasburg. We brung this from way above Richmond at all speed. That don't need to get in the hands of the Red Coats."

Henry gently took the pouch off as he lay the man back down. The man moaned one time and stopped. Henry felt for a pulse in the neck, finding none. Henry took the man's coat and covered his face. "He is dead. I'm sorry."

Oliver started sobbing. "Guess we failed our mission. Now the message will never get through."

Henry turned the collar of his coat, showing the man his badge. "We will take it on to Leasburg. We know Colonel Easton well."

Oliver said, "Thank you, thank you. I don't have a horse, or anything, now. They took everything." He was drained and depressed at having not fulfilled his mission to deliver the message.

Keeton took one of his pistols, a powder horn, and a hand full of bullets and gave it to Oliver. "Here, disappear in the trees. We must get this delivered as soon as possible. A mile or so down the road to the east are good Patriots. Go there for help."

"What about Kenny?"

Henry motioned to Keeton. "Help me. We will take him back in the trees and cover him until tomorrow." After they had moved Kenny back and covered him with leaves, Keeton said, "We need to wipe away traces of where they were."

Henry told him, "Go, hide out until this group passes, come back tomorrow, and bury him. Nothing else we can do at this time. Do you know how many was in the troop that ambushed you all?"

Oliver thought a minute, "Maybe twenty-five or thirty. We rode right in the middle of their camp without knowing it. But a whole troop is on the way here now."

Henry said, "Go!" and pointed to the south east. "Go, find the

Patriots, and come back tomorrow. We will deliver the message."

"Thank you," Oliver said, and quickly disappeared in the bushes with the pistol in his right hand.

Chapter 12

Henry said, "Nothing else here," and they got on their horses and rode.

It was nightfall by the time they got to the first sentry, who stopped them until he saw it was Henry. "Go on, man. The road is open."

Henry told them to be on alert. "The Red Coats are coming!"

In a short time, they reached the training camp at Leasburg and immediately went to the hospital tent. There they found Sergeant Major Ricketts and Doc Shults closing up for the night. Ricketts asked, "What brings you here in the dark?"

Henry told him, "We have a dispatch from General Greene up north for Colonel Easton."

Ricketts asked, "What is the dispatch?"

Henry held up the leather pouch. "We did not open it. It cost one good patriot his life trying to deliver it."

Doc Shults went into the tent, returning in a couple minutes with two mugs of hot coffee, and handed each a cup. "I can rustle up some food later."

Ricketts went off, almost running, to Colonel Easton's tent, returning with him in just a few minutes.

Colonel Easton walked fast to Henry. "What do you have?"

Henry handed the leather pouch to him. "We don't know, but it must be important!"

Colonel Easton took the pouch and went inside the medical tent. Doc followed and lit a couple lamps.

He opened the bag and took out a wax-sealed envelope, broke the seal, and read and read again. He handed it to Doc Shults. "Read it."

Doc Shults read, "This is from General Greene's aide, Colonel Cody. Says there is a full troop on the way to Leasburg training camp to wipe out the patriots. The Red Coats know the training there is the best and they want to erase that place from the earth. He expects at least 250 trained militia and Red Coats to be marching your direction at this time."

Colonel Easton asked Keeton, "How long ago did you get this dispatch?"

"We got it near the cluster of springs up in Virginia right at daybreak. We rode as fast as our horses could to get here."

Colonel Easton looked at Sergeant Ricketts. "Round the troops, be quiet, get them in uniform, rifles in hand, and be ready for an attack at daybreak."

Sergeant Ricketts asked, "Where do you think they will hit us?"

Henry said, "If it was me, I would come right down that valley from the north. It is a quarter-mile wide and runs maybe fifteen miles."

"Ready the troops. No lights. Get the two little cannons pointed in that direction."

The colonel turned. Moses Lark had heard and was standing by. "Moses, put on a large pot of coffee. See what you can fix for breakfast, and make it good. Gonna be a long night and day. We don't know how fast the Red Coats will be coming or when they will get here."

Moses said, "Yes, sir." He turned and started toward the mess tent.

Keeton kinda sunk down on a block of wood. "Now we can breathe?"

Henry told him, "Yes, for now."

Colonel Easton came back, in full uniform now with weapons in his belt. He paced back and forth. "OK men, you have been out there. Talk to me."

Henry told him, "We need to know when they will get here and the only way to send out scouts to watch and report back."

"Where do you suggest?"

Henry told him, "There are two routes, one by the road and the other in the valley. Now, there are trees up most of the valley. We would not see them until almost at the camp."

285

Keeton said, "The road is mostly open and almost a straight line here. If they are bringing cannons and wagons, they will come by the road. If not, they will come by the valley."

The colonel replied, "So we need eyes and ears out there?"

Henry replied, "I would suggest that, Sir. I'll go up the valley for about three miles and watch, reporting back if I see or hear them."

Keeton said, "I'll go up the road about the same distance."

Sergeant Ricketts had joined them. "Colonel, we have some good backwoods men trained. Why not send a couple of these men with Henry and Keeton? If something happens, at least one should make it back."

Keeton replied, "I like that idea. I gave one pistol to the man who had the dispatch. Do you have another?"

Sergeant Ricketts motioned to one of his men. "Go get this man one of the new pistols, some more powder, and bullets."

The man replied, "Yes, Sergeant." He returned in a couple minutes and handed it to Keeton.

Keeton said, "Thanks. I felt naked with only one pistol."

The colonel told Sergeant Ricketts, "OK, get four men, on horses, no uniforms and fully loaded. Two men for each team."

He replied, "Yes, Sir!" He turned and was gone.

Henry said, "Colonel, we will be coming down that valley in a hurry. Please tell the cannon crew to not shoot us."

The colonel replied, "Yes, yes, we will do that."

Daybreak came as the camp was stirring. Everyone got their

weapons loaded, ate breakfast and drank coffee. They waited, ready, just in case of the attack.

Colonel Easton told Sergeant Ricketts to get the camp in formation. "I'll tell them what we are facing."

Soon the entire camp was in formation as Sergeant Ricketts called them to attention.

Colonel Easton addressed the men. "Good morning, men. We have a dispatch from General Greene's command that a troop of Red Coats and militiamen are marching this direction to wipe us from the face of this good earth. We are not going to let that happen. Now, we expect they will come from one of two directions. From the road or from the valley from the north. We will split the company, with half watching the road and the other half watching the valley. Now, if there is an attack from either direction, do NOT leave your post, as they may try to draw us in one direction or the other. We are sending out scouts to try to determine the direction they will come. We have two cannons. I want both set up to cover the valley. Now, HEAR THIS, our scouts will be coming back fast in front of the Red Coats. DO NOT SHOOT our scouts. Wait until they clear the distance and shoot over them toward the Red Coats. We have some trenches already in the valley direction." He looked at Sergeant Ricketts, Henry, and Keeton. "Did I miss anything?" All three shook their heads. He continued, "Go, make ready! Dismissed!"

Men went running in all directions, to collect extra powder and bullets.

Sergeant Ricketts assigned two men to each team. "Please be careful.

Come ahead as fast as you can to warn us of the direction."

All mounted up. Henry and two went up the valley. Keeton and his two went by road.

Keeton and his two men had gone north on the road about three miles, to the top of a small hill where they could see most of a mile to the north. They dismounted and waited.

Henry and his two men rode north for about three miles and stopped. Henry told them, "Dismount, relax a minute. We should hear them coming half a mile away. Just be quiet and listen. One of you go up the right hill, the other the left. I'll stay right here in the middle. If you hear or see something, come running, so we can get back to alert the camp. Go!"

Without a word, the two men split, going up opposite hills, to wait, listen, and watch.

Henry checked and re-checked his weapons. Checked and re checked his saddle and waited and waited. He looked toward the sun. *Must be mid-afternoon*, he thought. About that time both of his scouts came riding down the hills. "I can hear them coming."

"How far out?" Henry asked.

"I'd say less than half a mile."

Henry said, "OK, let's wait, just to be sure it is the Red Coats and not some farmer." In a short time, they heard the squeaking of leather and the rattling of the harnesses on the horses.

One man shouted, "I see them!"

Henry and his two scouts went, running their horses back toward the camp. He turned and saw a dozen horsemen chasing them. One shot was fired but did no damage. They rode faster, down the valley. Half a mile from the camp they broke through the trees to clear ground. Henry looked back and saw at least fifty horses now chasing them. Up ahead, he could not see anything at the camp, as the men were in trenches and behind trees, waiting for rifle distance. All at once, he heard a *kaboom!* and saw smoke from the two cannons. He thought, *That is way too low.* Suddenly, all was black. He could feel himself falling, then nothing, nothing. Darkness closed in around him.

Keeton had heard the shooting and the cannons and came running from the road to help in the battle, but by the time he got there with his two men it was nearly dark. The Red Coats, in and out of uniform, were lying everywhere on the ground. The able troops were fleeing back up the valley. Several of the loyalist militia in no uniforms were dead or wounded. All the area was a bloody mess with humans and horses blown into bits by the cannons.

Keeton rode right up and jumped off his horse as Colonel Easton was talking to Doc Shults. "Did we lose any of our troops?"

Doc replied, "'Fraid so, yes. At least six and about that many wounded, some serious. Just glad we were ready, or they would have wiped us out. There must be a dozen or so loyalist militia and a few Red Coats dead too."

The colonel barked orders to get the wounded off the field and into the hospital tent. "Leave the dead until morning."

Keeton asked, "Where is Henry?"

Doc looked at Colonel Easton. He looked back. "We have not seen him."

Sergeant Ricketts came running, "Colonel, I think the right cannon fired too fast and too low. We killed some of our own men with friendly fire."

"What?" Colonel Easton asked. "Who was on the cannon? What about our scouts. Did they come on in?"

Sergeant Ricketts replied, "No, Sir. We have not found our scouts just yet. I was watching as the first shell hit near the retreating scouts. I will find out who fired the cannon." He looked at Keeton. "Come on, let's go find him!"

They mounted up and rode the short distance to where several horses and men laid dead, strewn around the valley.

Keeton said, "So much carnage, but I don't see Henry."

Sergeant Ricketts said, "Where is he? Did he chase the Red Coats?"

Keeton got off, walking around, and yelled, "Here is his horse! Dead!"

"Where is he?" Sergeant Ricketts was yelling too.

Several other troopers had followed them with a wagon. He instructed the men to take the wounded back to the hospital. They walked over the bloody bodies to get a wounded man and gently placed him in the wagon. They carefully checked and rechecked each man for signs of life, taking only the living men.

Keeton now was in a panic. "Where are you, Henry?" He checked and rechecked the wounded men in the wagon. Henry was not there.

The men collected all the wounded and returned to the camp for the doctor to help them.

Keeton told Sergeant Ricketts, "He must have followed the retreating Red Coats."

Sergeant Ricketts replied, "He must have," but his gut told him otherwise.

Keeton screamed as he picked up something and held it to his chest. "OH NOOO!"

Sergeant Rickets came to him, "What?"

Keeton handed him a leather strap with three bear claws. "This was around his neck, given by our Catawba friends." He sank down to the ground, in the mass of mangled human and horses, tears running down his face, unashamed. He pulled pieces of bloody clothing and stopped again. "Just can't be?"

"What?" Sergeant Ricketts asked.

Keeton held up part of a coat with Henry's badge still pinned to the collar.

They all went back to the camp. One of Doc Shults's men was checking and unloading the wounded on the wagon. The wagon would go back in the morning and collect the dead with instructions to lay them under a tree for burial tomorrow. Darkness closed in.

Colonel Easton was talking with Doc Shults, low, but Keeton heard. "Henry is dead. Apparently, the first cannon shot killed him, his two scouts, and their horses. It exploded right under their feet."

Doc said, "I just don't believe Henry is gone."

Keeton walked up and said, "No, he can't be gone. He just can't!" He clinched the three bear claws and Henry's badge.

297

That night, Keeton took a torch and went back, trying to find Henry or where he had gone. Sergeant Ricketts joined him, searching, turning and examining fragmented human remains, and turning over dead horses, looking for any clue.

The night was long and everyone was exhausted, but Keeton could not get any sleep.

Toward morning, the camp awoke as several medical wagons under heavy escort approached the camp. Doc went out to greet them.

One driver told him, "We were sent by General Greene with medical supplies. We knew the Red Coats were coming to attack the training center."

Doc Shults told him, "We were attack yesterday evening. We have lots of wounded. We can sure use the help and supplies."

When daylight approached, a wagon was sent back to the battle area to collect the dead. Others were digging graves. The first wagon returned in an hour or so with eight dead men. Some were mangled badly. They unloaded the dead under a huge ancient old oak tree so they could be buried with a ceremony later.

As the men unloaded the dead, one said, "Hey, wait a minute." He pointed. "That man's eyes moved. He ain't dead!"

Doc was treating one of the wounded soldiers sitting under the same tree and asked, "What did you say?"

"Look, Doc, that one's eyes is moving. He's not dead."

Doc screamed, "Get him in the hospital tent!"

They grabbed him by the arms and legs and took him into the

hospital tent. Doc told his staff, "We have one alive. See what we can do to help."

The man had gotten their attention by moving his eyes. It didn't seem that he could talk, hear, or move his limbs. He was placed on the cold wood table, and someone wiped blood from his face and eyes. His face was swollen, and his hair matted with blood—his own plus others'. The man opened one eye and looked around. Was he dead? He could not communicate as the doctor gently washed his face and hands and took off his bloody clothing to examine for wounds. His arms and shoulders were splattered with small wounds, with oozing blood. Blood was dripping from both ears. He laid there and could only move his eyes.

Doc said, "He seems to be searching for someone with his eyes. He keeps looking around."

One of Doc Shults' aides asked, "Who is he?"

Doc Shults replied, "I just don't know. He is swollen too much to recognize if he is on our team or with the loyalists. We will treat him as a human being either way."

For two days, he laid there, not moving. Both doctors examined him daily, gently washing the blood from the oozing holes. One took a damp cloth and washed his dried lips. There was no change. Doc Shults said, "He will be dead in a few hours. He is not getting any better. His pulse is low, his breathing is shallow. Let's just keep him comfortable. I wish we had better equipment to look inside to see what is broken."

The other doctor said, "I agree, and someday there will be good equipment to help the wounded."

On the third morning, as he laid there, the doctor examined him and changed his bandages and washed this face. His lips were dried and cracked. Some water got in his mouth. He coughed. He was breathing hard, a hoarseness coming from his throat. A croaking, broken sound came from his lips as he whispered something.

The doctor stopped and motioned to Doc Shults. "He just whispered something."

Doc Shults leaned down and asked, "What?"

The nearly dead man with the broken voice whispered, "*Abigail.*"

Doc grabbed the man and gave him a hug. "Abigail, this is Henry!"

She screamed and fell over Henry, crying. Tears finally came from Henry's eyes. With all his might, he tried to raise his right arm and put it around her.

Keeton heard her scream and came running. "What?"

Doc Shults said, "That is Henry. He is alive. He is alive!"

ACKNOWLEDGEMENTS

First, I would like to thank God for allowing me to reach out and help others.

I ask daily for faith, wisdom, knowledge and understanding and the ability to be of service to others.

I am thankful and blessed to have more and more people reading Henry's story, now from coast to coast, and asking for more books.

My old army buddies, Pruitt, Ricketts, and Ownby show up in every book now. They are a special breed. All veterans are special, as we stepped forward, signing a blank check to America to give as much as possible to protect our country, including death if necessary. We swore to protect against all enemies, foreign and domestic.

A special thanks to Sara Foust for the fantastic task of editing and formatting. And to my daughter, Becky Frisbie, who does the first editing and suggestions.

ABOUT THE AUTHOR

Arthur M. Bohanan is an internationally award-winning patented inventor, researcher, lecturer, author and a Certified Latent Print Examiner (only 980 in the world) with over 58 years in the study and practical application of forensics in thousands of violent crime scenes. He earned a bachelor's degree in criminal justice from East Tennessee State University (Legacy Award 2017) with further studies at the University of Tennessee, Knoxville. **Art** retired in May 2001 as a Senior Forensic Examiner with Knoxville Police Department (26 years) and twice received the Knoxville Police Officer of the year award plus the Legacy Award in 2018.

Bohanan was inducted into the International Hall of Fame in Atlanta (sponsored by the Inventors Clubs of America) with two distinguished awards plus a doctorate in science and technology for pioneering research involving children's fingerprints. He has responded to many major disasters, including the Columbia Space Disaster, The World Trade Center, Hurricane Katrina and six airline crashes to help identify the human remains. Art patented the use of superglue to develop fingerprints on human skin and discovered children prior to puberty have different chemical compounds in the fingerprints versus adult fingerprints.

Bohanan has invented a device to locate and gender lost graves.

Arthur M. Bohanan is a 6th generation Sevier Countian, a US Army Veteran (Viet Nam Era MP), who has truly been blessed by God over the many years of service to humanity.

MW01230975

Other Books in the Henry Bohanan's
Journey series:

Watauga

Pigeon Rivers

Volunteer Patriots

Hornets and Crowes

Guerilla Fighters

Two Deadly Enemies

Patriotic Duties

Return to Watauga

Protecting Our Assets

Left For Dead

Arthur M. Bohanan

ISBN: 978-1-7347056-7-6

Chapter 1

Tanner ran circles around the horses. He was ready for the road too.

Henry told him, "Don't think it's gonna get much warmer today."

West they rode. No one was out this early, and they had the dirt road to themselves. By noon, they had covered over fifteen miles.

Henry said, "Stop, we need a break, and the horses need a break." They got off, let the horses drink in a small stream, and walked around a few minutes before remounting.

Few words were said the first half of the day.

After noon, Keeton asked, "How do people live in Williamsburg? Can't even get out and shoot your gun for fear of hitting another house."

"Hey," Keeton said, "where is that stick candy?"

Henry opened the pack and took out two sticks. "One for me, one for you."

Henry replied, "They have huge plantations where they hunt."

"And they eat those horrible-looking oyster things. The crab was not good, but once I saw its shell, and it reminded me of a tiny turtle."

Henry laughed. "Well, guess it does in a way, has a shell."

They arrived back at the relay station just as darkness moved in. The old lady heard them and looked out the door and yelled, "You know the routine, jest help yourself." They unsaddled and unpacked the horses, turning them in the pasture with the others, and came to the house.

Tanner was right on Keeton's heels. "Hey buddy, I'm not going to

run off and leave you tonight, just chill out." The big dog just looked at him and turned toward the woods. "Guess he will find a warm supper tonight."

Henry asked, "Rabbit or squirrel?"

Keeton laughed, "Anything but a skunk." They both laughed.

Keeton did not bother to knock, just opened the door and walked in, carrying his rifle and two packs, which he sat on the floor just inside the door.

She said, "Don't got any coffee, how 'bout some tea with honey?"

Henry told her, "Anything warm and sweet." He looked at Keeton and asked, "Should I?"

Keeton read his mind. "Sure, couple would be good." He opened the bag and took out two sticks of

candy and laid them on the table. "We brought these just for you."

She turned from the fireplace, saw the candy, and broke into a wide, ear-to-ear smile. "Been long time since a man brung me candy." She picked them up, looked at them, smelled them, and then put the candy in a jar. "Them are fur later." She poured them the tea and sat down on the other side of the table. "OK, what is going on where ye all been?"

Henry laughed. "Being nosey or just curious?"

She smiled, maybe for the fifth time they had known her, and laughed. "Gets lonely out there. Reckon I'm a might nosey and curious too."

Henry told her, "We had a meeting with the governor, several military men and two friends, Pruitt and Dr. Neville."

She calmly listened while sipping the hot tea. "Wuz the meeting 'bout the war with the Red Coats?"

"Yes," replied Keeton.

She said, "Don't wanna know details, just are we gonna win our independence?"

Henry replied, "If we all do our jobs, yes, we will win."

She replied, "Been a'worryin' 'bout it. Got some hot head neighbors who will do anything to stop us."

Henry told her, "Lady, you are doing your part, just keep it up. We thank you."

She looked at him. "Now givin' me candy and now callin' me a lady. What next?" She finally laughed.

They enjoyed the time with her, and as they left the next morning, she asked, "Can I give you boys a hug?"

"Sure can."

She hugged both Henry and Keeton. "Stop by anytime back this way. You are always welcome, that is if you bring me more candy."

It was a long cold day back toward Buffalow Creek and Braton's house that day. By afternoon, the winds started blowing from the northeast. Keeton commented, "Are we going to make it back before snowfall?"

Henry replied, "Sure hope so. We don't know who is friend or foe out here, and that little tent is not much shelter in the wind and snow."

Keeton asked, "We are close to Rice?"

Henry replied, "Think we are there. See the four houses?"

Keeton replied, "Good. We are 'bout an hour from Braton's place." About that time, the first snowflake fell. The huge, white, fluffy flake

lazily came to the ground. It was not long until it was joined by many more, and the winds blew, bringing more. They pulled their hats low and their collars high and, without a word, kept going.

By the time they arrived at Braton's house the winds were howling, snow blinding, as they heard a horse calling out. "We are close. That may be Star calling out."

Henry said, "Or Ugly Horse. Think we will go on to Braton's now. We can take the horses back to Mr. Finchum tomorrow."

Keeton replied, loudly, as it was hard to hear because of the winds, "Maybe. Depends on how much snow."

The horses were laboring now as the snow was up to their knees as they approached Braton's place.

He came out to help. "Just put them in the barn. There is feed for them."

Henry told him, "Thanks. Made it just in the nick of time."

Braton replied, "Feared you all might be stranded out in the middle of nowhere."

Keeton took two packs to the house, and Braton carried the other two. "Be careful with that one with the red string. It's breakable."

They sat the bags down, hung their rifles on the wall pegs, and placed their pistols and knives on a high shelf, out of reach of the children.

Bobby and Susie just watched as they shook off the snow, took off their coats, and hung them up to dry too. Keeton took off his hat and shook it over the children, who went

screaming toward Lizzy. She laughed, "Snowing inside now?"

Bobby replied, "No, Mommy. Unke Key did that to us wid his hat."

"Come, sit by the fire. Want some hot sassafras tea?"

"Sure," both replied, moving their chairs closer to the fireplace and rubbing their hands together to get warm.

She brought the hot, steaming tea, and Susie said, "Mommy, me too, me too."

Lizzy got a cup of the tea, watered it down, and handed Bobby and his sister the cup. "Be careful, it's hot."

Soon they were warm. Braton asked, "Good trip?"

"Yes," replied Henry. "We delivered the letter and things are now in the works."

Lizzy asked, "Do you kids know what day it is?"

Bobby's eyes went wide, "It's Christmas?"

Braton replied, "Tomorrow will be and your uncles are here to share with us."

"Yeaas," the kids yelled. "Santa will come tonight? But the snow. Can he walk in that snow?"

Lizzy replied, "Yes, he is magic. He can go anywhere. He works in all kinds of weather."

"Yaa," both children yelled again.

Braton said, "Think they are excited?" and laughed.

"Aww, to be a kid again. Remember, many years ago we had snow and papa took us all up on the ridge, squirrel hunting?"

Braton said, "I do remember. He took one gun and never fired it,

but we came home with a sack of squirrels."

She asked, "Now how did he do that?"

Henry told her, "There musta been five or six kids stomping in the snow. We found a big tree with holes in it, one about three feet up. Papa had stopped at the corn crib and got some dried corn silks. He had us hold the sack over the hole and put the corn silks in another and struck a match. Lots of smoke. The squirrels, in a panic, ran out in the sack. Should have seen the kids screaming at the squirrels trying to get out of the sack."

Braton said, "And Momma had squirrel and gravy that night. Ahhh, what memories."

Lizzy asked, "So what kind of food did you all eat in Williamsburg?"

Henry replied, "Dee Pruitt had a huge beef roast for everybody and apple pie. Now back at Robbie's, we had crab and oysters."

Keeton said, "Yuck, the crab was not bad, but the oysters looked… well, just like you blew a blob out your nose."

She looked at him and then Henry. "Seriously?"

"Yes, seriously, and they tasted horrible."

They all laughed.

"OK, kids, bedtime, or Santa will not come. See, we have some presents under the tree, but Santa will bring more."

Both kids were excited to get to bed so Santa could come.

The adults sat up later, talking of the war and maybe the new country someday.

16

Early the next morning, the kids came screaming to the fireplace as Braton put two logs on to warm the house.

Henry and Keeton sat up, on their pallets on the floor, just to watch.

Several more presents magically appeared under the tree during the night.

Liz looked shocked. "Now where did these come from?"

Both Henry and Keeton replied at the same time, "Santa!"

The presents were handed out. She looked at one and then at Henry.

He smiled. "Said for you."

She slowly unwrapped and held up some beautiful blue cloth. "Wow! My favorite color. Where did it come from?"

Henry said, "Remember, you told the kids Santa would come."

17

She stood up, held the fabric to her, and twirled around, a huge smile on her face. There was a note. She read it, *I wish you all a most merry Christmas. Hope you like the color. There should be enough for you and your little girl a dress. -Santa*

"What, how?" She looked at Braton.

"Hey, not from me."

She held up a little bag and opened it. "Red buttons. Wow! And a dress pattern!"

She looked at Henry and Keeton.

Henry said, "Hey, we don't know ladies' things." Then he whispered to Keeton, "Musta been Dee. We must thank her next time."

Keeton whispered back, "And it made her day."

"OK," Braton said, "Couple more," as he handed one to Bobby,

who tore through the papers, pulling out a bright green yoyo and a green spinning top.

Susie quickly opened hers and squealed. "Oh, Mommy, a dolly, a dolly!" She stood up, hugged it, and went running to Liz. She kept looking at it. "Oh, Mommy, she has eyes just like mine."

Liz said, "Yes, green eyes." The little girl was beside herself.

Keeton said, "And one more thing," as he handed a box of stick candy to Liz.

She was almost in tears. "Thank you, thank you. This is their best Christmas. EVER!"

Henry smiled. "We just delivered Santa's package. We had no way of knowing what was in it."

"Serious, really?" she asked.

"Yes, we asked Dee to find something for the kids, and she had it packaged."

"Well, I owe her one," Liz replied.

Braton, grinning from ear to ear, said, "Thank you, brothers. Yes, this is one we shall never forget."

Henry laughed. "Now to catch some squirrels in a sack." They all laughed.

That Christmas was the best. Henry knew Abigail was okay but wondered where she was and Keeton wondered about Tina back at Watauga.

Winter was upon them. Little they could do outside except make a path to the barn to keep the horses and animals fed. Tanner decided to sleep in the barn on the hay beside Star. Seems he and the black horse, Star, had become good friends, as they

would be seen running in the snow almost daily, playing like two puppies.

The warm southerly wind finally came and melted most of the snow so they could take the horses back to Mr. Finchum.

Keeton rode Star, the black son of Ugly Horse. He commented to Braton, "I like this horse. Matches my dog too."

Braton said, "Well, why don't you just keep him? I'll trade even for Dusty. She is getting old and would make another good horse for the kids to ride."

"You sure, brother?"

"Yes, he needs out and running. I just don't have the time to work with him."

Keeton finally agreed. "But I hate to leave Dusty behind. She has been an excellent horse, but she is

now close to twelve years old, as best I could determine."

By mid-February, the weather cleared for a few days. Henry, now with cabin fever, asked, "Why not head back toward Fort Chiswell? We have the supplies for Sammy and Sally."

Keeton replied, "And the orders for Captain Whaley too."

They talked it over with Braton, thanking them for putting up with them for two months.

Liz replied, "It has been fun, and the kids really like the attention."

Keeton told her, "We love them as our own."

She smiled, "Well, maybe someday you both will have your own children."

Henry replied, "If this war is ever over, yes, we just might."

She smiled at Henry, "You know she will wait for you."

He replied, "Sure hope so. Seems a lifetime since we were last together."

They checked and rechecked their gear, the harnesses, and the horse's hooves and were ready to leave early the next morning.

Henry asked Liz, "What day is it?"

She checked her calendar, "It is February 20th, 1778."

He replied, "Thanks."

Braton said, "Just hope you don't get caught in another bad storm before spring."

Henry replied, "Spring is not a good time to travel, either, with the spring rains, the muddy roads, and floods."

Chapter 2

They were up and on the road by sunup the next morning riding west, along the Trader's Path toward Judge Lynch's place and onward toward the Great Indian Warpath and south to Fort Chiswell.

Tanner ran beside Star. Both seemed at peace with one another, as only animals know.

"How many days do you think, Henry?"

He replied, "With reasonable luck, we can be to Judge Lynch's by noon tomorrow."

"Hopefully we can find a place to let us stay in Appomattox midway to the judge's place."

They made good time and traveled fast as the weather was cool for the horses to travel.

They did find a relay station in Appomattox, but the owner did not have an old, ugly, red hound.

They were out early the next day and to Judge Lynch's place by afternoon. The hired hand just motioned them on in, as he knew they were friends of his boss.

They rode right in the barn, unsaddled, and fed the horses as the hired man brought them a couple loads of firewood for the little stove. He said, "Keep you fellers warm tonight. The judge is out and about. Don't know if he will be back afore dark or not."

Keeton told him, "We will see him when he brings his horse to the barn. Thank you."

The man replied, "Welcome. By the way, one of them men who was supposed to be hanged escaped. We did hang the other four though."

Keeton asked, "Which one escaped?"

"It was that crybaby, Clark."

"Now how did he escape? Henry asked.

"Well, that morning we was a'goin' to hang them. That darn Clark lay down in the corn crib and covered himself with corn husks. The men took the others out, thought they had everybody, as they looked inside seeing nobody else. When they walked up to the hangin' place, they counted only four, when they went back that sneaky Clark was done gone. We wanted to go atter him, but the judge laughed, said we will get him another day."

"So you all did hang the four?"

"Yes sir, they done their job a'crimin', so we done our job a'hangin'. See you fellers in the

morning." And off he walked, going home.

All was dry and warm for the night. They never heard the judge come in, so by morning, they were up, saddled, and on the road, west, toward Roanoke and then south toward Fort Chiswell.

Henry mumbled, "Three more days, if no more bad weather."

Keeton replied, "Well, it's still February. Expect anything in the weather."

"We have been lucky so far, so maybe we will make Fort Chiswell before the bad winds of March blows in."

Three days later, just at dusk, they saw the little village of Fort Chiswell looming in the distance. Lights were already on in the house and store as they arrived.

Keeton jumped off Star and stomped on the porch. "Ye done closed the store afore dark?"

Sam came out, laughing, "Well no one with any sense rides around in the dark. Put your horses in the barn and feed them. Hey, a new horse. What happened to Dusty?"

Keeton told him, "We retired her. She is getting old and deserves the retirement with Brother's kids."

"Who might we have now?"

"This is Star. Remember Ugly Horse?"

"Really? Ugly Horse had a colt that color?"

"Yes, solid black except the white star on his forehead."

They unloaded the pack for Sammy. "Carefully, it has bottles. Don't break 'em."

"Oh, he will be beside himself to finally get glass bottles."

Sam carried the pack inside the store. Polly and Sally came from the rear.

She asked, "You talking to yourself now, Sam?"

He laughed, "Well, sometimes I do, but Henry and Keeton are back. This pack is for Sammy."

Sally screamed, "He will be sooo happy! We did not have small bottles to put the medicine in."

"Where are they now?" Polly asked.

"They put the horses in the barn and their packs in the little cabin beside the church."

Keeton said, while unsaddling Star, "Hey, Festus looks good. The wound is mostly healed."

Henry looked, "It does but does seem a little raw around the edge."

Keeton replied, "Aw, he will be okay come spring. Sally will be riding him everywhere."

Soon Polly and Sam heard stomping on the porch, as Henry and Keeton stomped their feet to get the mud off. They walked in as Polly said, "We did not expect you two until spring."

Henry replied, "We got a break in the weather, so we took a chance. Anything going on at the mines?"

"Nope," she replied. "All quiet so far. Course we don't get much information in the winter."

Keeton said, "We have orders for Captain Whaley from the Governor to stay and keep control."

Sally asked, "What? Now who is Captain Whaley?"

Henry told them, "We discussed his work, and the Governor, with recommendations from General

Greene, promoted him. Course we put our two bits in for him."

"Well, that was fast." Polly laughed. "From a private to captain in a year."

"So where is Sammy. What is he doing?" Keeton asked.

Sally told them, "Sammy had turned his little house into a lab. He is running all kinds of tests on the herbs. He just don't sleep much anymore."

"Or eat," Polly interjected. "Brain just too busy."

Henry said, "Dr. Neville and the military will take all the medicine he can produce."

"Really?" asked Sally, "Just wow! Wait till he hears that."

Keeton said, "Boy, I'm hungry. Got anything to eat, Polly?"

She replied, "Yeah, got some oysters," and laughed.

"Now, how did you know I hate those snotty things? Rather eat a skunk."

She laughed. "Henry done filled me in. Of course I have food. Sally is learning to bake. She just baked fresh bread today."

Sally smiled. "And it is good."

Sam said, "I have to agree."

"So where is it?" Keeton asked, smiling and licking his chops.

They all laughed.

"OK, give us a few. Got veggie soup and bread with butter," Polly replied.

"Sure beats that foul oyster stuff."

"Take your coats and hats off. Put your guns in the usual place. Let's eat, I'm hungry," said Sam.

Soon they were all seated at the long table when they heard the front

door of the store slam shut. In walked Sammy, all red in the face.

Sally jumped up and ran to him. "What happened?"

He told her, "Think I used too much alcohol too close to the candle. It flashed up on me."

She slowly removed his hat. Most of his hair was singed off.

Sally hugged him. "Poor guy." And led him to the table. "Let's get your coat off."

She slowly took his coat off as he sat down.

"What do you need?" Polly asked.

Henry got up. "Medicine, my medicine bag."

"Where is it?" Sam asked.

"It's right behind the door. It's the black case."

Henry got up, went outside, and returned in a few moments with a

bucket of cold water, "Here, put a rag in it and hold to your face. I think it will take the burn away."

Sammy looked up at Henry. "Really, does ice help? Always heard use heat with heat."

Henry said, "Just try it for a few minutes."

Polly dipped the towel in cold water and gently pressed it to his face.

He said, "Aww, that does feel good."

She asked, "How long should I keep it on his face?"

Henry replied, "I'd re-soak it in the cold water every couple minutes. He asked Sammy, "So did it flame up?"

Sally had the cold wet towel completely covering his face. "Yhesss slur."

Sally giggled.

Sammy asked, "Wat do punny?"

They all laughed.

Henry said, "I think you are pressing the towel over his mouth too tight."

"Oops," she said, slowly removing the towel and putting it back in the cold water. "Do I need to repeat? How many times?"

Henry replied, "I just don't know. Do this for maybe five minutes and give him time to breathe."

Sammy looked up at Polly with big eyes, but no lashes or eyebrows. They'd all burned off. "Would you be my nurse?"

She hugged him., "Any day, Sammy." She looked around the room and blushed.

Polly said, "Now I think she needs a cold towel on her face."

Henry told them, "OK, give him a break while we eat."

Sammy told them, "I have no appetite, but I'll just sit and watch you all eat."

Sam said, "So fill us in on the trip."

Henry told of their travels, the relay stations and getting to Robbie's house. Keeton continued, "We went on a sailboat down this huge river where the water runs up hill."

Sam said, "Now you are telling one."

"Nope," he insisted, "When the tide comes it pushes the water back up the river."

"OK, I know of the tides," Sam replied.

"We got to Williamsburg, went to the Pruitt place, and stayed overnight. Dee Pruitt had a huge feast for us. We met General Greene and

saw General Morgan again. There were several other important people there."

Henry said, "General Greene wants us to enlist doing the same thing in the same areas we are in now."

Sam asked, "Now what is that?"

"He asked that we sign up to be in the light dragoons, scouting, gathering information, pestering the red coats, and shooting a few officers when we get a chance."

Polly said, "Ohhh, that sounds dangerous."

Sally laughed, "Well, that is just what we have been doing for the past couple years. Can I join up? Nope, guess bad idea. They don't want women a'fightin'."

Keeton laughed. "So we don't tell them you already been a'fightin'."

"So now?" asked Sam.

Henry told them, "We are to deliver orders to Captain Whaley down at the salt mines. I doubt the militia has made it this far with the deep snows and cold."

Sam told them, "I have seen no troops coming this way. A couple men did past through, going toward Kentuck they said. I did not like the smell of them."

Polly added, "They did stink!"

Sam replied, "They were not normal."

Henry continued, "Sammy, there is a high demand for your medicine. The militia needs it. Dr. Neville wants it and will be sending information and supplies to you on the next freight wagon."

Keeton added, "And Cousin Robbie said, whatever you need, just

send in the request. Might take couple months to get to you though."

"Wow, just wow," Sammy replied. He looked at Sally. "We got work to do, lady!"

Henry said, "Be right back," he went in the store and brought back his pack. He took out the bamboo tube of medicine and asked Sammy, "Let me try some of this on your face?"

Sally asked, "May I put it on him?"

"Sure," Henry said and handed her the tube. "Gently now, just a light coat."

She got down in front of him and gently applied some of the salve from the tube. By the time she finished he said, "Now that feels cooler, much cooler. What is it?"

Henry replied, "Now I know what that odor is. It is sulfur, pain

medicine from the birch and willow twigs, and beeswax."

Sammy got all excited, "Can we make more of this for the troops?"

"Sure," Henry replied.

Sam asked, "Now just what was you doing to get burned?"

He replied, "Well I had mixed some of the willow twigs in the alcohol to steep. I had just added a little of the sulfur powder when I got careless and turned a candle over on it. It went poof and flashed up right in my face."

Henry inquired, "Now do you think the sulfur steeped in alcohol and willow twigs is good for what?"

He replied, "That is what I have been putting on Festus the past month. It really made the sore heal much faster."

Sally added, "We have a whole list of other recipes or formulas,

whatever you want to call them, that we have worked on."

Sammy looked up at her, took her hand in his, and said, "It's been fun working with her."

Again, her face lit up, blushing red.

Polly said, "Enough for one day. Tomorrow is a new day."

Henry asked, "No freight coming in today?"

"Nope and don't know when I'll get another wagon. Depends all on the weather so you men have the little cabin all on your own."

They walked the short distance to the little cabin beside the church, went in, and built a fire in the fireplace.

Keeton plopped down on the bed and took off his boots. "Sure good to be home."

Henry asked, "Home?"

"Yeah, home away from home. Good to be back here where I'm comfortable. Just don't like a big town like Williamsburg with all their ways of doing things and so many people."

Henry pulled off his boots. "Yes, this is home away from home. You know, I do wonder if we will ever have a real home and family."

Keeton replied, "Well maybe you and Abigail. Not so sure about me."

"Why?" asked Henry. "Thought you and Tina had a thing going?"

"She has her doctoring business. Not sure she would have time for me and the business. Guess it's her call, sometime down the road."

"Get some rest, we will see what tomorrow brings."

They slept well after a hurried trip to Williamsburg and back. Winter was still in the air as they got up the next morning with clouds covering the sky and a cold dreary day. They tended their horses and walked to the store. Polly asked, "You men used to sleeping till noon?"

Keeton looked around. "Is it really noon?"

She laughed. "No, 'bout nine. That is late for you two?"

She handed Henry a cup of coffee.

"This feels just like home. We slept sound in our own beds."

Sally just looked at him for a minute. "Really, home?"

He replied, "Yeah."

She said, "Oh sorry, I forgot to ask last night with Sammy burned, did you get any information on Abigail?"

43

"Yes, Dee Pruitt had received a letter a couple weeks prior from her. She is well, in upper Maryland with the troops. She said just too much work and not enough doctors to help with all the diseases, injuries, and wounds."

"Good that you know she is OK. Does she know where she will be going or is she just staying in that camp?"

"No, the letter said she moves from troop to troop wherever needed."

"Set and eat. We already ate."

Keeton told her that Robbie's wife had a sweetbread she called a bear claw. It was really good with butter, sugar, and some sort of spice on it.

Sally said, "Did you ask?"

Henry laughed. "No, he had his mouth too full to ask."

They laughed. Keeton said, "I think she said cinnamon was the spice?"

Sally said, "I'll order some next time the freight wagon gets here. So, you don't want our biscuit covered with butter and brown sugar now?" She reached for his plate.

He jerked it away. "This is just fine."

She laughed. "Well eat up. Got plenty more."

Henry asked, "Where is Sally?"

"She got up early and is already gone to Sammy's place."

Henry told her, "Dr. Neville asked what was Sammy's last name. We could not tell him."

Polly just stopped, coffee pot in her hand, "Come to think, I never heard him say."

Sam chuckled, "Bet Sally knows."

"So, what today?" Polly asked.

"Well, guess first order of business is to go check on ole Amos at the lead mine. Are they being paid?"

Sally laughed. "Now, Amos's wife is a wiz with books. She is keeping them paid till the money on hand runs out and she asked if we would take a I.O.U. note until they get more cash. I told her we would honor the note if she signed it, so now she is taking care of that end. Not the day-to-day operation, I don't have a clue."

Keeton told them, "OK, we will saddle up and ride over that way. We will be back before dark."

"Anything you want?" Henry asked.

Sam replied, "Yeah, deer or elk meat would be good. We are running a little low on meat."

Keeton replied, "We will try our best to bring home the bacon."

Polly laughed. "Now, where are you going to find a pig?"

Keeton told her, "Well, you just never know."

Chapter 3

Soon they were in the saddle, Tanner running right beside Star, who kept prancing around, wanting to run, so Keeton turned loose the reins. *Run her out, boy.* Star jumped forward, and the race was on with Tanner right beside him. About a mile down the road, they slowed down. Keeton stopped to let Henry catch up.

They slowly approached the mine. Smoke was lazily spinning upward from three locations.

Keeton said, "I want to see the entire operations today."

Henry replied, "Yeah, me too."

As they approached the lead mine, a man came running out of the big building that the boss had used. He yelled, "Come on in, men."

When they got closer they saw it was Amos Rogers. "Git offa yur hosses. Come on in and meet the missus."

"How are you doing, Amos?" Keeton asked.

He replied, "Our production is up almost double compared to when the loyalists took it over."

Henry asked, "Now, just how did you do that?"

He replied, "Nothing. The men did. They are getting paid regular, no one to boss them around, and everyone works like family."

Keeton laughed, "Well, just how many family members do you have here?"

Amos just stopped, counting on his fingers. "Reckon 'bout ten, including me and the wife."

"So that's half the operation?"

"Reckon so," he said, with a grin from ear to ear. "Gotta take care of kin if they will work."

Henry told him, "I understand. Family comes way up front."

"Come on in, house is warm, and the wife is here."

They dismounted and walked into a warm room with the odor of some kind of tea.

Amos, smiling, said, "This is my wife, Mary. You folks introduce yourself."

Henry said, "I'm Henry, and," he pointed toward Keeton, "this is Keeton. We are brothers and we do take care of each other."

She replied, "So good to finally meet you. Thanks for trusting Amos and me. We aim to keep the operation going to supply our troops with the lead they need."

Henry said, "I'm just curious. What is that tea?"

She told him, "It is mountain mint with just a hint of sassafras root. Want some?"

"Sure," replied both men.

"Some honey to sweeten?"

"Yes," they both replied.

She poured the tea and handed it to them. Henry smelled it and took a taste. "Wow, that is good."

She just smiled, waiting on Keeton's response.

He looked at her. "Don't think it's good at all." She made a face as he continued, "It's fantastic. Wow! Best I ever had."

Henry asked, "Where do you get your honey?"

Amos replied, "From my brother. He got lots of bees."

"Does he have honey for sale?"

"Yeah, but most folks don't got any money to pay him."

Henry replied, "Tell you what. If you can get a couple jars, I'll pay him for it next time I'm here."

Amos smiled. "He gonna like that. Look around, folks. Everything is open to you two."

Henry told them, "We met with the governor and General Nathanael Greene. They are impressed with you all. I told them that you know everything of the operation."

Keeton added, "They are sending the militia to secure the mine and escort the lead and shot to our troops."

Amos just looked stunned a minute. "The governor knows 'bout us?"

"Sure does, and he wants you all to remain in operation."

Mary looked at her husband. "Well speak up, man." She laughed.

"Done told you when we first met that I know this from one end to the other and I'll do my best."

"Can you get us some lead? We want to see how good it is, just in case the governor asks."

"Yes," and he was out the door.

Mary asked, "You boys married?"

Both replied, "No," at the same time.

"Well," she said, cocking her head kinda sideways. "Wanna get married?"

Henry replied, "No, found my lady."

Mary asked, "Like maybe a girlfriend?"

Henry replied, "No, no thanks."

She looked at Keeton.

He just smiled, "Maybe, why?"

Mary told him, "My little sister needs to get married, purt nigh old maid."

Both men just looked at her.

"She'll be a'coming soon. She brings our lunch every day. Nelle is a good cook too."

Keeton asked, "Well, how old is she?"

"Nelle'll be 18 tomorry. She not purty like me though, kinda homey. Tall, skinny, no meat on her bones. Long, stringy hair too."

They thanked her and went out on the porch to wait on Amos to return with some lead they could test and shoot.

They saw a lady, slightly bent over, carrying two buckets. She had on a long dress, dragging the ground, some sort of shawl around her shoulders, and a huge bonnet.

She came up on the porch as Keeton asked, "Can I help you?"

She replied, "Jest open the door please." He opened the door, and she said, "Thank you," and walked in, then she kicked the door shut with her foot.

"That must be Nelle," Keeton said.

Henry replied, "Must be."

About that time, Amos returned with a wooden box and set it down on the porch. "Whew, that darn stuff is heavy."

Henry looked down in it and saw foot-long bars of lead. He picked one up and looked at it. "Looks good."

Amos replied, "All our lead is just like that. We do make shot of several sizes but mostly the lead bars."

Mary yelled from inside, "Come on and eat! It's on the table a'getting' cold."

Amos said, "Come in, boys. Nelle always brings us something good."

He opened the door. Keeton went in first. There was a spread on the table of meat, beans, and cornbread. And some sort of pie. He said, "Sure smells good."

About that time from another room came a tall young lady, long blonde hair, smiling from ear to ear. "Done cooked it myself. Sit down, dig in, boys." Her walk was like she was just gliding over the floor, not like she walked when carrying the two buckets of food.

Henry just sat down but he, like Keeton, could not take his eyes off Nelle. She was stunning with long straw-colored hair, eyes clear and

piercing, and a voice a man would never forget.

Mary saw them staring at Nelle. She stood beside her sister, put her left arm around her, and flipped her hair out of her face with her right hand. "See," she said, "not as purty as me."

Keeton was drinking tea and spewed it all over the place. "Sorry, folks, went down the wrong way." He thought there was no comparison between the sisters. Mary, short and plump, and Nelle, a real beauty.

They filled their plates, trying not to stare at Nelle. Keeton took a bite. "Wow, that is good."

Henry took a bite and stopped to savor the taste. "Wow, what is that?"

She replied, "Surprise. I try to surprise them every day with something different." She laughed.

Keeton just stopped chewing, to listen to the voice of Nelle.

Henry thought, *Gotta change the subject.* "Now, are the men all working well?"

"Yes, sir," Amos replied. "Turning out more than ever before. And they get along well with each other too."

"Good, good. Now we need to keep the mine protected."

Nelle kept passing platters of food around. "Now, you boys eat up. Don't want to take it back home for the pigs to eat."

Henry asked, "Really, do you all have pigs?"

"Yelp, whole field full. Pappy done got smoked hams ready for market, but there is no market."

Henry asked, "How 'bout bacon?"

"Yelp, the smokehouse is a'hanging full of hams and bacon. He smokes it with hickory wood."

Henry asked her, "So was that smoked ham we just ate?"

She laughed, the musical laugh sweet to their ears. "Yes, that was the hickory smoked. He uses different wood sometimes. He can't get much salt, but salt makes a different flavor."

Henry told her, "We can get salt."

Keeton asked, "Now, just how far do you live from here?"

She looked at Amos, "Don't rightly know. Takes me 'bout half an hour to walk up here."

Keeton looked at Henry and winked. "We did tell Polly we would bring home the bacon."

"Yes, we did." Henry looked at him and smiled.

They kept thanking her for the fine meal.

"See, done told you she could cook," Mary commented flipping her hair again.

"And I have to agree," Keeton said.

They walked out on the porch with Amos. "So what now?" Amos asked.

"Let us know when you have a shipment."

Amos replied, "We need a good freeze to harden the road. Can't ship much when the ground is wet. The wagons just get stuck."

"So what do you suggest, Amos? You been in this business a long time."

He replied, "'Bout the only way to get lead to the troops this time of year is horseback. They can't carry as much, but we can get the lead out.

60

Now, come summer, we can ship wagon after wagon."

"So, you think best to stock up the lead till after spring thaw?"

He replied, "Or later, after spring rains. Now if we can get pack horses, we can ship anytime."

Henry replied, "OK, I get it. I'm going to send a letter to Governor Henry suggesting you stay in charge and about the shipments in winter and summer. Is that OK?"

Amos smiled. "Sure, that will work. Just hope the lead don't walk off too much in the winter though."

"Walk off?" Keeton asked.

"Yeah, seems lots of lead disappeared last winter."

"And no real way to lock it up?" Henry asked.

"Nope. Maybe we need a well-secured place for it?"

Henry replied, "That will be our first project. Can you get lumber?"

"Not much, but we can get logs."

Henry said, "OK, find someone to hew them out. That will make a well-secured building."

Henry smiled. "Well, we know where some went."

"Where?" asked Amos.

"Remember the man who jumped in New River and never came up?"

Amos thought a minute. "You know, mighta had lead in his pockets." He laughed.

Henry noticed Nelle had walked out on the porch, talking to Keeton. Both were laughing. Nelle went back inside.

Keeton finally told Henry, "Think we might get some bacon for Polly?"

"Sure, want to go back with Nelle?"

"Guess so. When she is ready."

Keeton opened the door and told Nelle, "When you are ready, we will go back to buy some bacon from your folks."

Mary looked at Nelle and winked. They both giggled.

Keeton said, "Think I'll walk with Nelle, being's she has no horse."

Henry said, "OK, I'm gonna ride."

Nelle and Keeton walked. He led his horse. Tanner walked beside him, as usual. They talked non-stop until they got near her folks' house.

Henry, being higher on the horse, said, "Wow, whole field full of hogs."

She said, "Told you we got lots of hogs and more on the way."

They were met at the house by her father. "What ye a'doin' walking with my Nelle?"

Keeton held his breath. *The old man smells like pig crap.* Then he replied, "Mary told us that you had bacon for sale?"

He said, "Do," and looked kinda mean at Keeton.

"Come on to the smokehouse. Nelle, you best get inside, change your clothes, and take care of the sows getting ready for babies. Gotta get your choirs done, Nelle."

She replied, "Yes, Papa," as she waved at Keeton. "See ye round."

He smiled. "Maybe."

Her father asked, "What that all 'bout?"

Keeton said, "We are working with Amos to secure the lead for our troops."

"What troops?" he asked.

"Our men fighting for independence."

"Not so shore we need to be a'fightin' the mother country. They done so much for us."

Keeton looked at Henry.

Henry replied, "Well, we have militia coming to guard the mine. Think you might just sell them lots of pork?"

The old man replied, "Maybe. Still don't like us to go a'fightin'."

They bought a couple sides of bacon.

Henry asked him, "Mary said you have trouble getting salt to cure the hams. Maybe we can help?"

The old man just stopped, "Ye boys a'doin' this cause of my Mary and Nelle?"

Henry said, "No, forget it. We don't cause trouble with families."

They loaded up and started down the road.

The old man yelled, "Hey wait a minute! Maybe we can work something out, but you stay 'way from my Nelle. Don't got anybody else to help me." He held his hand out. "I'm Bob White." He shook both Henry and Keeton's hands.

Keeton said, "We'll be back in a few days. Maybe get more bacon, if you have it."

He replied, "Have it. Come on back. Bring some salt. Better than money to me."

They left the pig farm, as Nelle stood on the porch looking at them.

Keeton noticed she waved just a little so her father could not see.

"Whew, glad to get away from that ole man. He must be nuts." He smelled his hand. "Geez, my hand now smells like pig where he shook it."

"Or just protecting his assets," Henry replied.

"Assets? The pigs?"

Henry said, "Well, no and yes. He don't want Nelle to find a man 'cause he can't operate the pig farm alone."

"Ummmm," said Keeton.

Henry looked at him and laughed. "Now what is up your sleeve? As Mary said, 'She ain't so purty.'"

Keeton looked at Henry and said, "Think sister Mary is jealous or blind. Did not see one thing wrong with Nelle. Love her laughter too."

Henry smiled. "Wanna come back tomorrow for lunch? We can bring salt for more bacon."

Keeton just smiled.

Chapter 4

Henry and Keeton returned to Polly and Sam's store. Tanner had wandered off and arrived when they did, with a fresh-killed rabbit in his mouth.

Keeton, carrying the two slabs of bacon, walked into the store. "We brought home the bacon."

She replied, "Show me. Oh my, you did. You did! Now, where did you get this?"

He replied, "Over near the lead mine. Old man has lots of pigs."

"And…" Henry laughed. "And a very pretty young daughter too."

She looked at Keeton. "Serious? Are you being serious?"

He smiled and replied, "Maybe."

"We will have bacon, biscuits, and gravy tonight, if you all want?"

Henry replied, "We want. Where is Sam?"

"He delivered a load of goods. Should be back anytime."

"How is Sammy?"

"He appears fine. He came over near noon. Sally went back with him to work on a few formulas."

"We'll unsaddle the horses and check on Festus."

She replied, "Have supper in 'bout an hour."

"Good," Keeton said. "I'm hungry."

Henry laughed. "You was too busy gawking at Nelle to eat lunch."

Sally laughed. "Oh nooo. Bug done bit you, Keeton?"

He just smiled.

That night, Sally and Sammy joined them for supper. All was good, and the smoked bacon was fantastic.

Henry told them, "We need to be going on down to the salt mines tomorrow to deliver the orders for the new Captain Whaley. Wanna go, Sally?"

She looked at Sammy and back at Henry. "Don't think Festus is ready for a long trip just yet."

Polly just grinned at Sam.

"OK, we pull out first thing. Think we will take one of the slabs of bacon to trade for salt."

"What is that ole man's name?" Sam asked.

Neither Polly nor Sam had ever heard of him.

"Oh well. Nelle's Papa? He needs salt to cure the hams. Told him we would bring him some back."

Sam asked, "Did you tell him when?"

Keeton looked at Henry. "Guess we forgot to tell him might be a couple of weeks."

Henry asked Polly, "Do you have any salt? We can repay when we return from the salt mines."

"Sure do. Maybe twenty-five pounds. Can let you have twenty of that if you want. But are you going that way?"

Henry told her, "We might just go back and see Nelle's Paw to trade for more bacon to take to the salt mines. Besides, Keeton would like to have another look at Nelle." He smiled.

They all turned to look at Keeton. He just smiled. "She is easy on the eyes."

They all laughed.

Henry said, "Maybe we need to get there 'bout noon, as she brings the meal for Amos and Mary?"

"Now that is a good idea." Keeton grinned.

The next morning they got the twenty-pound sack of salt ready to start toward the lead mine.

Henry asked Keeton, "Wonder what she will have for lunch?"

Keeton just smiled. "Bet it will be good, no matter the food. Oh, wait a minute." He ran back inside the store, returning a couple minutes later and shoving a small bag into his coat pocket. "OK, now we go."

Henry laughed. "Now you need to eat just a little and let her see you. Yesterday, you just looked and did not eat."

Keeton just smiled.

Around noon, they arrived back at the lead mine, which was working

full force, with men going here and there on their jobs. Amos saw them coming and yelled, "Just go on in, Mary is there."

They hitched their horses to the rail, and got off, standing on the porch looking around as Henry said, "Is that Nelle I see coming up the road?"

Keeton did not reply, just jumped off the porch and went to meet her, taking the two buckets of food from her. He could hear her laughing and talking as they got closer. Of course, Tanner had to follow alongside. He heard Mary asking, "Is that you, Amos?"

Henry replied, "No. Me, Henry. Do you want Amos?"

"No, just tell him Nelle will be here soon with our dinner."

Henry replied, "She and Keeton are walking up the road now."

Mary asked, "What? Oh," as she came to the door and saw them. "Now ain't that a purty sight. Nelle likes him."

Henry asked, "What's for dinner?"

Mary replied, "Don't know, but it will be good."

Keeton, carrying the two buckets, walked up on the porch behind Nelle. Both were laughing and having fun.

"Sit it on the table, Nelle. We got work to do. Amos'll be here in a few."

Nelle took the food from the buckets and set it on the table, all but one bowl.

Henry asked, "Now, what is in that bowl?"

Nelle got it out and hid it behind her back. "This is just for Key. He gonna like it."

75

Mary looked at her and winked.

Amos stomped up on the porch, came in, and hung his coat and hat on a wall peg. He sat down to eat.

Mary said, "Don't you know your manners? 'Posed to wash you hands before eatin'."

He mumbled, got up, went outside on the porch, and came back in a few with wet hands, slinging water everywhere. "No darn rag to dry on out there."

Mary replied, "That darn dog done got the rag to play with again." She went outside, returning in a few minutes with the drying towel, handing it to Amos. "Now, dry your hands. You folks sit down. Let's eat."

Nelle sat down beside Keeton. Henry noticed real close to him, as she was giggling and laughing.

Mary passed the bowls of food around, all except the one. Everyone

ate, except Keeton. He seemed occupied by the closeness of Nelle, her long, straw-colored hair, her knock-out figure, and the sweet laughter.

Nelle jumped up, got the hidden bowl, and placed it in front of Key. "This is just for you. Wuz a'hoping you would come back today."

Mary asked, "Now, what special did you bring him?"

Nelle smiled. "Sweet tater pie. Do you like it, Key?"

He replied, "Hang on, let me get a spoonful." He did and smelled it, then placed it in his mouth. "Yummy, that is sooo good."

Amos asked, "Nelle, did you bring enough for all of us?"

"Maybe, when Key gets what he wants first."

Keeton pushed the bowl across the table for Amos, who took out a large portion and pushed it on to Mary. "Get some and send the rest to Henry. He might like just a little bite."

Mary told them, "Sorry don't have any coffee. Done run out. Maybe next time to the store."

Henry said, "If I had a'known coulda brought you a pound or two."

She asked, "When air ye a'coming back this way?"

Henry replied, "May be a month or so. Going down to the salt mines to check on things. All depends on the weather."

Amos replied, "Spring just round the corner."

"And high waters, lots of rain too, I expect," Henry said. "We brought twenty pounds of salt to trade for some bacon to take down to the salt mine folks."

Nelle just stopped and turned toward Key. "Air ye gonna walk me home?" She giggled.

Keeton put on the charm. "Well, if you want me to, lady?"

Mary looked at both and said, "She wants. She wants you to walk her home. Jist don't get on the bad side with my brother. He can be like a fightin' hornet when he gets mad."

Henry thought a minute. "And just how can we keep him on the good side, Mary?"

She looked at Amos and replied, "He do like money and don't like boys a'comin' round to see Nelle."

"Why?" asked Keeton.

"Well, cause he ain't got no boys, and Nelle is the only help he can get."

"Not fair to her," Keeton told them. "She is a lady. Needs to do lady

things from time to time." He took out the little bag, opened it, and handed her a blue ribbon.

Her eyes got big. "No boy never brung me anything, never!" Nelle hugged Keeton and gave him a kiss.

Mary just smiled.

"Air ye a'trying to win her over, Keeton?" Amos asked.

Mary laughed. "Think he done done that."

Nelle held up the blue ribbon.

Mary asked her, "Want it in your hair?"

Nelle asked Keeton, "Think it will look good?"

"Sure," he replied, smiling.

Nelle walked around the table to Mary, who pulled her hair back into a ponytail and tied the blue bow in.

She swirled around. "What you think, Key? Does it match my blue eyes?"

He put on a huge smile. "Love it, love it."

She kept turning round and round.

"Happy Birthday."

Nelle just stopped and looked questioningly at Mary, who nodded. "Yes, it's your birthday, Nelle. You are eighteen today."

They finished their meal as Henry thanked them for the fine food. He kept bragging on Nelle and the excellent cooking she had brought.

Mary said, "'Bout time you head back, Nelle. Brother gonna be a lookin' for you."

Nelle blushed, "Guess so," as she jumped up, got the bowls, and put them back in the two buckets. She

turned to Keeton. "Ye a'goin' to carry these heavy buckets fur me?"

Mary said, "But we et the food, the buckets are… Oh, never mind," and smiled.

Henry and Amos walked out on the porch as Amos said, "Sure a good day. I like the sun."

Henry replied, "Sure is, just don't know from one day till next what will happen."

Nelle came out the door, followed by Keeton carrying the buckets, with Mary following.

Mary winked at Nelle. "Now, you behave. Don't get my brother all stirred up."

Henry thanked them again. "The militia should be here in a few days. Make them welcome. They will not get in your way, just helping to protect the mine from the loyalists."

Amos replied, "Come on back when ye get back from the salt mine. Bring us some salt too."

"Wish we had pepper," Mary added.

Henry walked out in the yard by a weed patch. "Here, Mary, pepper grows right in your front door."

"Where?"

He pulled the seeds from a weed and handed a couple small black seeds to her. "Take a bite, chew."

She did and spit it out. "Now, that is hot pepper. What is that stuff?"

"That's wild pepper. Has a purple bloom in the summer. Been used by Natives for thousands of years."

She said, "Nelle, come here a minute."

Nelle, standing beside Keeton, asked, "Now, what yu a'wantin'? I'm kinda busy."

Mary motioned to Nelle. "Come here, girl. Gonna show you we have black pepper a'growing wild and never knowed it."

Nelle walked the few steps as Mary held out a couple black seeds.

"Bite one."

Nelle did, spitting it out. "Whew that is hot. Ye shore it's safe?"

Henry laughed. "Yes, very safe."

Without another word, Nelle turned back to Keeton. "'Bout time we started a'walkin', I guess."

Henry looked at Mary, who just rolled her eyes and giggled.

"See ye when we get back. Just be safe," Henry told them.

Henry decided to walk the half-mile, leading his horse and Star, Keeton's horse, with Tanner following along.

84

Keeton and Nelle walked and talked, laughed and she giggled, till they were in sight of the pig farm.

Henry asked, "Now, where would your father be now, Nelle?"

She just stopped, froze, and moved away from Keeton. "He here 'bout somewhere." About that time her father, Bob White, came from a low-covered pig barn. He just stopped and stared at them and walked to meet them.

"Ye boys back again? Thought I done told you to stay away from Nelle. Where did you get that blue ribbon?"

Nelle lied, "Mary got it for me for my birthday. Did you remember it's my birthday, Papa?"

He removed his ole hat, scratched his head, and said, "Plumb forgot."

Henry replied, "We checked on Amos and Mary and walked back to trade some salt for bacon. That is, if you have any?"

The old man replied, "Ye got salt. How much?"

Henry replied, "Twenty pounds and want it all in trade to take to the salt mines tomorrow. We can bring you more salt for trade."

"Ye tolt me the militia would be a'comin' and needing pig. Where air they?"

Keeton replied, "They are on the way, Mr. White. Should be one troop here and the other going to the salt mines."

Nelle was standing off to the side, holding the two empty buckets. She slowly set them on the ground.

Mr. White said, "Come on in the smokehouse. Give you one side of bacon for five pounds of salt."

Henry said, "Nope, two pounds of salt for a side of bacon."

The old man replied, "Ye a'tryin' to steal my bacon. That's way too cheap."

Henry thought the old man was playing a game with him. "Nope, two pounds of salt or we take our business elsewhere."

Mr. White smiled for the first time. "Now, where are you a'goin' to find another pig farm?"

Keeton said, "Bottom price, two and a half pounds of salt for a big side of bacon."

The man instantly stuck out his hand, shaking both. "Deal."

Henry said, "If you are happy, we are happy."

"How many ye a'wantin' today?"

Henry turned to Keeton. "We did not discuss this."

87

Keeton said, "If it's OK with you, we will take four sides of bacon and you can credit us the rest till next time?"

Mr. White, now smiling, said, "Ye a'trustin' me?"

Keeton replied, "Seems we have no choice, Mr. White."

Nelle was silent as a fly on the wall, listening and trying to study Keeton's face, Henry noticed.

He got the four sides of bacon and wrapped them in a cloth. "Here, makin' you a rope to tie to the saddle horn. Ye all be careful and come back."

Henry looked at Keeton, who said, "You askin' us to come back?"

"Yelp, just don't get too friendly with my Nelle."

Henry laughed. "Well, now Mary is trying to get Nelle married off."

Nelle told her father, "Why don't you take Henry and show him around?"

Bob White smiled. "Ye wanna see my pig operation?"

Henry replied, "Sure, never seen anything like this in my life." He looked at Keeton, who winked at him.

"Well, come on. Got several pens and lots, try to keep the males separated so they don't inbreed."

Henry said, "I understand that," as they walked down toward a small creek. Henry looked back, not seeing Keeton or Nelle. He thought, *You devil you, done gone to get some lovin'*.

The man talked a mile a minute, filling in little details of the operation. Henry finally asked, "Where did you get this breed of hogs?"

The man stopped, looked around, and replied, "Got a cousin down in Charles Town who sent me a couple sows and one boar. Course I had to find more to keep the blood line separated."

Henry asked, "Do you have good records of what you have?"

Bob replied, "Nope, mostly in my head. Mary is good at writin' and addin', and all that. She keeps good records for me."

"How many pigs could you produce a year?"

He replied, "Depends on the corn I can grow or buy. I mostly trade hams for corn. Course the chestnut trees there on the side of the mountain air good in the fall. Puts lots of fat on the pigs."

Half an hour later, he said, "That's about it," as they turned back toward the house. Henry noticed that

Keeton and Nelle were sitting on the side of the porch, talking and laughing. The blue ribbon in her light hair was a bright contrast.

Bob did not stop talking till they got back to the house. He suddenly stopped when he saw Keeton with Nelle. "He know anything 'bout hogs?"

Henry almost laughed. "Of course he does. But not on as large a scale as you are doing. He is strong too, very strong. Look at his shoulders. Why?"

"Oh, just thinking out loud."

They got the bacon loaded on the horses.

Keeton asked, "Is that a wolf down there at the creek by the pigs?"

The old man asked, "Where? Darn, can't lose more pigs." He grabbed a hoe and started running down the hill. Nelle smiled and went

to the other side of Star, hugging Keeton, as Henry could only see their feet and legs under the horse.

He almost laughed out loud. "Hey, we better get going before he gets back."

Keeton got on Star and reached down to hold Nelle's hand.

"You comin' back?"

Keeton smiled. "Yes, I surely am. You are most beautiful and sweet."

She blushed.

"And I'll bring red hair ribbons next time. OK?"

She replied, "Just come back, please." Smiling that sweet smile with lips puckered out as in kissing.

They turned the horses back toward Fort Chiswell and the store. Tanner was right by their side, easily keeping pace.

Keeton looked back as they crossed a ridge. He waved his hand, and she returned the wave.

Henry laughed. "You are sneaky, sending her Paw on a wild wolf chase."

Keeton laughed. "It worked." He was grinning from ear to ear. "Did you find out about the hog operation?"

Henry laughed again. "Now, did you put Nelle up to me getting a rundown of the place?"

Keeton laughed. "No, that was her idea, and it worked."

Henry said, "Now I can't get those smelly pigs outta my brain. TMI I guess."

They rode back to Sam and Polly's store. Henry took the bacon to the little cabin where they slept.

They fed their horses and walked back to the store.

Chapter 5

Polly met them at the door. "Well, I see you two did not get shot."

Henry laughed. "We found a soft spot with the pig farmer. He even asked us to come back. He saw how strong Keeton is. Think that was a plus for us?"

Polly, holding a broom, just stopped and said, "What, he asked you to come back? Oh no. Now we done lost Keeton to a pig farmer's daughter." She laughed.

Sam overheard and asked, "What is his soft spot?"

Henry laughed. "Money, the man likes money."

Sam asked, "Did you work out a deal on the salt for bacon?"

Keeton replied, "We did two and a half pounds of salt for a whole

large side of bacon. We would have gone to three pounds, but he was happy with two and a half."

Sam replied, "That is a bargain, being's there are few pigs hereabout. How did you bring all that back?"

Henry told him, "We got only half. He put us credit for the remainder next time."

Polly smiled, looked at Keeton, and said, "There will be a next time too. Did she like the ribbon?"

Henry answered for Keeton, "She sure did and looked just beautiful."

They all looked at Keeton, who slightly replied, "Yeah, she did."

Sam looked seriously at Keeton. "You get some lip sugar?"

Henry laughed. "I'm sure he did. When we got to Nelle's place, she had her paw take me on a tour of

the pig farm. Of course Keeton and Nelle disappeared."

They all laughed.

Henry told them, "OK, tomorrow we get an early start for the salt mines. Anything you want us to deliver?"

Polly replied, "I think I'll send a little doll for Fredrick's daughter Polly. Will you take it for me? Can we send coffee too? We will take trade for salt when you return."

Keeton replied, "Sure will, and the dolly should make the little girl happy."

Sam said, "Why not take the newspapers? They are old but sure Whaley has not seen them yet."

Polly replied, "I'll make some extra biscuits for the road if you all like. Maybe throw in some bacon. Is that OK?"

Henry replied, "Yes, that would be very good."

She laughed. "Well, you all did bring home the bacon."

The next morning was cold and clear as they loaded the pack horse with the sides of bacon, their tent, and their camping gear. Goodbyes were said as they saddled up and turned south toward the salt mines. There was no one on the Great Indian War Path that runs down south all the way north to New England. A couple hours out Keeton said, "'Bout time for a break."

They stopped and noticed the horses were breathing steamy air out in the cold.

"Think it will warm up today, Henry?"

He replied, "May not. Look at those heavy, low clouds that are moving in from the south."

"Snow?" asked Keeton.

"Maybe or just a cold day. Most of our heavy snows come from the north or east."

Two days later, they turned north through the cut in the mountain where a sign pointed to salt.

"Another more miles, now," Keeton said.

Henry replied, "Yeah, notice how the clouds are coming from the east now?"

Keeton replied, "Yes, been watching that for some time now. Seems the wind is getting colder too."

Henry replied, "Yeah, glad we are close to shelter. Don't want to be out in the cold tent with lots of snow. No real way to stay warm."

An hour later, they approached the salt mines. Seems everyone had a job and was working.

"Hello, Mr. Henry," Abraham yelled from one of the huge steaming kettles.

"Well hello, Abraham. Things OK here?"

"Shore is, we jist a working like bees. Mr. Whaley good to us. He 'preciates a good day's work."

"Where is Fredrick?" Keeton asked.

"He up at the big house, I guess. Seed him walk that way earlier with his little girl. Think Mr. Whaley is there too."

They rode the short distance to the larger house, which served as an office too. Henry yelled, "Anyone at home?"

The door flew open, and Sergeant Russ Whaley walked out. "'Bout time you got back. No one to talk to here 'bout the war. Got any news?"

Henry replied, "We brought the newspapers out of Richmond. It's old, but it has lots about the war."

He said, "Come on in. I'll get one of the men to take care of your horses." He whistled, and a black man came running. "Ro, will you take care of these gentlemen's horses?"

"Shore thing, Mr. Whaley."

Henry told him, "Hang on a minute. Let's get our saddles and packs off first. Can we put them here on the porch?"

Whaley said, "Just bring them inside. Gonna snow tonight."

Henry replied, "I have to agree on the snow."

He untied sacks and handed them up on the porch to Whaley. "We brought you some bacon, if you want it?"

Whaley replied, "We want, we want! Been a long time since we had good bacon."

Fredrick came out on the porch with his little girl, Polly. Henry gave her a little wrapped package. "This is for you, Polly, from Polly."

The little girl was hesitant until Fredrick said, "Go on. You can have it."

She held her hand out to Henry, who put the package in her hand. She gently opened it and screamed, "A dolly, a dolly!" She looked at Henry. "Jist for me?"

"Yes, Polly, just for you."

Fredrick told them, "That is the first real store-bought dolly she has ever had, and Ms. Polly sent it for her?"

Keeton replied, "Yes, she did."

He almost cried, "And I tried to take things from them without paying. I'm still sorry over that."

Henry told him, "Hey, it's forgotten. OK?"

Fredrick shook hands with both Henry and Keeton. "Thank you so much for making my lil' girl happy."

Sergeant Whaley said, "Come on inside. Got a pot of herbal tea on. Don't have any coffee."

Henry got the days' old newspaper from his saddle bags along with another letter and walked inside the warm cabin.

"Russ, we have news for you, directly from Governor Patrick Henry."

Russ just stopped. "Oh no. What did I do?"

Henry told him, "We informed Governor Henry of your work here, and, on the recommendations of

General Nathaniel Greene, you have been promoted to Captain." He handed the sealed envelope to Russ Whaley, who froze, gently took the envelope, and opened it.

"I'm without words. What? How?"

Keeton said, "We explained what you are doing here for the war efforts. They are in agreement this is an important asset for the war efforts. You will be getting a team of militia in the near future to help keep control of the mines."

Whaley looked at one and then the other. "I don't know what to say." He took a deep breath. "Thanks to both of you. I would be back with Doc Shults emptying bed pans if it wasn't for you two. How can I ever repay both of you?"

Henry replied, "Just keep up the good work and keep the salt,

saltpeter, and sulfur for the home team. We fear, as they do, that the loyalists will try to take it back over like they had it. That cannot happen. Period!"

The now Captain Whaley said, "You know I will do my best," as he took out the captain's bars and carefully examined them. "I never dreamed of being in the militia, and it blew my mind to be promoted to Sergeant and now a captain. What is my family gonna say?"

Keeton replied, "They are going to be most proud of you."

Little Polly looked out the window. "Poppy, it's snowing." She held the doll at her little arm's length and then hugged over and over again.

Henry replied, "Just got shelter in the nick of time."

Whaley said, "You fellers make yourself at home. We will have bacon

tonight. Fredrick, go tell the men to stop and to cover everything 'cause it's gonna be a deep snow. Cut part of a side of bacon and take to your house, get some help, and give two sides to the working men. They gonna eat good for a day or two."

Fredrick smiled, "Yes, sir. Can do that, and thank you, men."

Keeton said, "Oh, almost forgot," as he got a bag and handed it to Whaley. "We brought you some coffee too."

Whaley said, "Been a month since we had some. Is this Christmas or something?"

Henry laughed. "That was a couple months ago."

They settled in the house for the night as snow fell and the winds blew and whistled around the house. By morning, a foot of snow had fallen. Henry got up, stirred the fire,

and put more wood on it as Captain Whaley came out of his room. "You fellers sleep OK last night?"

Keeton opened his eyes. "Is it daylight yet?"

Henry laughed. "Don't tell me you have been dreaming about Nelle?"

He snuggled down under the blanket and mumbled, "Did it snow or did I dream of it?"

Whaley replied, "Yeah, it snowed."

Captain Whaley put on a pot of coffee and relaxed by the fireplace, talking to Henry. "Now, who is Nelle?"

Henry replied, "According to her sister, Mary, she is tall and skinny, and 'not nearly as purty as me,' Mary said."

Whaley laughed. "Well, is Mary purty?"

Keeton, still under the blanket, said, "You know, Russ, beauty in the eyes of the beholder?"

Henry told Whaley, "She is a willowy blonde with big sky-blue eyes and a knock-out figure."

Whaley said, "Wow, you do find a few beauties. I never been that lucky. Where does she live?"

Henry said, "She is a sister to Mary Reagan. Her husband, Amos, is in charge of the lead mine at Austinville. Nelle is Mary's sister. She just turned eighteen last week and got a blue ribbon for her hair."

Whaley kicked Keeton's cot. "And who might have gotten the blue ribbon for her?"

He laughed. "Reckon I did. She liked it too, but she had to lie to her paw that Mary got it for her. He is a pig farmer. We got the bacon from him."

107

Henry added, "And Mr. White noticed Keeton's broad shoulders and how strong he is. Think he would make a good pig farmer, Russ?"

Russ laughed. "I'm not getting into this argument. Bacon for breakfast?"

"Sure," Henry replied. "It's smoked not salted, as he had no salt. We plan on taking him salt for more ham when we return. Had any problems here, Russ?"

He replied, "Not much. Seems a couple men came in and tried to get the black men upset. They told the two men they never had it so good and they were no longer slaves, that I had set them free. That did not go well with the white men."

"Where did they go?" Henry asked.

"Don't know and don't know if it was some of the loyalists who was here before or not."

Keeton, now fully awake, said, "How long ago was that?"

"Two or three days. Did not find out about it till right before you all came yesterday. Abraham came and told me. He was very upset."

"And you believe him?" Keeton asked.

"Sure do. He is trustworthy, a good worker, and the men respect him."

Dark, low-hanging clouds covered the area. "Not much to do in the snow except stay in and stay warm."

Whaley spent several hours going over the newspapers from Richmond, stories of the war and some goods for sale. "I see here that Patrick Henry or should I say,

Governor Patrick Henry, said, 'Give me liberty or give me death,' during a speech. And another paper has Nathan Hale saying, 'I only regret that I have but one life to lose for my country.' Those are strong words. Did you all meet Nathan Hale?"

Henry replied, "No, but we heard the same thing. And the British hanged him. Course you know we have met Governor Henry. I met him a couple years ago at the meeting with the General at McGruder's house."

Whaley laughed. "And The General borrowed your little knife to whittle on his teeth?"

Henry laughed. "Sure did."

Keeton sat up. "That is where they named him Hornet for knocking down the hornet nest on a couple spies. Wonder if they ever identified them?"

110

Henry replied, "You know, I just never thought to ask. Bet WAP or Doc Neville would know."

Keeton replied, "You know, some day we will be able to talk to people like that at long distances."

Whaley replied, "Now that would be nice." He walked out on the porch to check the weather and finally came back, sat down, and talked to Henry and Keeton, who were just relaxing by the fireplace. "We never found out who threw the rocks when we got here." He got up and retrieved a couple from the fire mantle. "Here are two of them, both about identical in weight and size."

"OK," Keeton asked, "Now about Fredrick's right arm. Has it been hurt? He has some type of bandage around it."

"Not that I know. He is left-handed though. Why?"

Henry said, "Remember Daniel in the Bible with the sling? We know one other person who has leather around his wrist. He uses the slingshot. It's very effective. Even killed a couple of bad men with it."

Whaley paused. "Think we should ask Fredrick?"

All was silent for a few minutes.

Keeton said, "Why don't we just act like we know nothing? In time, he will talk or not talk. That's his secret."

Whaley replied, "Good enough for me. What's happening with you men and the war efforts?"

Henry told him, "The militia will be here when the weather permits. Do you have any place to house them?"

He replied, "Just part of the shed we use to store the salt. How many are coming?"

Henry replied, "I think maybe a dozen or less, but if you read your orders, you are in charge of them when they get here. They are only for protection of this asset. How much salt, saltpeter, and sulfur do you have now?"

Whaley replied, "We have a good wagon load but can't get it out until spring now. We will need horses, wagons, and barrels to keep them dry."

Keeton replied, "We need to return to Fort Chiswell as soon as possible. Can we take fifty pounds of salt?"

"Sure can, and tell Polly to get us more bacon and ham from Keeton's father-in-law to send on the wagon."

Henry spewed out his coffee and laughed. "Did I hear that right?"

Keeton said, "I heard that, no way."

They all laughed.

Not much to do for several days till everything froze solid. Henry and Keeton were getting restless.

Keeton asked Henry, "Think we might start back tomorrow?"

"Yeah, guess we better. We will only have to camp for one night on the road."

Whaley told them, "Sure gonna miss you fellers. You are good people and true Patriots. I shall never forget what you have done for me. From Private to Captain in under a year. I promise to do my best."

"We know and trust you, Captain Whaley."

Captain Whaley looked seriously at both. "I will always be just Russ to you two. OK?"

Both replied, "OK."

Chapter 6

Two days later, they had returned to Fort Chiswell. New horses were in the barn and the saddle pole was full.

Keeton asked, "What the?"

Henry replied, "Must be the militia going down to the salt mine?"

Keeton replied, "Must be."

They walked the short distance to the little cabin, opened the door, and were met by several men.

"Who are you?" one asked.

Henry replied, "I'm Henry Bohanan. He is Keeton Fretwell. And who are you?"

The man replied, "I'm Sergeant Hopewell of the Virginia Militia, and I know who you two are. We have orders from the governor to assist you two any way we can."

Keeton asked, "How many men do you have?"

He replied, "I brought six. Sergeant Smithton has six at the lead mine now."

Henry said, "Good, good. We just came from the salt mine and brought fifty pounds of salt to trade for bacon if you want to wait a day or so and take several sides down that way."

He replied, "Sure. We will need something to eat."

They talked for a few minutes. The little cabin was crowded.

Henry asked Keeton, "Why don't we just stay in the store tonight?"

Keeton replied, "Sure, won't be the first time."

Sergeant Hopewell asked, "Are we taking your beds?"

Keeton told him, "It's OK. It's warm here. We can bed down in the store. You know the Wythes are good friends with the governor?"

The sergeant smiled. "No, did not. We will be good to them." He laughed.

"You will report to Captain Russ Whaley at the salt mine. He is in charge there."

He replied, "Never heard of him. Who is Captain Whaley?"

Henry told the men, "He was promoted to Captain a couple weeks ago by Governor Henry on recommendations of General Greene. He is a good man. We have known him for months now. He has black men working for him at the salt mine. They are free to come and go as they please. They wanted to stay and help, to get paid, and to help the cause for independence. You will meet

Abraham Lark. He is a brother to Colonel Easton's right-hand man at Leasburg."

The sergeant replied, "Yes, we have heard of Colonel Easton. He is a good man."

Keeton told him, "We will bed down in the store. You men can have the cabin. You all can just relax tomorrow, if you want. We will take a couple of your packhorses and get the bacon and hams."

Sergeant Hopewell replied, "I'd like to come along, to learn the area, if it's OK with you two?"

Henry replied, "Yes, it's OK with us. We will go by the lead mine on the way to the pig farm."

"Good enough for us. We will head out at daybreak."

The next morning, Henry and Keeton were up, saddled, and ready to travel as Sergeant Hopewell came

leading a couple packhorses down to the store. "Ready?" he asked.

"Yes," Henry replied. "Keeton went in the store. He'll be back shortly."

In a couple minutes, Keeton ran from the store and almost jumped on his horse, Star. He looked at both of them. "Well, we going or not?"

By noon, they had reached the lead mine. Henry got off and went in the house now used as an office. He came out a couple minutes later, laughing.

"What's so funny?" Keeton asked.

About that time, Mary came out on the porch. She looked at Keeton and told him, "I have sad news for you, Keeton."

He asked, "What?"

She replied, "I'm so sorry. We all liked you. You are a good, decent man."

"What?" he asked, anxiously.

"Nelle ran off while you wuz gone. Her paw is furious. Gonna kill the man if he can find him."

Keeton, in shock, feebly asked, "When did this happen? I thought she liked me?"

Mary replied, "She did like you but reckon you wuz not here and, well, you know 'bout women."

Keeton looked seriously at her, "No, apparently I do not, so what happened?"

"This sharp-dressed man came in, asking about the lead shipments and such. She was here with lunch, and they sorta connected, I reckon. He really honeyed up to her. All the charm I never seed before."

Henry asked, "And he was a loyalist, I just bet, trying to buy lead for the Red Coats?"

Amos walked up and overheard. "You are right on that. How did you know?"

Keeton told him, "We know the patriots who will be dealing with you, not some shyster from the other side." He took out the little bag and handed it to Mary. "This is the red ribbon I promised her, you can keep it or give it to her tomorrow."

Amos replied, "No, she can't give it to Nelle. We don't know where he took her, but she did not return home. She done gone away with him."

"Did he have a name?" Henry asked.

"Yes, Rodney Turpin. Why?"

"It all makes sense now. Remember the man who drown in the

river when we first got here? He was Turpin from Richmond. Bet he was kin."

Amos took off his ole hat, scratched the side of his head, and replied, "I otta remembered that name."

Henry told them, "This is Sergeant Hopewell. Where is the militia?"

Amos said, "They are up by the place, fixin' it up to stay out of the weather."

Keeton turned to Henry, "Why don't we give the salt to the sergeants, let them deal with Mr. White? Don't think I want to face him after Nelle running off."

Amos looked at both. "Good idea. I'll ride over there with them."

Henry took off two bags of salt, handing them to Amos. "This should get several sides of bacon and ham.

Now remember our deal was two and one-half pounds of salt for a large side of bacon or one ham. Hold him to it."

Sergeant Hopewell shook both their hands. "Good to meet you two men. Where are you off to now?"

Henry replied, "We will go back to the store, pick up our supplies, and start toward Judge Lynch's place. See if we can do any good there. You know the way to the salt mine, so good luck to both your troops." They turned and rode away.

The ride was silent most of the way back to Fort Chiswell and Polly and Sam's store. Finally, Keeton laughed. "Easy come, easy go. Sure glad we did not get hitched. Don't think I could become a pig farmer."

Henry looked at him. "Don't think so either, but you do smell like a pig sometimes."

They both laughed.

124

By late afternoon, they had returned to the store. Sally was on the porch, sweeping, and yelled, "Come on down. We need to talk."

"'Bout what?" Keeton asked when they got closer.

Sally informed them that Sammy had sold all the medicine he had bottled and now was waiting on more medicine bottles.

Polly came out on the porch, joining Sally. "So why back so early? Where is Sergeant Hopewell?"

Henry told them that Keeton had been shot out of the saddle. "Nelle had done run off with a loyalist who was trying to buy lead from the mine."

Polly looked shocked. "Nah, don't tell me that. Keeton, I thought you two had a thing going?"

He replied, "Thought we did too."

Henry laughed. "And now he can't become a pig farmer."

They all laughed.

"So what now?" Sally asked.

"We are going to head out first thing in the morning, going to Judge Lynch's place to see where we might be needed. Are you going with us, Sally?"

She looked down at her feet. "If you don't mind, think I'll hang around here and help Sammy. He needs my help."

Henry cocked his head sideways. "Do I hear a church bell ringing?"

They all looked around.

He laughed. "Thought I heard a wedding bell ringing."

Sally threw the broom at him and spooked his horse. They all laughed as he finally got his horse back under control.

Sally said, "Sorry, Henry, did not mean to do that. I do like Sammy. He is a kind and gentle man."

"Not what I saw," said Keeton. "Remember he had Fredrick down and in a hammer lock not so long ago?"

She smiled. "Think he can protect me?"

"Might be the other way round," Keeton said.

Sammy joined them for supper at the Wythe's table that evening. All had a great time, good food, good friendship, and lots of pig farm laughter by all.

Polly said, "You all bed down in the store. I'll have breakfast early if you want."

Henry replied, "If it's not snowing. We do need to get back to work."

Sam replied, "Thought that was what you all have been doing."

Keeton told them, "At some point in time, we are going to join the militia. General Greene has a place for us in the light dragoons and we will be working near the Virginia-North Carolina line, along the traders north-south route."

Sam asked, "If it's not a big secret, how many Hornets are out there now?"

Keeton told them, "As you know, Henry was the first. We don't have a clue. We know Bear, Nathan Wright, Thomas Ownby, and Oscar King are part of the group. We have no idea who else has joined but would expect nigh a hundred by now."

Sammy said, "Don't leave till I get back in the morning. I have some medicine you men maybe can use on the road to help yourself or others.

I'm making little emergency kits. Hopefully, most men in the militia can carry one in their packs."

Sam asked, "Now who's idea was that?"

He looked at Sally. "Her idea. She knows Henry has the little bamboo tube with a healing salve. Every soldier needs one."

Henry looked at Sally. "Thank you, and I think the governor will be impressed and order several hundred. Can you supply that many?"

Sammy looked stunned. "Yes, yes, of course. We need someone to sew the little pouches."

Polly replied, "We have an older lady who likes to sew. Maybe you can buy them from her. She buys the cloth here in the store from us."

Sally asked, "Do you have oil cloth on hand? We need a pouch that don't leak, that's waterproof."

Polly replied, "We do have some, but I can order more next freight wagon here."

Henry told them, "Make up a list, we can pass it on to Williamsburg or Hopewell as we are going that way."

The next morning, Henry and Keeton said their goodbyes to their special friends Sam and Polly. Sally had already left, going to Sammy's place to help make more medicine.

The air was cold and crisp as they headed north on the Great Indian Warpath toward Roanoke and east on the Trader's Path toward Judge Lynch's place. Few words were spoken as each was deep in their own thoughts. A couple times they passed a wagon or riders going south. Several houses were springing up near Roanoke now that people were exploring the area.

Late on day two, they approached Judge Lynch's place. Several men were present as they rode right up to the barn. One of the men, who they had met before, motioned and yelled, "Come on to the barn, take your saddles off, and make yourself at home."

Henry asked, "What is going on?"

The man replied, "This Red Coat came by here this morning with a young lady. She was not happy at all, but we did not interfere.

Henry asked, "Your name is Albert?"

"Yes," the man replied.

Keeton asked, "What did the judge have to say?"

"He was not here is why we are here now. Do we interfere or not? We don't like to meddle in other people's affairs."

Henry asked, "What did he look like?"

Albert replied, "He was a sharp dresser, latest coat and hat we think."

"What did she look like?"

"She was a real beauty, long light hair, tiny voice, scared to death, was crying and takin' on."

Keeton asked, "Did you hear her name?"

"Nope, he would not let her talk. Had her riding a man's saddle on an old hag of a horse."

Henry looked at Keeton. "Has to be Nelle."

About that time, Judge Lynch arrived in his buggy. The men ran right up to the buggy and would not let him off until Albert told the story and asked what should they do.

Judge Lynch looked at Henry and Keeton. "Why did you men not do something?"

Keeton told him, "Judge, we just got here about ten minutes ago and put our horses in the barn."

"Have any idea what is going on?" the judge asked.

Henry replied, "Maybe, just maybe. Can we talk in private?"

The judge told Albert to put his buggy and horse in the barn and to feed his horse good too. "Go on home when you're through. We will figure out something."

"Henry, you and Keeton come on up to my house. Let's talk."

"Sure," both replied. They walked beside Judge Lynch to the house. Tanner just followed. The judge turned and asked, "How you doing, boy?" He patted him on the head. Tanner just wagged his tail in return. "You men know where to put your guns. Come on in the living

room. I need a hot cup of coffee. How 'bout you two?"

Henry replied, "Yes Judge, now that would be good. Was a cold ride up from the salt mines."

Soon they were seated around the large fireplace. The judge sat down in his rocking chair. "OK, lay it on me."

Henry started, "We think this is Nelle White. She and her paw run a pig farm down near the lead mines. Her sister and brother-in-law run the lead mines. Doing a really good job too. The militia arrived a couple days ago and will protect that asset."

Keeton told him, "Her sister, Mary, told us two days ago that Nelle had run off with a slick-talking man who was trying to buy lead from the mine. Amos would not sell to him. Apparently he put on the charm, and

they thought she just ran off with him."

"Any idea who the man is?"

"Yes," Henry replied. "Rodney Turpin, I bet he is kin to the Red Coats from Richmond. There was another Turpin who fell in the New River and drown. Thought he had lead in his pockets."

The judge just stopped rocking, got his pipe and filled it, got a coal from the fire, and lit the pipe, blowing smoke upwards. "Sure you don't want to smoke?"

Henry replied, "No thanks."

"OK," the judge replied. "So maybe she did not leave on her own with Turpin? I know the Richmond Turpins. Bunch of Tories, love the British."

Keeton replied, "Either that or she got cold feet a little while later

and wanted to go back. He would not let her."

Henry interjected, "Or…"

"Or what?" the judge asked.

"Maybe he is taking her, holding her against her will to get lead from the mine in trade."

Neither had a comment for a few minutes.

The judge replied, "You know, you may be right. He was sent to secure the mine and the man would not sell him any. Basically, ran him off. So..."

Keeton asked, "What shall we do?"

The judge said, "Why don't we eat?" He asked the housekeeper if soup was ready.

She replied, "Yes, tater soup with sausage."

"Not much we can do until later. Stay the night and start out early

in the morning. You may be able to catch up with him. The old mare she is riding is slow, according to my man at the barn."

The soup was excellent and hit the spot with red pepper sprinkled over it.

After they had eaten, Henry told the judge, "Thanks, we will start out at daybreak. See if we can catch him."

Judge Lynch told them, "And you bring the rascal to me, either way. If he did take her against her will or she wanted to go back, that is kidnapping. We will have a rope ready for him."

They thanked the judge and walked the short distance to the barn and the tack room. Keeton opened the door, "Wow, warm in here."

Henry walked in and shut the door. "Yes, very warm. We need to thank Albert in the morning."

At daybreak the next morning, they were saddled up. Henry asked Keeton as he was putting his bedroll on the horse, "Did you get any sleep last night?"

Keeton replied, "A little, troubled sleep at best. Think we will catch them today?"

Henry told him, "We need to, or once he gets back toward Richmond, he might disappear and we never see him again."

Keeton mumbled, "Don't care so much 'bout him. I just don't want Nelle to get hurt, if in fact he did take her."

East they rode, slow at first and picked up the pace. Soon they met one of the freight wagons going west.

Henry stopped him. "Did you see a man and a woman anywhere along the road? Her horse was an old wore out hag."

The driver stopped a minute. "Do I know you?"

Keeton replied, "Maybe. We are kin to Robbie Fretwell."

The man smiled. "Thought so. You are his cousin. This is his freight wagon, going all the way to Fort Chiswell if the weather holds."

Keeton got off his horse, stretched, and replied, "Hope you have medicine bottles to deliver."

The man replied, "This is the main reason I'm going. Got a load with direct orders from the governor to deliver as soon as possible. Do you know what will be in the bottles?"

Henry replied, "Yes, Sammy and Sally have made medicine for the troops. If you stay overnight, they

might fill them to return to our fightin' men."

The man replied, "Mister, if I need to stay two days, I will. Got a brother working with a doctor who really needs all the medicine she can get."

Henry just stopped. "She?"

"Yelp, Buster is working for some lady doctor who is taking care of our troops."

Henry asked, "Do you know her name?"

The man replied, "Well, he done tolt me, but I plumb forgot. Why?"

"Would it be Dr. Abigail Carter?"

The driver excitedly said, "Yes, yes. That is her name. You know we don't have many lady doctors. The men have the utmost respect for her."

Keeton smiled. "Mister, you have made Henry's day. That is his lady friend. Do you know where they might be now?"

He replied, "Nope, somewhere up Maryland or maybe New England. I just haul the medicine back to Hopewell. They send it north as soon as possible."

Henry shook the man's hand. "Thank you, thank you. Yes, you have made my day."

Keeton asked, "OK, now have you seen the man and woman?"

The man replied, "Nope, saw two men, one smart dresser, other all wrapped up in a blanket, coat, or something. He was ridin' an ole wore out horse."

"Could that have been a woman?"

The man replied, "Maybe. Could not tell, all covered up with a man's hat."

Keeton said, "Thanks, I bet that is the couple we are looking for. When did you last see them?"

"'Bout two hours ago, going east. He waved at me when we passed."

"Thanks," Keeton replied.

And off they went at a run, toward the east. They rode fast, trying to catch up. By noon, they stopped to let the horses rest. Men were working on a barn close to the road. Keeton said, "Wonder if they saw these two people?"

"We can ask," Henry replied.

They walked to the barn.

One man said, "Howdy, can we help you?"

Henry told the men they were looking for a man and woman. The woman may be dressed like a man.

"Why?" one of the men asked.

"We believe she was kidnapped down near the lead mine."

One of the men said, "Ain't none of our business."

Keeton said, "Well, if it was your daughter, would you care?"

The men mumbled at each other.

One man finally said, "Nope, we ain't seen any two people like that."

Henry thanked them and walked back to their horses. "What do you think?"

Keeton replied, "Well, they may or may not be telling us the truth. I saw a little British flag hanging on the house behind the barn."

"OK," Henry told Keeton, "Let's ride another half mile and check the horse tracks in the road. We know there should be two sets going east."

They rode over a little rise in the road and down a hill where mud had collected. Henry said, "Stop. That mud will tell us the horse sense."

Both dismounted, walked to the muddy area, and looked. They saw deer tracks, dog, and a horse or two, but not two going in the same direction since the last freeze.

Henry stood up, "OK, we passed them somewhere. Now, where might that be?"

Keeton said, "Why did we not check horse tracks back down the road?"

Henry laughed. "Just guess we focused on finding them soon."

So they backtracked past the barn. The men working on the barn just stopped and stared but said nothing. Henry waved at them and yelled, "Thank you!"

Keeton asked, "Thanking for what?"

"Apparently they had not seen two on horses going east today."

West toward Judge Lynch's place they rode, checking tracks in the road frequently.

About five miles later, they picked up the tracks, going west, not east.

Keeton asked, "What the? Did he turn around? If he did, why?"

"Maybe Turpin missed the cutoff to a friend's house and he is going back to find the house."

A short time later, Henry said, "Stop, look, the tracks are going south now."

Keeton said, "I see that, and do you know who lives that way?"

Henry instantly replied, "Yes, the Rust family where we caught the others who had held the Rust family hostage."

"Don't tell me they are involved again?"

"Seems to be," Henry replied.

"OK, same routine or do we just ride in?"

"All depends, do you think Turpin did not know we wiped out the loyalists?"

"Maybe he don't, but we do have one man still missing that was not hanged. Remember Clark?"

"Yeah, he hid in the corn crib and escaped hanging." Henry paused. "Would it be possible that Clark has a new crew and has retaken the Rust house? Look, two fresh horse tracks going that direction."

"Geez, I sure hope not. One time kidnapped is enough."

"Let's just approach like we did before, go to the top of that hill, and look over."

"Sounds good to me."

A short time later, they tied their horses beside the road on a tree limb and quietly walked to the top of the hill and looked over.

Henry said, "You gotta be kidding? Look, several wagons at the barn now, all painted that ugly green."

Keeton replied, "Yes, darn. Bet they took over the family again. What do you suggest, Henry, with only two of us?"

They quietly walked back down the hill to their horses. Henry said, "Let's swing west, tie our horses well back in the trees, and go to the house first. If we can free the family first,

we can take care of the others. Main thing is the family is safe."

Slowly they walked west, circling to the rear of the large two-story house. They tied their horses well and then checked and re-checked their rifles, pistols, and throwing axes.

"All set?" Keeton asked.

"Sure."

They slowly approached the large house from the rear. They could hear men talking in the barn and someone banging on metal with a hammer.

Henry sneaked up to a window and looked inside, seeing the Rust family by the fireplace and Nelle to the back, maybe watching them. He motioned to Keeton to come look.

"What do you think?" Henry asked him.

"I don't know. Is Nelle actually watching them?"

"Maybe, just maybe, but why?"

Henry replied, "Maybe she did leave on her own?"

"Don't know, only one way to find out. Why don't you go watch the front of the house and barn. I'll peck on the window."

He gave Henry a couple minutes to walk toward the front of the house and pecked on the window.

The Rust family heard first. Mary Rust held her finger up to her mouth and mouthed, shhh.

Keeton tried to read her thoughts but could not. Mary Rust got her husband's attention and had him look. Both could see Keeton out the side of the window, but Nelle could not.

Mary Rust got up and told Nelle she had to go to the outhouse. Nelle raised a pistol and told her not to try anything funny.

Mary came out the back door, right beside Keeton. As she came out, she whispered to Keeton, "She is part of the gang," and walked on toward the outhouse.

That startled Keeton for a minute, waiting on Mary to return, which she did in couple minutes. She opened the door, and Keeton followed right behind her and saw the surprised look on Nelle's face. She raised her pistol to shoot Keeton, but he was too fast and grabbed the gun, pointing it upward in her hand as it went off, making a loud noise as he wrestled her to the floor. She kept screaming, trying to bite him, and kicking at William Rust who came to the rescue.

Keeton told them, "Control her, I must go help Henry," and out the door he ran, facing five men who came running from the barn. One raised his rifle to fire. Henry shot him.

He fell to the ground. A second pointed his pistol at Keeton, who sidestepped and fired, knocking the man to the ground. Tanner was barking wildly, running toward the last three. They gave him their attention as Keeton and Henry moved forward and got control of them, telling the three to drop their guns and raise their hands, which they did, all but Turpin, who turned from Tanner to fire. Keeton shot him flat in the chest. He fell face-down and did not move. They heard screaming and here came Nelle, falling on Turpin, screaming and crying at the same time. William and Mary Rust came running and collected the guns. It was all over in a matter of seconds. Keeton looked at Henry. "You OK?"

Henry replied, "Yeah. Are you?"

Keeton just stopped, looked around, and finally turned to Henry. "What just happened?"

Henry replied, "I don't know, but the good guys are OK."

Mary interjected, holding a gun in each hand. "And the good gals too!"

There was only two left, and one was Clark, who had escaped hanging the first time. He just sat on the ground with a shocked expression on his face.

Henry told him, "Second time we meet Clark. Stand up, and don't try anything. I have one pistol still loaded, and Tanner would be delighted to bite you a few times."

Clark scrambled from the ground. "Please, don't shoot me, mister. I had nothing to do with this!"

Keeton laughed. "Sure you did not, and you did not help hold the Rust family hostage again either?"

William Rust came right in front of him. "Why don't you run, just run, and see if you can't outrun this bullet in your rifle."

Clark whimpered. "Nooo, that bullet is faster than I can run. Please don't shoot me, please."

Mary Rust just stood, looking at the crying Nelle. "What is wrong with that girl. First she told us that he had kidnapped her, and the next few minutes she was taking up for him, holding us at gun point."

William Rust replied, "I have read of such things, where they actually feel for the kidnapper and change sides."

Henry asked, "Is that possible?"

Mary Rust replied, "We just seen it with our own eyes."

Keeton asked them, "Where are the kids?"

"They went to visit my sister just down the road. I hope they are OK."

Henry told them, "Why don't you go check on them? We have this under control. Can we borrow a wagon and couple horses, take them two and the three dead ones to Judge Lynch? Let him deal with them."

"Sure can, but the five horses beside the barn don't belong to us anyway and the two green wagons were stolen. Just take them, you don't have to return 'em. Tell Cousin Charles, this is twice, and it's getting old."

Soon they had a team hooked to the wagon. They made Clark and his buddy pick up the three dead men and put them in the wagon. "OK, now we go west."

Clark pleaded, "Please, don't do this to me, please, he will hang me."

Nelle was setting beside Turpin, holding his dead hand, crying from time to time. They could hear her talking to the now-dead man.

Henry and Keeton just looked on, not saying one word at her actions.

Keeton told him, "You beat the hanging noose once. Think they will hang you this time. You ran off once, but the judge said you would be back."

Henry and Keeton collected their horses, and both followed the wagon driven by Clark toward Judge Lynch's house. Back on the Trader's Path they saw a freight wagon, stopped it, and told him to follow them.

He said, "Gladly, and that is one of our wagons they are on. Been painted looks like."

Three hours later, they arrived at Judge Lynch's place. Albert came out to meet them. He looked at Clark. "Oh, you again!" Albert went to the side of the barn and rang a large bell for a minute or so. This brought Judge Lynch down the hill from his house.

He stopped beside the wagon. "You again, Mr. Clark? This time you will hang. What happened, Henry?"

"We followed Turpin and Nelle, lost their tracks, came back, and found them at William and Mary Rust's place. They had held both at gunpoint. Their kids had gone to visit her sister down the road."

The judge stopped. "OK." He held up one finger. "Kidnapping times two, holding them at gunpoint times two. Don't need to count more. All

that is hanging offenses. Albert, go get the hanging ropes."

Albert went into the barn and brought out two nooses. "We just got two, judge."

The judge replied, "All we need. What about the young lady?"

Keeton said, "She was holding guns on the Rusts in the house. First told them that she had been kidnapped by Turpin but changed her story and held a gun on them. Mr. Rust said he had read stories of such."

The judge scratched his head. "Yeah, me too. There is a term for it, but I forgot. What shall we do with her?"

Keeton replied, "Can you get someone to escort her back to the lead mine and her paw's place? He is worried crazy about her."

"Sure can. Tomorrow."

About that time, four men came riding their horses in fast, asking what the bell was for. One looked at the two prisoners. "We remember that one." He pointed at Clark.

Henry asked the judge, "Do you need us anymore?"

Judge Lynch replied, "No, we can take it from here. Please go back and tell my cousin their troubles are over."

Keeton and Henry looked at Nelle. Had they not known her before they would not have recognized her. She had changed that much with the crying and the disheveled look on her face.

Judge Lynch said, "OK, men, throw up the rope over the hangin' limb."

Clark and the other man starting crying, "Wait! Wait! We've not been tried and found guilty!

The judge replied, "Clark, you was convicted not too long ago and escaped. Now, what is your name, for the record?" the judge asked the other man.

The man turned. "Please, judge, please."

Clark said, "Oh, hush you was with us all the way. If I hang, you will too."

"Well, what is your name?"

The man finally got out a name of Rob Pihl.

"Was you kin to the Pihl who was down in North Caroline and went AWOL?" Henry asked.

"Reckon so. He is my brother. Where is he now?"

Clark told him, "Forgot, he was kilt back at the farm last time I was there."

Keeton turned to Nelle. "Go on back home, make something of yourself."

She just looked at him, not saying a word and with no expression on her face.

Chapter 7

Four days later, they returned to Braton and Liz's house, to the delight of the two little red-headed kids.

They came running out to meet them as Keeton yelled, "Anyone home?"

Liz followed, giving them both a big hug. Dusty horse came to the fence, looked over, and whinnied for Keeton. He went to her, rubbed her face, and hugged her neck. "How are you doing, girl? Enjoying retirement?" She kept rubbing her nose and face on his arm.

Keeton asked, "Where is Braton?"

"He will be back later. He is out delivering mineral water. Put your horses in the barn. There is feed for both of them."

The kids had both stopped in front of Tanner and kept shaking his paw with their little hands. He seemed delighted to get the attention. By nightfall Braton had not returned.

Liz told them, "Now I'm worried. He is never out this late."

Henry asked her, "Where did he go?"

She replied, "He was delivering mineral water to the Black and White community."

Keeton asked, "As in white and black folks?"

'No, no," she replied. "There are two taverns, one owned by a man named Black and the other owned by a man named White."

"How far is that?" Keeton asked.

"A day's ride, round trip with the slow wagon. I just don't know the miles."

Henry told her, "We are going to saddle up and go find him. How many roads to that community?"

She replied, "Just one. Along the Trader's Path toward Petersburg and Hopewell."

Keeton replied, "Seems we did see that wide place in the road a couple times. We will find him, wherever he is."

"Do you think something happened to him?" The two kids, now clinging to her dress, sensed the fear in her voice.

Henry assured her, "It may be just a broke wagon wheel or something with the horses."

In the darkness, they rode eastward with only dim light to show the road. The trees and grass beside the road were black, with only maybe an outline of a tree here and there. Tanner was out front as usual, head

high in the air, sniffing the various odors only a dog could smell.

Both were quiet in their own thoughts, and finally, Keeton whispered, "I don't like this, don't like it at all."

Henry replied, "How far do you think to that community?"

Keeton replied, "Must be near midnight, no moon shining, so just guessing as the hours we traveled."

Suddenly Tanner stopped and gave a soft bark as he sat down in the road. As best they could determine, he was looking to the south side of the road.

Keeton whispered, "What is it, boy?"

The dog made a small woof. Keeton and Henry dismounted, guns ready for anything.

"Darn," Henry said. "Wish we had some type of light to shine.

Someday, someone will make a shining light."

Keeton said, "Here," as he gathered some dried grass from the side of the road. He got some gunpowder, poured it on the grass, and made a spark. Poof, there was a bright light. Keeton said, "Better hurry, this will burn fast."

Henry replied, "Hang on, let me find some wood for a torch."

Keeton walked to Tanner. "What is it, boy? Find."

The dog, ears pointed ahead, slowly went down into a ditch and out the other side into some pine trees and stopped. They followed and heard someone moaning.

Keeton took the torch, following the sound. "Hey, it's Braton!"

Henry came running. "Here, let me hold the torch."

Keeton got down to examine his brother.

"What happened, brother?"

Braton's teeth chattered. "Brr, it's cold. Done got robbed. They surprised me right before dark and hit me on the head, and took my wagon, horses, and even my coat. Cut these ropes, then they tied me to the tree, apparently, after I passed out, 'cause I don't remember that. Where am I?"

Keeton replied, "You are about 100 feet from the Trader's Path." He took off his coat and wrapped his brother in it as he cut Braton's hands and feet free.

Braton started to resist. "Now you will be cold." He tried to hand the coat back to Keeton.

Keeton replied, "No, I'll get one of the blankets from the horse. Wear my coat, get warm."

Henry asked, "Did you see who it was?"

"No, no, but I would know that Irish accent any day. He was back at the last delivery of White Tavern. Besides, he will be wearing my coat."

Keeton asked, "So what did they get other than the horses and wagon?"

"They got my gun and the money bag where I collected money from both taverns."

Henry asked, "Are you hurt bad?"

Braton, rubbing his head, replied, "Feels like a hen egg on my head where they hit me."

Keeton asked, "Can you stand?"

"Maybe. What time is it?"

Keeton replied, "Near midnight best we can tell."

"Oh no. Liz will be worried. Plumb worried."

Keeton told him, "We stopped by there. She told us you was missing. Here, let me help you up. If it had not been for Tanner, we would have missed you." Keeton held the rope Braton was tied with up to Tanner, "Sniff it, boy. We must find who did this."

Braton patted Tanner on the head. "Thank you! Thanks for finding me. Might have froze to death if you had not come along."

Henry asked, "OK, how far to the tavern from here?"

Braton rubbed his head. "I just left, had not been gone half a hour. Why?"

"It's closer than going back home tonight. Let's go find a warm place."

Braton replied, "The tavern is closed by now. Where will we find a place?"

Henry replied, "Just leave that up to us." He helped Braton on his horse and started walking, leading the horse with Tanner again out front, sniffing along the way.

Half an hour later, they arrived in the little community of Black and White. No lights were on. Henry asked, "Where is that tavern?"

Braton replied, "It's the one on the right. The White Tavern is on the left."

Henry walked up to the door, took his pistol, and beat on the door, knowing the owner lived in the back of the place. He kept beating until he heard a man yelling, "We are closed."

Henry yelled back, "We know you are closed. Open up! We have an injured man here that needs help."

A couple minutes later, they saw the reflection of a lamp being carried toward the front of the tavern. The voice said, "How do I know you ain't gonna rob me?"

Henry replied, "We are officers of the House of Burgess. Open up or we will open it up for you!"

The man replied, "You don't have to be rude."

A moment later, the man opened the door. Henry showed him his badge. "We are officers and need your help."

The man replied, "And what if I don't wanna help you?"

Keeton replied, "You can explain this to the judge, the judge in Hopewell or Judge Lynch back down the road."

The man said, "Hey, I don't want anything to do with Judge Lynch. Do you know him?"

Keeton replied, "We do, and took two men to him a couple days ago, He hanged them right on the spot."

"Come on in, come on in." He held the door open and helped Braton inside.

Braton said, "Howdy, Lester, remember me?"

The owner said, "Yes, yes, what happened, Braton? Should have told me it was you."

Braton replied, "That Irish man that was here when I left last evening robbed me and took my wagon. He had a couple other men with him."

Lester replied, "I never saw him before, just felt he was trouble. I'm so sorry. Come set. I'll stir up the fire."

Keeton told him, "If we had not come looking for him, he probably woulda froze to death. They beat him

on the head, took his coat, and tied him to a pine tree."

Henry inquired, "Do you know where this man might hang out?"

"No, no, his last name is O'Bridge. He's trying to pick a fight with the patriots here. The other tavern is the loyalists, so we kinda respect each other. Ain't been no trouble so far."

Lester put some wood on the fire. "Hang on, I'll make some coffee to warm you up. So sorry, Braton, so sorry."

In a short time, Braton's teeth stopped chattering. Keeton asked, "Are you OK, brother?"

"Yes, finally getting a little warmer. Thank you, Lester."

Lester replied, "You are good people, Braton, always treat us right. Hate it happened. Do we need to

notify the sheriff when daylight comes?"

Henry replied, "You can, but we will take care of this. Where might they have taken his wagon?"

Lester thought a minute. "You know kinda hard to get rid of a wagon. I'll get the wife up. She can make us some breakfast. Not much we can do till daylight anyway."

Braton said, "I agree. Know my wife must be worried sick, me missing overnight and now you two did not return. We need to get word to her."

Lester told them, "There is a freight wagon in town, going past your place. Maybe you can hitch a ride with him, being's you have no horse."

Keeton replied, "Good idea, 'cause we gonna find your wagon and horses soon. Bet there was no other

wagons coming from the west since they took yours, so should be easy to follow."

Lester's wife came in. "Want some grits and coffee, boys? 'Bout the only thing I got handy."

Henry told her, "Anything warm will do."

Soon she had grits boiling in the pot, as they drank coffee and just waited till daylight.

There was a knock on the door. Lester opened it. "Come on in." The man came in. "Folks, this is Charlie. He is driving the freight wagon."

Braton said, "I know you, Charlie. You work for our cousin Robbie Fretwell."

The man looked at him. "I do. What happened? I seen the horses out front?"

Braton explained that he had been robbed.

Charlie replied, "Thought they was after me. That is why I stayed the night here. Don't need to be on the road after dark."

Braton asked him, "Can I hitch a ride with you back to my place?"

"Sure can, be glad to have your company."

Daylight finally came. Henry and Keeton went outside where Tanner was waiting. They walked across the dirt road a couple times and came back inside. Henry said, "Looks like the wagon went south from here. What is south, Lester?"

Lester replied, "Not much of anything till you get down in North Carolina. Couple wide places in the road."

Keeton asked him, "Are they patriots or loyalists down that way?"

Lester replied, "Mostly loyalists. Why?"

175

Keeton told him, "Maybe O'Bridge is taking the wagon and horses down that way for them to use. We bushed up a couple gangs that was taking freight wagons, painting them green, and giving 'em to the loyalists cause. Are you OK, Braton?"

"Yes, I'll survive another day."

Keeton told him, "Go on home, brother. Let us take care of this. We will bring your wagon and horses home later. Here is one of my pistols." Henry gave him one too. "Now you are armed if you need be."

Charlie laughed. "Well, you sure are confident, Braton."

Braton looked at Charlie. "I am confident. These are my two brothers, and they are law officers under the House of Burgesses."

Charlie looked at both. "So you are the two who has brought some justice to the thugs that have been

robbing, pillaging, and stealing from our families?"

"Yes, they are," Braton proudly replied.

Lester and his wife overheard. He came toward them and held out his hand. "We just want to shake both you fellers' hands for doing right by our patriot families." His wife joined in thanking them too.

Charlie paused. "But we heard a huge appaloosa mule was part of the team?"

"He is. That is Festus. He got shot but is recovering. Down at Fort Chiswell now."

"Hurt bad?" the wife asked.

"No, not so bad he cannot come back in service later."

Henry told them thanks, and went outside, checked his horse, and saddled up.

Keeton joined him. "Go on home, Brother. We'll be back before dark if we don't find a nest of hornets."

Keeton got the rope that had tied Braton and let Tanner smell it. "Remember this," Keeton gently said to the big black dog. Tanner sniffed and wagged his tail.

They followed the wagon tracks south. From looking at the horse prints inside of the wagon tracks, the figured a couple horses were following the wagon. "Wonder if these horses are part of the gang or just going the same way?"

Keeton said, "You know, we never asked Braton how the men got him stopped. Were they on foot or horses?"

Henry replied, "Oops, yeah we did forget that minor detail."

Keeton laughed. "Would be good to know now."

Tanner was out front, head high, from time to time sniffing the air. Other times his nose was to the ground.

A couple hours later, they came to a crossroad. The tracks turned left, which was east. Tanner was getting excited about half a mile later. The tracks left the road and went toward a low barn used to cure tobacco in.

Henry asked Keeton, "OK, what do you suggest?"

"Apparently the wagon and horses are in the barn. Why don't we ride up to the house and see if anybody is home?"

Henry replied, "I see smoke coming from the chimney, so guess they are."

About that time, a couple of dogs came barking toward them.

179

Tanner just stopped, hair raised on his back and neck as he stood his ground. One of the dogs came to a screeching halt at the sight of the huge black dog. The other came on toward Tanner to within a foot of him, when Tanner lunged forward, growling as both dogs made a hasty retreat back toward the house. Henry and Keeton checked their weapons and slowly rode toward the little log house. About that time a man opened the door, holding a gun, and yelled, "Go away, don't like strangers here."

Keeton replied, "We are not strangers, and that coat you are wearing belongs to my brother."

"No, it don't. Better git or I'll shoot."

Keeton told him, "If you even start to point that gun toward us, my dog will tear you apart."

The man then noticed Tanner was only a few steps from him. He looked toward Tanner, making eye contact, and the huge dog jumped, grabbed the man by the leg, and pulled him down the two steps onto the yard. The man panicked and shot the gun up in the air. He started screaming in pain as Tanner had a death hold on his right leg.

Keeton told him to stop moving and the dog would let go. The man finally stopped kicking, and Tanner just stood over the man, teeth bared, a low growl coming from his throat.

Suddenly two men went running from the back door. Keeton whistled. Tanner jumped over the man and went chasing the two running away. He grabbed one by the arm as the other turned to shoot the dog. He did shoot, but he shot his partner. Tanner turned him loose and

jumped on the man who fired. The man was screaming in pain as Tanner had him by the right arm. The gun dropped and both went to the ground.

Henry kept the man in the yard covered while Keeton went toward the man Tanner was holding. Keeton whistled and Tanner stopped, turned loose, and backed away. Keeton ordered the man, "OK, you can stand up, but if you try anything my dog will get you again."

The man, with fear in his face, slowly got up, eyes focused on Tanner. "Dat a big dog. Please keep him away frum me."

Keeton checked the man lying on the ground. He was dead. He brought the other man back to the front of the house.

Henry asked, "OK, which one is O'Bridge?"

The man wearing Braton's coat said, "None of yur business, and we aim to get the sheriff. You done comed here to rob us."

Henry replied, "Oh, really, and where did you get that coat?"

The man replied, "Found it side of the road."

Keeton asked, "So if we check the barn, are we gonna find a couple horses and a wagon that was stolen?"

The man looked shocked. Finally, he feebly replied, "Don't rightly know. Was asleep last night.

The other man chimed in, "Me too, me too."

Keeton told them, "Henry is gonna keep you two here. I'm going to check the barn." He walked the short distance to the barn and came back in a few minutes with Braton's wagon and two horses.

Henry told them, "You are under arrest for attempted murder, leaving a man tied to a tree to freeze to death, and stealing his wagon and horses. Besides, he had money hidden under the wagon seat."

Keeton checked the wagon. "They did not find the money." He held up a bag, shook it, and listened to the jingling. "Get on the wagon. Sit in the back. Henry will follow us, and my dog will be watching."

The man Tanner had attacked in the back yard yelled, "See! Done tolt you we could not get away with this. You, O'Bridge, done got us caught."

Henry looked at the man wearing Braton's coat. "So you are O'Bridge? And the Irish accent is strong about you. Maybe the judge will hang you two for these crimes."

Keeton replied, "Yeah, just like my brother tied to a tree, to freeze to death."

O'Bridge yelled, "Ain't no man gonna hang me. I know the judge here 'cause he is my cousin. He gonna turn me loose." He rubbed his dog-bitten arm.

About that time, a group of militiamen came from the north, down the road toward them.

Henry told the me. "Just sit tight on the wagon. I'm gonna see who is with the militia."

Henry walked to the road, waiting on the dozen or so militiamen walking south.

Henry said, "Howdy, fellers. Where you all a'goin'?"

One man in the front called a halt to the men. He asked, "Who is askin'? Hey, wait a minute. You are

the doctor who brung us medicine. Thank you, Doctor Henry!"

Henry looked him over. "Who are you? When did this happen?"

The man replied, "I'm Lieutenant Cook, part of Colonel Taylor's team from Leasburg."

Henry shook his hand. "Good to see you men."

Cook turned to his men. "Men, this is the doctor I done told you about who kept most of us alive with herbs down at Leasburg."

Henry asked, "Where are you all going now?"

"We have been ordered back to Leasburg to help train the other men. We done been in a dozen skirmishes."

Henry asked, "Where is Colonel Taylor?"

"He is up north of Richmond. A place they call Camp AP. He is doing OK."

Henry explained about the two men they had in custody and what happened.

Lieutenant Cook smiled and winked at Henry. He yelled, "Men, we need a firing squad!" The entire militia came forward and got in a long line.

Henry yelled at Keeton, "Bring those two murderers down here and stand them in line. We gonna take care of business right here and now."

Both men started to resist, telling Keeton, "Hey, this ain't legal. We ain't done nuttin' to be shot for."

Keeton had to prod both men with the end of his gun to make them walk forward.

Lieutenant Cook got their attention. "I'm Lieutenant Cook. Before becoming an officer, I was a Justice of the Peace under the House of Burgesses here in Virginia."

Henry motioned him to the side, gave him his written authorization in Virginia, and showed him their badges.

Lieutenant Cook read and reread the paper, handing it back to Henry. "I had no idea you two were working here in Virginia."

Henry told him, "We were requested by Governor Patrick Henry."

Lieutenant Cook replied, "Well, that says lots about our governor."

Henry said, "My friend Governor Henry asked us to do this, and General Greene gave his blessings. We will be joining General Greene's Army for defense south of the James River soon."

Lieutenant Cook turned back to his detachment and loudly announced, "Men, you will serve as jury for this

case today. Now, Officers Bohanan and Fretwell will provide the proof."

Both outlined what had happened, and the fact that they had taken a man's coat and tied him to a tree to freeze to death got their attention real quick.

Henry walked over to O'Bridge and yanked Braton's coat off him. "Don't want a bullet hole in this coat."

O'Bridge said, "Hey, man, I'm gonna freeze."

Lieutenant Cook asked his men, "OK, what is the verdict?"

All ten men yelled, "Guilty, shoot them!"

Both men sank down to their knees, "Please, please don't shoot us. We will do anything but be shot."

Lieutenant Cook ordered them, "Stand. There is one thing you can do not to be shot."

The two men scrambled to their feet.

O'Bridge told him, "Anything, man, just anything."

Lieutenant Cook told them, "OK, raise your right hand and repeat after me. Say your name."

Both men did.

Lieutenant Cook continued, "This day, I voluntarily enlist myself, as a soldier, in the American Continental Army, for one year, unless sooner discharged; And I do bind myself to conform, in all instances, to such rules and regulations, as are, or shall be, established for the government of said Army. So help me God."

The men repeated after him.

Lieutenant Cook boomed, "Now take one step forward."

Both men kinda jumped forward a step or two.

Lieutenant Cook winked at Henry. "OK, now they are my men."

O'Bridge asked, "Whut? Whut just happened?"

The other man, Smithy, replied, "Think we done messed up real good this time."

Lieutenant Cook told them, "You just volunteered for the militia and took a step forward to defend against all enemies, foreign and domestic."

The two men looked at each other.

O'Bridge said, "Hey, we did not know about the step."

Henry laughed. "I heard him ask you to take a step forward. Now you both are in the Army and will be shot if you go AWOL."

Lieutenant Cook asked, "Who was the leader?"

Smithy pointed to O'Bridge and said, "He planned it all."

Lieutenant Cook asked, "Who tied the man to the tree?"

Again, the man responded, "He took his coat and tied him up real tight."

Lieutenant Cook turned to Keeton. "What do you suggest we do with them?"

Keeton asked, "Just a minute. Let me talk this over with Henry." They moved to the side and whispered. He came back and said, "Take them down to Leasburg, have Sergeant Major Ricketts deal with them. You got pits, ditches, and graves needing to be dug. Put them at hard labor for a good cause."

Lieutenant Cook turned toward Henry, "Do you agree?"

Keeton laughed, "Lieutenant Cook, they belong to you now. Do as you see fit or just shoot them now."

Henry said, "Lieutenant Cook, they need to dig a grave for their dead friend in the rear of the house. I'm sure they will have more practice in digging graves."

Lieutenant Cook told them, "OK, go dig a grave for your partner in crime. We will stay here and make sure it is long and deep. Doc Henry, thank you for your service, and you may take the stolen wagon and horses back to Mr. Fretwell."

They went in the house and retrieved Braton's gun and other things that had been in the wagon. Henry came back out with a blue and red scarf, holding it up to Keeton. "Have we seen this before?"

Keeton replied, "Sure looks familiar, but where and when?"

Both agreed they had seen the scarf before, but they could not remember where. Keeton said, "I'm going to take it. We might remember, and they won't be needing it in uniform."

Henry laughed. "Don't think Colonel Easton will let them wear it."

Chapter 8

By late evening, they were back at Braton's house. He came out to meet them, shouting for Liz. "They are back!"

She came running, tears streaming down her cheeks. "I am so glad you got Braton back alive and safe. I was worried sick last night, the not knowing."

Keeton told her. "We took care of business."

She replied, "Hungry?"

Keeton looked at Henry. "Hey, we forgot to eat today."

They rolled the wagon into the barn and turned the horses in the field with corn and hay to eat.

Henry got Braton's coat, shook it, and gave it to him. "We did not put any holes in it."

Braton asked, "What?"

"The militia was about to shoot both in front of a firing squad. Now they are part of the squad." Henry explained what happened to the two men who had robbed Braton. At first, he was puzzled until Keeton added, "They did take a step forward." They all laughed.

Dusty horse had to be petted by Keeton. He rubbed her back and talked to her a little while. He told her, "I'm so glad you are retired with a good home. Know you must miss the excitement though."

As darkness rolled in, they were inside Braton's house, playing with the two little red-headed children. Both wanted attention at the same time as Keeton bounced one on his knee then the other. They laughed until Liz announced, "Supper is ready."

The kids jumped off his lap and raced to the table.

Liz asked the blessing before they ate. "Guess you all like squirrel stew?"

Henry and Keeton replied, "Yes, where did you get them?"

She replied, "Braton has a trap out by the corn crib, catches lots, and they don't go to waste."

They all laughed as little Bobby squinted his face like a squirrel. Keeton told him, "Now your face will look like that after eating supper."

He looked at his father, who laughed. "No, son, he is just kidding."

The children were put to bed as the adults gathered around the fireplace, relaxing after a hard couple of days.

Liz told them, "I would not have known what do if you guys had not come along."

Braton told her, "I probably would not be here. They had me tied to a tree, and it was cold."

She almost cried. "Please don't tell me that."

"And they took my coat."

Henry said, "No details, all is well with us tonight." He paused for a few moments.

Keeton said, "He is thinking about Abigail."

Liz told them, "I pray every night that she is OK. Do you have an idea where she is, Henry?"

He replied, "No, not really. Last we heard she was up north of Baltimore."

"Stay the night, we will see what the morning brings," Braton told them. "I have a wagon coming in a couple days. You guys can help me load it and give the horses a rest."

Keeton told them, "Seems like we are on the run all the time. Don't rightly recall the last time we had a break. Maybe go hunting tomorrow, bring home some deer meat."

Liz replied, "Now that would be a good change."

They loafed around for a couple days, cutting firewood and helping. Keeton did bring in a deer, which they all enjoyed. He enjoyed seeing his horse Dusty again. The kids were delighted with her and her gentle spirit as they climbed on her, between her legs, and did anything they wanted to do.

One sunny afternoon, the kids were outside playing with Tanner, chasing him around the yard, as a freight wagon came in.

The driver yelled for Braton, who came out. "I have several boxes for you. Think they are empty."

Braton replied, "Yeah, I ordered some to ship chemicals down to Williamsburg."

The driver helped unload and said, "Oh, almost forgot. I have a letter for a Keeton Fretwell and or Henry Bohanan. Robbie told me to deliver it here if you see them."

Keeton stepped from the workshop. "I'm Keeton."

"Good, good," the man replied. "I'll tell Robbie to pass on that you got it."

Keeton slowly opened the wax-sealed letter, read it, and handed it to Henry. Liz came outside with the kids. He read it while Braton looked on. "Well, what does it say? "

Henry told them, "The letter is from Governor Henry. Seems the Red Coats are using the King's Road lots more now. That was once the main north-south trade trail traveled by the

Natives for maybe hundreds of years. It goes way down past Charleston and Savannah and way up north into New England. They have heavy guards transporting materials from Charlestown up to Richmond and beyond. They want us to try to stop some shipments. They are especially looking for letters, maps, or troop movements."

Keeton asked, "Wonder where the other Hornets are and what they're doing. That is right up their alley."

Braton asked, "How many guerilla fighters are out there now?"

Keeton told him, "We have no way of knowing how many or who. I know we helped train the Swamp Foxes down south, and Henry helped with the Hornets near Williamsburg."

Henry read the letter and folded it, then he handed it to Braton. "Will you take care of this for us?"

"Sure will. When will you all be going?"

Keeton replied, "Guess we better head out in the morning. We can get far as Wilson to our contact there for the night. Maybe she has picked up some information we can use."

Late the next day, they approached their three ducks contact outside Wilson. They rode into the barn lot, unsaddled the horses, and put them in the barn, where they fed them some corn. There were no other horses in the pasture.

Henry asked, "Not like the lady to not come out to greet us. Wonder if she is sick?"

Keeton replied, "I get a funny feeling here now. Remember last time there were several horses to swap out. I don't see a one. And where are the ducks?"

Henry grabbed his rifle and checked his pistols and throwing axe, as did Keeton. "You take the front of the house. I'll go toward the back. I don't see any smoke from the chimney." Tanner was right by Keeton's left side, alert for any signal from his master. Slowly, they approached the house, one from the front, the other from the rear. No sound; nothing was close.

Keeton yelled and knocked on the front door. No one answered or came. Henry approached the back door and knocked. Nothing. He yelled to Keeton, "I'm going in." Just a moment later, he opened the front door. From inside he yelled, "Come on in, there is trouble."

They searched the little house, finding the Mrs. Wilson had been beaten and robbed. She was in the

bed, blankets almost covering her face.

Henry whispered, "Is she dead?"

Keeton got down on his knees and carefully shook her. "Are you OK?"

"No," she moaned. "Can hardly move. They even took my firewood."

"Who?" Henry gently asked.

She tried to sit up, moaning. "One man came, said he was working for the Patriots, but he did not have an old red hound, so I knew he was one of them loyalists. He made me sit in a chair, tied me up, and opened the door, bringing two other men in. They ate my food and carried off whatever they wanted. I kind of lost time, as they kept beating me and pulling my hair, looking for some message for the Patriots. I kept telling them I did not know anything about a message or

envelope. Did not matter, they did not believe me."

Keeton asked, "How long ago was that?"

She mumbled, "Few days. They stayed here that night, left me tied up. The fire went out, and I finally got loose and got in bed to keep warm."

Henry said, "I'm gonna build a fire. It's cold in here."

Keeton felt her head, She was cold to the touch and kept moaning. He examined the old lady. One eye was black and almost shut. There was bruising on her arms and legs, which indicated she had been beaten with a small stick or limb.

Henry went down to the little barn, finding a few sticks of firewood and bringing them back. He built the fire and came to look as Keeton covered her back up. "I'll make some hot tea. Maybe that will warm her

up." He saw some round river rocks on the fireplace hearth and moved them closer to the fire. "I'm going to warm the rocks and put them in bed with her, maybe warm her up faster. Can she drink now?"

Keeton replied, "Don't know if she is able to drink or not. Let's just get her warm first."

Henry muttered, "Now, who in the world would be heartless enough to beat an old lady that way?"

Keeton looked around, "She is right. She was robbed too. Look, everything is a mess like someone was searching for something." He started putting things back in place.

Henry added, "Hey, now I remember. She had that red and blue scarf like we found at O'Bridges' place. I don't see it anywhere here now."

They lit a candle as it was getting dark outside.

Keeton said, "I'm glad Tanner is out there on guard. We know not what or who did this or why."

Henry told him, "Could be robbery or could be because of her ties to the patriots and independence. I'm going to make us some soup." Liz had packed them a go-bag with potatoes and some beef jerky. He got this out, washed the potatoes, and put them in a pot of water over the fireplace. "Let them cook awhile, and I'll add some of the jerky for flavor."

An hour or so later, darkness had settled outside as they heard her moan and mumble something.

They moved to the side of the bed, just being quiet and listening. She opened the one good eye and tried to smile. She whispered, "Told

them you boys would come take care of me."

Keeton, concerned, held her hand. "Can you tell us who did this?" She tried to talk but could not, nothing would come out.

Henry asked her, "Think you can drink a little warm tea?"

She just nodded. He brought a small cup of tea sweetened with honey. She took a sip or two and could not drink more. Keeton told her, "Rest. We are here. OK?"

She weakly nodded and either went to sleep or passed out.

Henry said, "Not much else we can do. There are no real doctors close by. Guess she will be better in the morning or..."

Keeton said, "Don't say that word."

Henry replied, "I'm not, I'm not."

They settled down for the night. Everything was deathly silent. Toward morning, they heard Tanner growl low as he scratched the door. Outside was slowly breaking daylight.

They armed themselves. Henry said, "I'm going out the back. you cover the front."

Keeton said, "Just be careful. We do not know who might be there or how many."

Keeton quietly opened the front door and slipped out, to stand in the dark spot on the porch. He could not hear or see anything, nothing. He whispered to Henry, "Anything out there?"

Henry replied, "Nothing, just too quiet."

Keeton again whispered, "Something gave Tanner the alarm." He looked at Tanner, who was looking down the road to the east.

Quietly, Henry to come to the front. Both watched as Tanner kept looking to the east, head high, sniffing the air. From time to time he would sniff the air and the hairs on his neck would raise.

Henry said, "Something there he don't like."

Keeton replied, "Wonder what it is, man or beast?"

"Guess we just wait."

About that time, they heard talking in the house. Keeton slowly opened the door, seeing no one there. "It's her talking to herself again."

Henry asked, "What is she saying?"

Keeton replied, "Can't understand, but at least she is talking. I'm going in to warm some tea for her."

Henry replied, "I'll stand watch, and see what comes down the road."

Keeton did warm some tea, enough for all of them. He found the jar of honey to sweeten it, made a cup for Henry, and handed it out the door to him. "Anything?"

"No," Henry replied. "Makes no sense. We know Tanner was alerted to someone or something."

A short time later, Keeton silently opened the door. "She is awake."

Henry came inside, and both went to her bed. Keeton had a hot cup of tea for her. She opened the one eye, looking at him, and asked, "Got any tea for an old lady?"

Keeton laughed. "No, but I got hot tea for a friend. Think she can drink some?"

She told him, "Get me up. Light a'comin' through the winder and I'm still in bed."

Keeton laughed, "Well, this is your day to stay in bed if you want."

She said, "You boys don't look. I'm a'comin' outta this bed." They turned their head, hearing her moan as she sat on the side of the bed, pulling down her long dress and apron. "OK, help me to my chair by the fireplace."

They got her by both arms and helped her to the chair. She slowly sat down. Keeton handed her the tea. She took a sip and said, "Ahh, that is good."

She asked, "What day is this?"

Keeton replied, "Think it is Thursday. Why?"

She moaned, took a sip, and replied, "Reckon I was tied up for two days. Finally got the ropes off. The

house was sooo cold. Did not have strength to go find some firewood."

Henry told her, "Slow down, tell us who and what happened." He looked at Keeton. "Had to have been five or six days ago."

She took another sip. "This man, a'talkin' funny, think Irish, came in, said he was a'workin' with the patriots and needed shelter. I asked him if he had a dog. He replied, 'Nope, kilt the last one I had,' so I knew he was lying to me. He demanded food and money. Told them I had two friends who would make this right. They laughed, said no one would find me alive." She looked around. "Don't know what else is missing."

Keeton told her, "So sorry. There are no ducks or horses at the barn."

"Darn, just darn," she replied. "Makes me real mad."

"We can get you more horses."

She tried to laugh. "No, mad they took my ducks. Hard to get more ducks round here."

Henry asked, "Did they ask for anything in particular?"

She took another sip of the hot tea and said, "Yes, yes, they kept asking about a letter, a special sealed letter. Told them I know nothing about a letter."

Keeton when outside. He retrieved the red and blue scarf from his saddle bags and brought it in. "Is this yours?"

She replied, "Yes, yes, where did you find it?" She held it to her face.

So Keeton and Henry had to tell her about O'Bridge and his partners.

She told them, "Wow that was quick. Wonder where they are now?"

Henry laughed, "Oh, we forgot to mention. They volunteered for the militia, the Patriot Militia, and will be digging graves and ditches for at least a year."

She looked shocked. "Now how in the world did you make that happen? They wuz true loyalists, for the Red Coats."

Keeton laughed and told her, "It was that or the firing squad, so they sort of volunteered."

She laughed, for the first time. "Serves them right. I could have died tied to that darn chair." She got up, got the chair, and flung it in the fireplace. "Let that bad memory burn!"

Henry laughed again. "We do have friends in high places, and we did get the letter from Keeton's

brother. We are headed to the King's Road now to take care of some Red Coat business."

She said, "Not heard of the King's Road."

Henry told her it was the Indian Path, going north and south.

She said, "Well, I know that road, but I did not know they had named it for the King? Onlyist thing I ever knew was the Indian Traders Route north and south."

Henry asked, "How far is it?"

She sipped her tea and said, "Don't know how far but takes a couple days of good travel to get there. Been on it a few times going into North Carolina when I was younger."

Henry told her, "We can get you some horses back for the cause, but I don't know about the ducks."

Keeton told her, "We will leave you some food. Liz packed a go-bag for us. We have some money too for you to restock. We need you, lady! The cause for independence needs you."

She looked at both. "Thank you both for coming to my rescue. Next door neighbors don't really care. Do have friends down the road who can help."

"Tell us where, and we will tell them tomorrow as we pass that way."

She said, "Stay the night, and if you don't mind, bring in some firewood. Don't think I'll be doing much for a few days. I'm just too sore."

Henry said, "I have some herbs in my pack. I'll leave some to help."

She replied, "Thank you, Henry."

The next morning, they saddled up and left, going east. Half a mile later they approached the house, where she said they would find help.

Henry told the people about Mrs. Wilson. They were alarmed and said they had told her not to live alone, that it was just too dangerous.

They said they would go now and check on her. Keeton laughed. "She worries about the ducks. Can you take her a few ducks or chickens?"

The reply was yes.

Chapter 9

Onward they rode. On day two, they bypassed Tarboro and by day three they were near Williamston and the King's Road.

Keeton commented, "We might as well go into the camp and see if any of our friends are there."

Henry replied, "Yeah, if any of them know us. We have not been there in couple years. The place may have changed."

They went closer and stopped at a country store. Henry said, "Hey, Lee Morgan owns this store. I remember him. We should take some grub, being's we will be there a few days."

They dismounted and tied their horses to the hitching rail. Henry

walked in first and saw the place was much larger. "Anybody home?"

A man came from the back, "Well, if it's not Henry Bohanan. What brings you here again?"

"We have work to do. This is Keeton Fretwell."

"Welcome to our store."

Henry told him, "We need some supplies and will be going into the camp."

Morgan said, "Not a good idea. That place was discovered by you-know-who and is not used anymore."

"Do you know where we might stay a few days?"

Morgan replied, "Yeah, I saw Catawba Bear a week or so ago. He told me if I saw you to send you just short of Jamesville, turn northeast at two huge old oak trees. There is a little path, takes you a couple miles down to the Roanoke River."

"OK, we need coffee, bacon, cornmeal, and several things, and we have money to pay. Oh, and a couple bags of corn if you have it for the horses?"

"Yeah. Thanks," Morgan replied. "I'll bag it up for you. Just be careful going down to the river. You might spook someone you may or may not know."

They thanked him for the supplies, loaded up, and rode east until they saw the two ancient old oak trees. They followed a small path through heavy oak and pine trees. The path kept making turns and twists. Suddenly, a man stepped out in the road, holding a rifle, in front of them.

"We don't like people a'comin' here. Go back."

Henry whispered to Keeton, "Do we know him?"

Keeton replied, "Nope, never saw him before."

Henry replied, "We are friendly. Do you know our aunt Oddy?"

The man lowered his rifle at them, "No, and go or I shoot."

About that time, they heard a man laughing back in the brush. "Is that you, Henry?"

The man came out.

Henry said, "Is that you, Bear?"

"Bear in person. Matthew, this is Henry Bohanan. Do you not remember him?"

Matthew replied, "Guess not. Sorry, man. I did not know you."

Henry replied, "Well, it has been a couple years."

Bear said, "Come on. The house is just around the curve."

Keeton laughed. "The road sure is curvy."

Bear laughed. "You was just over there on one turn, fifty feet away. This way we know who is coming before they get here."

Henry laughed. "Sounds like an Indian trail."

Bear just grinned.

A short distance away, the wooded area turned into a large grass field that went all the way down to the river. Set back from the river was a huge house with a wrap-around porch. There was a low barn with several horses nearby.

Henry said, "Neat, just a neat place. How long have you all been here?"

Bear replied, "Just a few months. Our cover got blown at the other place. We had to leave with some supplies still there."

"Know who it was?"

"Nope, we will find out though."

They unsaddled and unpacked the pack horse. Henry told Bear, "Take these sacks of supplies to the house."

Keeton placed his saddle on a long saddle pole in the barn. "Look, Henry."

Henry put his saddle beside Keeton's and looked at the dozen or so saddles already there. All made by Ole Zeke.

Bear said, "Come on in. I'll introduce you to the others." They walked the short distance to the house where several men were loafing around on the porch, smoking or drinking coffee.

Bear introduced Henry and Keeton to the men.

Henry told them they had orders to step up the attacks on the Red Coats along the King's Road.

Bear grinned, "We been doing that, but now we have some problems."

"What?" Keeton asked.

"Their spies knows our horses by sight. We cannot go into any town or village here 'cause they all know the horses. We can change clothes, but we can't change horses."

Henry laughed. "Well, maybe we need to do some horse trading? No one knows our horses."

Bear asked, "Where is Festus? The word sure spread about that appaloosa mule."

Henry replied, "He is way down at Fort Chiswell with Sally and Sammy. He got shot, nothing serious, but we thought it best to keep him outta sight for awhile."

225

Bear told them, "Put your things in the rear room. We have plenty of room here for everyone, for a while that is."

"Who owns the house?" Keeton asked.

Bear replied, "We do, bought it with money taken from the Red Coats. We got a whole room of guns too if you all want one."

"Really?" Henry inquired.

"Yes, we keep what we want and trade the others for food or horse feed. We had one rifle that showed up three times here."

Keeton laughed, "If only that gun could talk."

"Relax, get some rest. We will talk more in the morning. We have a team out now, down in North Carolina causing a little fuss. They should be back in a day or two."

Keeton asked, "What happened to Orange Hair or, rather, Nathan Wright?"

"He is part of the team out down toward Charles Town."

They rested well with friends, good food, and a warm fire.

The next morning, they were eating breakfast when the team returned. Nathan had been wounded in his left arm, but it was nothing serious.

Bear asked Henry, "Can you swim?"

"A little. Why?"

"We have a new way of pestering the Red Coats. Down this river and turn left is Albemarle Sound. Just up the sound a few miles is a strong hold of the Tories. They come and go there by boat and land. We noticed several smaller ships going that way and followed them in

227

our little boats. They landed there and offloaded supplies."

Keeton asked, "What kind of supplies?"

"We think gunpowder, guns, and uniforms."

"So?"

"We might go, lie in wait till dark, and torch a boat or two. We can go pretty fast in our rowboats if the weather is right, and they can't catch us."

Nathan replied, "Yeah, easy this time of year with the dry grass and hay in the barn."

Henry and Keeton remained at the house while the others took the boats for a raid. They returned well after midnight.

They finally settled down for the night, or what was left of it. Morning came as someone made a big

pot of coffee out in the yard over the fire.

Bear came out of the house with two sacks of bounty from the last evening. He opened the sack and started taking out pistols. "Wow, these are the latest. Nice, really nice."

Henry picked one up, "Yes, these are the latest officer's Elliot .62 caliber." He handed it to Keeton.

Keeton examined it. "Yes, nice, very nice."

Bear told them, "These are issued only to officers and the dragoons on horseback."

Nathan added, "And now we have them too." He brought the other two bags out and counted. "Looks like we have a total of forty-five pistols."

Henry asked, "Now what? I'm happy with the two pistols I carry now. They are reliable and shoot good."

Keeton told them, "I'd like to trade my two in, if it's OK?"

Bear laughed. "Take two, keep yours for trade later if you want."

Nathan interjected, "OK. One question, if we are seen with these pistols, how do we respond?"

One of the other men said, "You can tell them that you got it off of a burning ship."

They all laughed.

Keeton said, "Now that would surely work."

Henry said, "Seriously, we sell, trade and buy all the time. That story should work, we got them off a couple of drunk Red Coats. They wanted more whiskey, so even trade."

All was silent for a few minutes. Bear said, "That does sound truthful. That is the story we will tell."

Keeton asked, "What will you do with the remainder?"

Nathan told them, "Let our Hornets get what they want, and we can trade the others for horses, food, or supplies. There is a huge demand for pistols all over the place."

Henry said, "Wait a minute. We don't have bullet molds for the .62 caliber? Our rifles shoot the .65, .69 or the .75 caliber."

Running Bear's partner, Noah, said, "I know someone who can make that mold for us."

"How much will he charge?"

Noah replied, "He is a true Patriot, but if it's OK, I'll take him one of the new pistols."

Nathan said, "Great. We will need three molds."

"No problem. I'll go check with him tomorrow."

The remainder of the day was spent resting and checking on equipment. Noah had left to get the

new bullet molds made. Tanner enjoyed the lazy time to sleep and just lie around, but by mid-afternoon he sat up and whined. Henry and Keeton both noticed he was on alert. Henry whispered to Bear and the others, "Someone is close."

One of the men, Rex, slowly got up, grabbed his rifle, and told Matt to follow. "The rest of you men just melt back into the brush till we know who this is." No questions were asked, as each grabbed their guns and disappeared back into the wooded area. Rex and Matt had gone in the direction of the trail and hidden, awaiting the unknown threat.

Henry was with Keeton and Tanner, who was silent beside Keeton. "Wonder who it is?"

"Don't know, may be friend or foe."

A few minutes later, they could hear laughter coming from the house. "Guess all is OK?" Keeton asked.

"Guess so." He and Henry walked back to the house. There on the horses were Oscar King and Thomas Ownby.

Thomas looked at Henry. "You sure are hard to find."

Henry laughed. "Didn't know I was missing."

Thomas got off his horse, shook Henry and Keeton's hand, and gave both a bear hug. "Good to see you all again."

Henry noticed several bags tied to both their saddles.

The others had come from hiding and wanted to know the two strangers.

Henry told them, "This is Cousin Thomas Ownby from the

233

mountains and his cousin Oscar King. They are Hornets too."

Everyone shook their hands with a welcome to their camp.

Bear questioned, "How did you find us?"

Oscar replied, "We saw Noah back up the road. He told us how to find the camp. Glad he was there, or we would have gone to the old camp."

"So what is going on?" Henry asked

"We got bored at Hunting Camp with the Harrisons. Just wanted a little action."

Oscar looked at Thomas, "No, that is a lie. Nane had him roped and wanted to get married. We escaped when we got the chance."

Everyone laughed.

Bear told them, "Welcome to our camp. Go put your horses in the

field. There is plenty of grass and corn for them."

Thomas told them, "We brought chickens for supper." They took off the bags. "Should be enough for all of us."

They made a big pot of chicken dumplings for supper. All the men gathered as Thomas asked the blessing. All the other men said amen at the same time.

Dusty told them, "Dig in, there is enough for all of us, and we might even find a leg bone or two for Tanner," who was setting watching the kettle.

Keeton laughed. "Don't know if he ever ate a chicken leg bone or not."

Bear was the first to get his bowl of dumplings. He dug down in the dumplings and found a bone, tossing it to Tanner. Tanner smelled

235

of it, grabbed it, and turned away.
Crunching of the bone could be heard.
They ate their fill and had molasses
on the biscuits. All was excellent.

They laid around, close to the
kettle and the fire as the air was
getting cooler.

Henry asked Bear, "What is on
the calendar for tomorrow?"

Early the next morning, one of
the men came in to awaken the camp.
"There is a boat with four men
prowling around the shoreline."

Henry asked Bear, "Who are
they?"

Noah told them, "Don't know,
but I think they might be looking for
us from up at Merry Hill. What shall
we do?"

Bear replied, "We just lay low.
If they land and come this way, we
will take care of business. Did we
hide the boats well?"

Nathan replied, "Yes, I don't think they can see them unless they come up the little creek and look in the reeds good."

Each man got their weapons, just in case. Two went to protect their horses, while the others moved behind some brush and trees where they could watch the men in the boat.

By mid-morning, the boat was seen going back north toward Merry Hill.

Keeton asked, "Do you think they made this camp?"

Bear replied, "Don't know, but we need to find a second place soon anyway."

"Where would you look?" Henry asked.

"We need to get away from the river for a while, maybe go west."

Henry told them, "We have a good patriot in Scotland's Neck.

Morgan might know of a place. It is near the intersection of several crossroads."

Nathan said, "Good, good. That way we will be closer to the north-south King's Road."

Thomas added, "We have friendly people there. Look up the Duggan place. I think it does back up to the river. They might do some horse trading too. Let's go out in the yard. I'll draw you a map in the sand."

All the men walked outside to look at the dirt map. Thomas said, "See the river makes a huge curve here." He pointed to the dirt. "This is about halfway from Scotland's Neck and Palmyra to the north. I think the Duggans own that entire area of several hundred acres."

One man asked, "Is the Roanoke wide there?"

Thomas replied, "Don't know, but there should be lots of cane breaks along that area."

Henry told them, "We can ride up that way, see what is available. Is this the same Roanoke River here?"

Bear nodded.

Keeton told them, "We will be leaving. If there is a good place, we can get word back to you all. Do you have funds if needed to rent or buy?"

Nathan laughed, "Oh yes, we do have funds directly sponsored by the Red Coats."

Henry told them, "So it is settled, we will find a second place for you all to hide." The matter was settled, and the men were anxious to get back to work.

Bear replied, "We might as well ride up the King's Road, see if we can cause any discomfort to the King's men. Maybe two teams, one

going north and one going south. I think the Merry Hill bunch will be looking for us to hit again. We will wait a few days and sneak back in on land. It's hard for them to watch the waterfront and all the land at the same time."

Henry asked, "Is it a training camp?"

Bear replied, "Maybe, but mostly for the officers to come and retreat and plan on some next moves."

Bear looked at Nathan. "Guess we need to find some more black walnuts for his hair?"

Keeton replied, "Yeah, don't need the orange hair showing. Too many people looking for that."

Henry added, "But we have chickens, maybe some black chicken crap would change the color real good," and laughed.

Nathan looked at them, "Just try that, and I'll make you eat some."

They all laughed. Bear said, "It's good to laugh now and then. Hey, where is your lady friend, Henry?"

He replied, "Last we heard she is way up past Baltimore."

Bear replied, "Just hope she is OK. When are you two gonna step forward?"

Keeton told him, "We have talked this over. Seems General Greene wants us in the light dragoons, doing what we are doing now."

Henry added, "Governor Patrick Henry wants us to be for defense south of the James River. Guess we will be doing the same thing we are now, but under the militia. The governor assured us that we would get all the equipment we need. But I told him we already have

that. I think when spring finally gets here, we may go back on the Trader's Path toward Roanoke and work that area. Seems several loyalists keep getting our supplies and killing off the freight drivers."

Keeton told them, "We already had six to hang, and one even tried to swim in the New River with lead in his pockets."

Bear laughed. "Bet he went straight down."

"He did, not even a bubble came to the surface, but the river was running cold and deep."

"Rest, we will make plans in the morning."

The next morning, Thomas told them, "Think we will go over to the less-traveled road going north up through Scotland Neck, Roanoke Rapids, and into Virginia by way of Skipper."

Bear asked, "Why that route?"

Oscar told them, "We picked up information that the carriers are going that way to attract less attention, taking the loyalist routes and the mail on to Richmond. They know that the King's Road has been a problem by you men."

Henry, now curious, asked, "Now, how did you get that information?"

Thomas told them, "We kinda found that information by accident. You know Henry Harrison's place is huge. One night a rider stopped, asking quarters during the last big snow. Of course, Mr. Harrison let him stay in the tack room. When he got there, we was already setting by the fire. He came in and placed his saddle bags beside the fire, as it was wet and snow covered. He asked if we were friend or foe. Oscar announced that

we were pure loyalists. The poor cold man took it as the truth. He got dry and warm and fell to sleep right there on the floor."

Thomas said, "His saddle bag kinda fell open and there were letters and orders for eyes only for the top Red Coats in Richmond. Of course, being nice like we are, we closed the bag and let the poor man sleep. He stayed around for a couple days till the snow melted and went on North.

"Mr. Harrison, of course, asked questions and laughed at Oscar for being a loyalist."

Henry asked, "So is Lilly and Nane still working for the Harrisons?"

Oscar responded, "Oh yes, they have sort of adopted both. They found a good home, well, until Thomas has the courage to pop the question to Nane."

Made in the USA
Columbia, SC
08 October 2022

68834292R00170